COILED VENGEANCE

An Eomix Galaxy Novel

CHRISTA YELICH-KOTH

This book is a work of fiction. All characters and events portrayed in this book are either products of the author's imagination or are used fictitiously.

COILED VENGEANCE (An Eomix Galaxy novel)
First Printing: November 2018

Copyright © 2018 by Christa Yelich-Koth
www.ChristaYelichKoth.com

All rights reserved.

Published by CYK Publishing
Oregon, USA

ISBN: **978-0-9883470-8-3**

Cover art: Creative Alchemy Inc and CC Covers

THANK YOU

First, thanks to you, the reader, for wanting more.

Thank you to everyone who helped along the way with this journey. *Coiled Vengeance* had its own journey and so many helped to get it to where it is today.

Sandra Yelich: For being a soundboard and editor through multiple versions.

Jessica Therrien and Kat Ross: For your fantastic feedback and edits.

Stu Tighe: I'm sorry you had to punch your truck, but the edits were great.

The SCWC: For helping me turn my story into the best written version I could make it.

Creative Alchemy Inc. and Conrad Teves: For your help to create a beautiful cover.

Look for other books by CHRISTA Yelich-Koth
www.ChristaYelichKoth.com

The Land of Iyah trilogy
THE JADE CASTLE
THE JADE ARCH
THE JADE THRONE

Eomix Galaxy Novels
ILLUSION (Book 1 of 2)
IDENTITY (Book 2 of 2)
COILED VENGEANCE

The Detective Trann series
SPIDER'S TRUTH
SPIDER'S RING
SPIDER'S QUEEN

Graphic Novels
HOLLOW

Comic Books
HOLLOW'S PRSIM SERIES
(6 issues total)
Issue #1: *Aftermath*
Issue #2: *Reunion*
Issue #3: *Alliance*
Issue #4: *Trigger*
Issue #5: *Revelations*
Issue #6: *Fusion*

CHAPTER 1

WHITE.
White everywhere.
Lights, eyes, clothes, skin.
Machines, needles, doors, locks.
Even the toys.
All white.

Exarth's eyes snapped open and adjusted to the hotel room's dim light. They focused on the domed cream-colored ceiling above her and locked onto the empty metallic light socket in the center. Twisted shadows seemed to be caught mid-crawl along the peeling bits of paint.

It was just a dream, she thought, willing her breaths to slow. *You aren't in that hospital anymore. Only a dream.*

She shifted her view and looked at the individual lying next to her, his blue skin having paled and puckered throughout the night. Red, vacant eyes stared up at nothingness atop his face, which expressed a mixture of pleasure and shock. His uncovered chest and arms were dimpled and scratched—souvenirs from a sexual conquest he would never get the chance to brag about.

"Ughhh…." Revolted, Exarth pushed the corpse away from her. The rigid body slid ungracefully off the bed and landed with a sick thud onto the floor.

Exarth threw off the covers and shuddered when the cool air met her bare skin. She made her way through the bedroom to the washroom, using the inklings of light that seeped around the edges of the opaque curtains to find her way. She didn't know the exact time, but it didn't matter. Her next appointment wasn't scheduled until that afternoon.

She entered the washroom and stood before the reflector unit, admiring her naked body—small, but by no means frail. Taut muscles rippled when she moved. Any teeth marks and bruises on her skin from her enthusiastic partner had vanished, her body having repaired itself during her brief sleep. Her icy white skin, a stark contrast to her long, dark locks, remained smooth and supple as usual.

Exarth slid her delicate fingers over her hair, which hung straight to her waist. Light in the washroom glinted off its surface, revealing subtle multi-colored tones among the inky blackness, like an oil spill made of silk. She popped in a pair of black contacts to hide her color-changing eyes, which at the moment swirled between the greens and blues of pleasure.

She dressed quickly, turning her back toward the room with her recent lover's corpse. She hadn't even been that attracted to this one, but her fury at the news she'd received the day before prompted her to vent her frustration, which led to…whatever his name was. The few moments of sexual gratification, however brief, gave her an escape from the rage that swelled inside her. But then he'd looked at her as if she meant something to him—his eyes full of joy and adoration after their pleasurable physical act—and she'd snapped his neck without a second thought.

Not that she would have kept him alive anyway, but still. *Why do they always have to spoil the moment by getting emotional?* she thought.

Still, her climactic release and solid few hours of sleep had done wonders for her mood. Though often quick to anger, Exarth now felt focused, ready to deal with the bad news she'd received. One last look around the room confirmed she hadn't left anything behind. She pulled a small circular device from her jacket pocket, set the timer, and lobbed it onto the bed.

As she exited the building, the device detonated, blowing apart half the hotel. Chunks of debris flew around her. Dust spewed through the sun-streaked air as bystanders shrieked in fear, protecting their heads, and running for cover. Pieces of shrapnel hit her body, tearing into her skin. She didn't care. The wounds wouldn't take long to heal.

Exarth smiled.

It was going to be a good day.

CHAPTER 2

NESS OPUTE FELT dwarfed by the size of the room, a feat not easily accomplished. He sat in a government building in the capital city, Wolina, of the planet Sintaur. His large, muscular frame made the hand-carved brit tree chair he sat in creak as he surveyed the space. Across from him, lounging comfortably behind a large desk, sat an old acquaintance of his, Nuis Weri.

Nuis smiled at Opute's amazement, his white teeth dazzling against his auburn face, even in the brightly lit room.

"Yes," he said, "it's really my office."

"No question," Opute said, indicating the elaborate additions.

Nuis stretched his fingers and slid his hands across the top of his red-stained ivory desk, its edges rimmed with clear crystal, the drawer handles made of polished, black stone. He breathed in the perfume-scented air and raised his eyes toward the giant chandelier that hung above them. Its golden-white light bathed them in rays that rivaled the planet's sun.

Thick, plush, crimson curtains hung across the window,

tied up by golden-laced cords. The oval rug underneath the desk and chairs matched the curtains, a thick-knapped deep red color with a delicately woven gold spiral pattern that became busier as it pulled away from the edges toward the center.

Nuis's grin widened. "Show me where it's written a man can't be comfortable where he works."

Opute snorted a laugh and rubbed a hand across his shorn haircut. "The set-up I understand, but the job? I never figured you for the governmental type. And it's not like you need the paycheck."

Nuis shrugged at Opute's reference to his vast inherited fortune. His dark blond shoulder-length curls bounced at the motion. "I'm not really sure myself. I guess I got tired of sitting around all day doing nothing. It may sound odd, but after what the Sintaurians went through last year, it felt good to stay and help. Besides who can pass up the chance to have the title 'Dignitary of Off-world Affairs?' It's so classy."

Opute shook his head. "I just can't believe you've gone respectable."

"Playing the rich kid got old." Nuis paused. "So what about you? I haven't heard from you since everything happened last year. You sort of disappeared."

"I'm not one for the spotlight. Besides, I don't think having my face splayed across news vidlinks would help my career."

"That's why you should get out of smuggling and into something legit, like me."

Opute picked at his teeth. "Funny you should mention a change."

"Is that what brings you knocking on my door?"

"In a way. Mostly looking for money," Opute said, his usually stony face spreading into a grin. "Legitimate this time though."

"What do you have in mind?"

"How much would the government of Sintaur pay to increase its attack cruiser complement by six ships?"

Nuis frowned. "I'm not really sure. We're focusing more on rebuilding efforts right now, not military vehicle replacements."

Opute leaned in toward Nuis. "What if they were six ships from Exarth's personal fleet?"

Nuis let out a soft whistle. "You're selling them? I thought they were your prized possessions after you stole them from her in the first place."

"They are, but I can only pilot one ship at a time. I'm keeping the lead ship for myself and selling the rest."

"Well, I can pretty much guarantee Sintaur will be interested in that type of purchase. If nothing else, we may use them as symbols and put them on display for the crowds." He tapped his fingers on the desk. "I think I can swing the deal. The treasury is still recovering from the losses they suffered last year, but I know having those ships would help boost morale. I bet I can convince them it would be a good investment." Nuis quickly put together a message to set the deal in motion. While he sent it to the correct department, he continued to speak. "If you don't mind my asking, what's the money for?"

"I'm going after Exarth."

Nuis's voice caught in his throat. "Exarth? Again? I thought you'd decided she wasn't real, just a made-up persona."

"I talked with someone who's seen her."

Nuis chuckled and shifted awkwardly in his chair. "Who? Some client of yours? I mean, come on Opute, if she's real, she's the scariest thing I've ever heard of. She'd have to have fingers, tentacles, or whatever she has, in everything: governments, industries, utilities, education, hospitals, you name it. Spread over dozens of planets. I've dealt with some of her companies and I doubt one woman can do all that."

"The source is reliable." Opute rubbed the back of his thick neck. He didn't feel like divulging his informant was a telepath who'd seen Exarth through the mind of a war criminal.

Nuis pursed his mouth. A few moments of silence passed.

"How do you plan to find her?"

"I have a few ideas," Opute said, relaxing. He laced his fingers and pulled his arms behind his head.

Nuis chewed on his lip. "Maybe you should just let this one go."

Opute clenched his jaw, trying not to let his anger get the best of him yet again. "It's not just the fact she killed Lang, or even that she joined up with the Aleet Army. It's more complicated than that."

"How so?"

Opute hesitated. "Let's just say Lang wasn't the only death on Exarth's hands. You don't know all I did to try and find her…for five years I tracked her down, from her illegal ops like debris dumpers and twig pushers to her corporate shell companies and medical facilities." The anger flared in his belly, red hot. "I couldn't find anything. I found *less* than anything. All I heard were stories. No one had ever really seen her." Opute slammed his hand on the desk. "No one!"

Nuis jumped, his eyes wide.

"I started to believe Exarth *was* a myth," Opute continued through clenched teeth. "So I gave up. Got my life back together, what was left of it. Then as soon as I'd settled back into my own business and began to get comfortable…Lang got murdered."

Opute gripped the chair arms. "She had Lang killed because he was in the wrong place at the wrong time. And I got to find his body, fresh with a circular scorch mark the size of my head in his chest."

Opute forced his hands to unclench at the apprehension in

his friend's face.

"I should never have stopped looking for her. If I hadn't, Lang would still be alive."

Nuis's mouth softened and he tilted his head to the side in sympathy. "Lang's murder is not your fault. I'm sure you did everything you could to find Exarth."

"If that were true, I'd have her head hanging on my wall!" Opute stood abruptly, bursting out of his seat. The chair flew backward and broke against the door.

Opute's eyes cleared and he looked around the room, realizing what he'd done. "Sorry," he mumbled. "I'll pay for that." Embarrassment washed over him.

Nuis went and poked the chair with his foot, which had broken into three pieces. His face pinched together for a moment before he cleared his throat and waved a hand at the chair as if it were unimportant. "Don't worry about it."

Opute cringed. "It's expensive, isn't it?"

"Priceless, actually. It's a one-of-a-kind Mussoilah design. She died last year." He paused. "Ah well, this gives me an excuse to get something new. Now listen," he started slowly, "I have no love for Exarth either, but are you absolutely sure about this? It seems you already spent a lot of time looking for her and couldn't find her. What makes you think you'll have more success this time?"

Opute's steely gray eyes bore straight into Nuis's. "Because this time I'm going to find her from the inside out."

Nuis's eyebrows contracted. "What do you mean?"

Opute hesitated about telling Nuis his plan. He didn't want Nuis to be involved, but something felt final about this, like Opute may not come back. And even if he did, he wouldn't be the same man anymore. "Last time, I kept trying to find her through others in her organization with threats, pain, or whatever happened to be necessary. But this time, I'm going to infiltrate her organization from the inside, and work my way up in the ranks until I gain her trust."

"How is that going to work? Doesn't she know who you are?"

"Not if I'm not me anymore."

Nuis lifted his eyebrows in understanding. "That's what the money is for, isn't it? You're going to change your appearance."

Opute nodded. He stood with his arms crossed, regretting that he'd broken the chair.

Nuis sat back down behind his desk. "Have you already found someone to perform the operation?"

"An old client of mine, a Grassuwerian, is going to help me out. And don't worry, she's trustworthy enough."

Nuis thought a moment about the insect-like creatures. "I didn't know Grassuwerians *could* perform surgery. Don't they only have one arm?"

"Yes, but most of the surgery will be performed by a machine."

"Oh."

Silence lengthened between them. Nuis jumped when the chimes to his office rang. He laughed away a bit of the tension in the room and asked whomever it was to enter. A young message clerk walked in, eyeing first the broken chair and then the gruff, imposing figure of Opute, before handing a datapad to Nuis. Nuis thanked the clerk and dismissed him while turning on the datapad. He read it quickly and smiled at Opute.

"You're in luck. Sintaur's Treasury of Military Weapons and Vehicles has approved the transaction to purchase your ships. They cut three percent off the price you wanted, since they have to retrieve the ships from off-planet and transport them back here, but overall, I think it's a good deal." Nuis handed Opute the datapad.

Opute briefly looked over the contract and signed it. "It'll do. I'll still have enough after the surgery to refit my own ship so Exarth can't recognize that either."

Nuis nodded at the datapad. "Just take that to room B-four-twenty-six, which is the Treasury Department and talk to Ufi Ro. She'll get your money for you."

Opute and Nuis stood and clasped wrists. "You ever need my help," Nuis said, "for anything, you know where to find me."

* * *

Opute made his way to room B-426. A sparse room compared to Nuis's office, with a single desk, two chairs for visitors, and a data storage shelf across the back wall.

He drummed his fingers on Ufi Ro's desk as she read through the contract on the datapad. Her short, spiked, coppery hair looked sharp enough to puncture skin.

"This all looks in order," she said with a slight drawl. Ufi stood and walked to a square, metal machine behind her, which spewed forth a small piece of plastic.

Ufi grinned. He noticed her slightly crooked front tooth.

"This card has been charged with the amount of money agreed upon by the contract. Please sign here," she said, handing him a different datapad, "signifying you received your payment."

Opute signed the datapad quickly and took the plastic card from her.

"Thank you for doing business with the government of Sintaur. Have a pleasant and productive day!"

Opute grunted and left the room.

He made his way to Wolina's main docking bay. A few supply barges and a couple personal shuttles made up the entire day's incoming and outgoing vessels, a vast difference to the hustle and bustle on his homeworld, C-Sector 9.

As Opute headed toward his docked ship, flipping the little plastic card over and over in his hands, he couldn't help but think about how his cruiser measured above and beyond everything around him. Not that the planet Sintaur could be blamed. They'd done what they could since the devastation they'd suffered the year before, but some things took longer to rebuild.

Opute pocketed the card as he arrived and entered his cruiser. He sat down at the controls, sinking into the pilot's chair, and took a moment to settle in. He'd never owned such a beautiful ship—her sleek black lines, her state-of-the-art weapons system, her powerful engine—and her beauty shone even more because of the circumstances in which he'd stolen her.

He started her up. The seat vibrated with a smooth purr, and he left the dock, pushing through Sintaur's atmosphere on a course for Grassuwer. His feet up on the console, Opute got comfortable for the standard weeklong trip.

He did his best to ignore the nervous ball in his stomach at the thought that in a week, he'd be a completely different man.

Then he remembered the soft curve of his wife's face and the thought of her, alone and scared, when her ship exploded.

The friendly smile of his friend, Pierze Lang, whom he'd found murdered, a gaping hole blown through his chest.

Opute ground his teeth, steeling his resolve.

He'd get it right this time. He'd find Exarth and she would pay for what she'd done.

CHAPTER 3

EXARTH RAISED HER chin a centimeter before the sleek white doors opened in front of her. The appearance of self-control radiated from her pores, though she roiled with both anger and anticipation within. She walked out of the air-propelled ovule, which could transport any crewmember around the entire building, and made her way toward the head of a long table. Her shoes clicked on the smooth, black tiles as quiet conversations in the room withered away. She knew the silence revolved around the fact that no one in this room had ever seen her before.

Exarth kept her true identity a secret to all except two individuals. The members of the room drank in every detail, from her starched white skin and long, dark hair, to her completely black eyes. They believed this to be an honor, that they'd somehow ascended the ranks to be admitted into her inner circle. A mistaken assumption. Many others had seen her, but none of them remained alive to reveal that information. Just like those in this room eventually wouldn't.

Before she reached her seat, she stopped for a moment and

slid a long-fingered hand onto the back of the chair next to it, occupied by a red-skinned male Aq named Fa'tay.

Fa'tay swiveled his head toward her, his dry skin crackling in the silent room. Being from an extremely humid planet, members of his species constantly oiled themselves to keep their bodies moist when visiting other worlds. He'd apparently been in such a hurry to get to the meeting that he'd forgotten his oil.

Exarth continued to walk, pacing behind her chair. She paused in front of the office's large windows—her black eyes stared at the gray sky, fluffy with dark cyan clouds, a sure sign a methane storm brewed outside the city's protective bubble. She turned and brought her attention back to the room, eyeing the bounty hunters. Six sat around the table: the dry-skinned Aq in the seat in front of her, a mated pair of Corenthians, with their stinger-tipped tails wrapped around themselves and their single eye's gaze fixed solely on her, a female Vorr, so short she needed to stand on the seat to see above the table, a gender-free individual that appeared robotic, but with dark, beady eyes that glistened through its metallic mask, and a female Slithe, a reptilian species, whose lean body lounged provocatively in her chair.

"As you all know," Exarth began, her deep, sultry voice echoing through the room, "there has been a traitor in our midst for several months now. Someone stole sensitive information saved on a disk, and foolishly allowed that disk to fall into the hands of a defenseless, ignorant store clerk on the planet C-Sector Nine.

"That store clerk is now dead." The clouds behind her through the windows swirled and funneled, darkening the sky, matching the edge in her voice. Exarth slowly walked around the table. "However, the disk never returned to me and instead came into possession of the forces opposing Commander Xiven's army. This made him no longer a valid business partner." Exarth sneered, her eyes now reflecting the storm outside. "I would like to take this opportunity to remind all of you that stealing from me is…unwise."

With a quick step, Exarth came up behind Fa'tay. Before he could turn his head to follow her, she raked one of her long fingernails across his throat. Fa'tay gurgled and tried to swallow. Several members of the group backed away from the table as black, viscous liquid sprayed forth from the open wound. Fa'tay clamped his hands over his neck in a vain attempt to stop his vital fluids from gushing out of his body, but after a few moments, his hands went limp, and he flopped over onto the table.

Exarth felt a feeling of satisfaction as the life dimmed from his eyes, but kept her demeanor cold. "Ladies and gentlemen," she said, as if nothing more unusual had happened then a brit tree spilling its sap, "if you'll follow me, we will finish this meeting in the room next door."

Exarth led the group one room over after contacting a clean-up crew to dispense with the body and they all sat themselves at the new table, with one seat empty.

During the scraping of chairs, the Vorr leaned over to the robotic-like creature next to her and whispered that she couldn't believe Fa'tay would have betrayed Exarth.

"And why not?" Exarth asked, having heard the comment. "He saw a profit to be made and a way to undercut my authority. Can you deny that you wouldn't have done the same thing?"

The Vorr's eyes widened. "Of course I wouldn't have," she blubbered. "I am loyal only to you."

"Today, perhaps," she answered, her eyes narrowed.

The Vorr gulped.

Exarth pressed a button and a simulated image of an attack cruiser popped up in front of them. "This," she said, indicating the ship with her upturned hand, "is one of my top fighting battle cruisers. Stolen, along with six others." The five remaining beings peered at the ship. "As you have just witnessed, stealing from me is unacceptable. I want whoever is responsible for this to be brought to my door, alive. They are also responsible for the deaths of several members of my businesses as well. He or she prevented a very important corporate arrangement from taking place, stole my payment, and took my ships. There is even a rumor that he or she disposed of Kircla."

A few raised eyebrows and several audible gasps occurred at this statement. Kircla's skill as an assassin was unequaled in the sector. If this thief killed Kircla….

Exarth leaned back in her chair, placing her fingertips together. "You have been chosen as the remaining top trackers and bounty hunters," she said, referencing the loss of Kircla, "and I will handsomely pay the first one who brings me the responsible party, *alive*. If the individual dies, your payment is forfeit, as is your life. No exceptions. That is, however, the only condition." She paused. "Anyone interested?" Each of the five beings raised a hand or limb into the air.

Exarth nodded. "Good. Stop across the hall to fill out your contracts and receive any pertinent details. You are all dismissed."

Exarth watched the bounty hunters clear the conference room and then walked back to the air-propelled ovule which brought her to her office. She pursed her lips at the thought of killing them. They could prove very useful in the future on other projects, but her identity must be protected. She also knew that if she wanted to catch this thief, she needed the best in the business.

When she arrived at her office, harsh white lights glared off the black polished floor, walls, and ceiling. Her glossy, metallic desk had only a datapad, a monitor, and a black chair behind it, with arms made of smooth, blood-red glass. No chairs for visitors, which seemed perfectly reasonable since only two individuals ever came into her office, and one of them couldn't even sit down.

When Exarth entered, she frowned at one of those individuals waiting for her.

"I don't want a lecture," Exarth told the woman, who stood rigid like a bleached marble statue.

The associate's completely white eyes widened slightly, but she said nothing.

Exarth plopped down into the chair behind her large desk. A few moments of silence passed while the associate stood there, staring…wherever she stared. Exarth could never tell since the associate's eyes were completely void of pigment. Exarth finally broke the quiet. "Coresque, what do you want?"

Coresque's face remained stony, but an air of amusement tinged her voice. "I want to lecture you."

Exarth rolled her eyes, grimacing at the pain her contacts made.

"Why don't you take those out? I know they are uncomfortable when your eyes change color."

"Uncomfortable?" Exarth muttered, rubbing her face. "I wish. It feels more like little flames licking my eyes." Exarth paused for a moment. "Whatever." She blinked and the two black contacts popped out. She caught them deftly in her hand before sliding them in a carrier in her desk drawer. "Happy?"

"Of course."

Exarth hated how she felt like a child dealing with a schoolteacher every time they conversed. It always made her defensive, like she would soon be punished. "All right then. Get it over with. Tell me how foolish I am for starting this search." She bared her teeth. "This never would have happened if Iry hadn't lied about killing him in the first place and when Iry returns from his business trip…" Exarth's threat hung in the air, dripping with malice.

"Are you sure it is Ness Opute who stole your ships?"

Exarth's eyes changed into a dark red, symbolizing her defensive frustration. "It has to be him!"

"Then why did you keep that information from your trackers? It would be easier for them to find him if they knew who to search for."

"Because if for some reason they come back with a different name, then I'll know my insider lied and I will deal with it."

"And if they come back with Opute's name?"

Exarth's eyes violently shifted into an intense red, rimmed with a dark purple. "I'm finding him and finishing him."

Coresque hesitated before speaking. "My sources say he has disappeared."

Exarth's eyes changed to the orange of surprise. "What?"

The albino woman sighed. "His name crept back up a year ago. Your insider was correct. Ness Opute was involved in the Aleet Army incident after he stole your ships."

The redness returned. "First Iry lies about killing him and now you tell me you've known he's been alive for over a year? Coresque, how could you keep this from me?"

Coresque shook her head slightly, a grinding noise issuing from her stony neck. "I did not think telling you would help. He is not the monster you think he is."

Exarth stood, trembling with fury. "Oh really? I think I've had enough experience with monsters to know one when I see one. Or have you forgotten the "doctors" who raised us?"

Coresque's lips pressed together tightly and, though colder, her anger equaled Exarth's. "I can never forget. You may have been unconscious during your experimental sessions with the doctors, but I was not."

Exarth sat back down at Coresque's words. She'd never seen her associate angry, *ever*. She was also unaware her friend remembered the procedures performed on them in the hospital they both grew up in.

Coresque continued, her anger melting away. "So no, I have not forgotten what monsters are and I do not believe Opute is one of them."

Exarth clicked her long nails on the table. Her eyes filled with purple, denoting concentration and thinking. "I didn't think he was, either. I believed in him. I *loved* him. But I was wrong. He helped that hospital. He deserves to die."

"How can you be sure he even knew what he supplied?"

"Two reasons," Exarth said. "One, Iry told me he saw Opute talking with the "doctors" at the hospital. He remembered seeing him speak with Arew, and as Iry can read lips and *never* forgets anything, I believe him when he says they conversed about what the supplies were for, multiple deliveries, and payments. Two, Opute was around fifteen standard years old when he made those supply drops. Plenty old enough to understand what occurred and to know the offense."

"Fifteen standard years old for his species may not be the equivalent to ours. We were aware of things on levels no children should have understood."

Exarth looked up at Coresque, putting the black contacts back into her eyes. "Regardless, he is not a child anymore and Iry said he showed no remorse for what he'd done. On top of that, he is still interfering with my life. He has stolen my property and interfered with my business plans. Opute made fools of us all. It is time to find him and end this."

Coresque let out a short breath through her nose and turned to leave. As the door opened, Exarth called out.

"I trust you are still on my side, Cor. I expect any news on Opute from your own sources to be relayed to me immediately from this moment forward."

A pause. "Of course."

* * *

Coresque made her way to her own office, thinking about her promise. Though she said she'd tell Exarth if her sources found out anything about Opute, she hadn't agreed to tell if she *herself* made contact with him. At this point, she didn't know what other path to take. She was unable to lie. From an early age she learned that whatever process allowed others to say something contrary to the truth, she did not possess it. She used to try, opening her mouth and willing herself to say something trivial, like a circular desk was a square, but felt as though something held back the words, and they wouldn't release until she made them tell the truth. Exarth knew this, so Coresque couldn't use her sources to discover any more about Opute.

Coresque knew the only way to contact him would be to use her Dream-Access, allowing her to penetrate into someone else's dream to communicate with them. Not exactly the easiest way to send a message, as she'd learned at a young age. Many individuals either didn't remember their dreams or interpreted her message the wrong way.

She leaned against a softened section of her office wall, since her solid body couldn't bend at the waist to sit in a chair. Her granite-hard skin prevented her from injury, but it came at a cost. Her limbs stuck inside themselves like a ball-and-joint socket made out of rock. She could swivel and turn, though usually accompanied by horrific grinding noises, but she couldn't bend.

Coresque let out a sigh. No matter her restrictions, she still had to warn Opute.

But how? In order to connect with someone mentally, she needed to have physically touched them first. She didn't understand the exact science, as she'd been too afraid to ever tell anyone about it, but when she came in contact with another's body, her skin picked up and stored the other being's unique mental signature, allowing her to follow the wavelength back to its owner's mind.

The problem remained that none of her sources could find him. As if he'd simply disappeared.

CHAPTER 4

HE COULD SEE HER.
She looked so beautiful.
She smiled at him and waved goodbye, headed for her ship to do one more cargo run.
Just one more and they could live happily.
They could be together.
And have a child.
He saw her, waving goodbye, her eyes alive with love for him.
He tried to tell her not to go. He had to warn her. She needed to know what would happen. But nothing came out of his mouth. He wasn't really there. He existed as someone else, watching the inevitable, watching as she caught on fire.
She still smiled as the skin melted off her bones.
She still smiled while Opute screamed.

Opute awoke with a start, jerking upright in his pilot's chair, a scream still in his throat. He took in a deep breath to dispel the nightmare only to jump again at his ship's proximity alarm. He peered out his viewport at the approaching planet,

Grassuwer.

As he entered its atmosphere, he never would have thought anyone lived on the barren sphere. There were no visible cities, buildings, or unnatural formations. The northern section of the globe contained a scattering of active volcanoes that blew smoke and ash into the sky, creating a gray haze around the upper hemisphere. The southern side consisted mostly of rock, with lava flows weaving throughout like rivers of liquid fire. But, as Opute well knew, looks could be deceiving.

Opute guided his ship just north of the equator to the city of Garvid. He led his cruiser into a large canyon, flying deeper and deeper until he saw a carved-out portion that wasn't natural. Flying into it, he docked.

Opute unconsciously tapped his fingers on the low ceiling of his ship before stepping off, an old superstitious habit he'd had for years. The theory stated that touching the ceiling before you disembarked let the ship know you planned to return, so she didn't leave without you. He didn't actually believe it, but he'd done it since his first cargo transport assignment and he wasn't about to take any chances now.

Opute paid the docking clerk and made his way down four flights of stairs to the visitor's lounge in the station to wait for the underground transport. Less than an hour later, a long tubular-shaped vehicle pulled up before him. Opute boarded the rust-covered monstrosity and found a place to sit. The seat sat very high, as Grassuwerians were much taller than his own species, and Opute felt a bit foolish as his feet dangled several centimeters from the floor—like a child sitting in an adult's chair.

The vehicle lurched forward and Opute frantically grabbed at a large pole, which hung down from the ceiling. Once he got comfortable with the turns, Opute stared out his window. Unfortunately, since Grassuwerians lived underground, he traveled through a tunnel, and his view consisted of a dirt-packed wall. To keep himself from getting bored, he looked around his compartment and studied the other passengers.

Opute's compartment seated twelve, but only seven seats contained occupants. He didn't recognize the species of one of the passengers, but the other five were Grassuwerians, all male, which he could tell due to their light-green coloring. Opute had only met a couple of Grassuwerians in his life: one in a neighboring city on Grassuwer during a business interaction, and one on his home planet, C-Sector 9, C-9 for short. Opute had been surprised at the meeting on C-9, since most Grassuwerians never left their home planet, unless they travelled with an entire colony.

Grassuwerians lived similarly to hive insects. Their queens connected the colonies through telepathy and their males were workers or breeders. Female Grassuwerians made up about one in ten million and each one led a different faction. They were fiercely protected and not allowed to leave their homeworld. The rarity of finding a male Grassuwerian off-planet paled in comparison to meeting a female.

So when Opute had first met Zarsa, a female Grassuwerian living by herself on C-9, he couldn't help wondering about her story. After they'd worked together several times, Opute finally asked. He remembered Zarsa smiling and telling him she admired his restraint at not asking sooner. Most wanted to know right away.

Zarsa told him about her genome defect. After her birth, the queen disowned her when she discovered Zarsa had no telepathic abilities.

"I didn't know some females don't have those abilities," Opute had told her.

"It's a highly guarded secret. Most queens are ashamed to give birth to one. They believe it shows weakness in their gene pool and can be viewed as a good reason for the other queens to use it against her and her position. Since my queen, which is what you would call my mother, had such a high ranking, she didn't want to lose her position."

"So what happened to you?"

"They changed my skin color to light green, that of a male. They erased my memories and I became a worker. At an older age, I realized what they'd done and changed my skin back. For some reason, my memory wipe failed."

"What did you do?"

"I confronted my queen. She denied the truth and sentenced me to death, but I escaped and left the planet."

"No going back home then?"

She feigned a grin, baring her teeth. "Not unless my mother dies. The use of telepathy is the only thing that keeps the queens in power. Millions of years ago, males lost their ability to connect telepathically. The queens took that opportunity to build themselves an empire, certain their retention of those genes meant they should lead. But I think our species is evolving not to have telepathy as a trait. I believe telepathy will eventually bleed its way out of our society. If that happens, we'll have to change everything about the way we function."

As he rode the shuttle, Opute felt glad to be seeing Zarsa again, and wondered if her mother had died, since she now lived back on her homeworld. He felt himself getting lost in some of their happier moments together, when a sudden halt of the shuttle at his stop brought him back to the present.

The platform he stepped onto looked exactly the same as the one he'd left. A brief moment of panic struck him at the idea he had gone in a circle. To his relief, he saw the new platform number posted above him.

Opute walked through several underground passageways, trying his best to ignore the stares from the Grassuwerians around him. He finally came to his destination, entered, and headed toward the elevator. He instructed the elevator to take him to floor 3G7, per Zarsa's instructions, and grasped tightly to the handle above him for support as it took off in a horizontal direction. The handle hung high above, forcing him to stand on his toes to reach it. The elevator stopped just as suddenly and Opute stumbled out, muttering apologies to the Grassuwerian male he bumped into. The Grassuwerian sneered as the doors closed between him and Opute.

Opute forced his clenched fists to open. Already frustrated with his surroundings, he itched for a fight to vent his anger. He wiped his hands on his shirt, much more aggressively than he needed to, and made his way to the front desk. A young Grassuwerian male looked up.

"Hello, off-worlder. How may I assist you today?"

"I have a meeting with Zarsa ..." Opute trailed off. He had no idea if Zarsa had a surname. Either she didn't, or it didn't matter, because the Grassuwerian behind the desk nodded his head.

"Of course. Zarsa is expecting you. I will call her to let her know you have arrived."

"Thanks."

Opute began to sit in one of the chairs when he heard a soft voice behind him.

"Late, as usual."

Opute felt the grin spread across his face before he straightened and turned around. He took a few steps toward Zarsa and then stopped, not sure how to greet her. They had parted on...uneasy terms. Zarsa caught his tentativeness and motioned for him to follow her toward her office.

"It's good to see you again," he mumbled as they walked through the high-ceilinged corridor.

Zarsa flashed him a smile. "You, too."

Opute watched her walk in front of him, admiring her curvy thorax. She stood about a third of a meter taller than him, but it made for a great view. Flashes of past intimate nights with her flittered through his thoughts.

Zarsa led Opute into her office. They both sat down and faced eachother, although Opute did so without as much grace on the elevated seat. Zarsa spoke first.

"It surprised me to hear from you after all these years."

"I know. Sorry it's been so long. I've been ..."

"Busy," she finished for him. "Some things never change."

Opute cleared his throat. "How have you been?"

"I've been all right. Business died down since the Aleet Army incident last year. Smugglers weren't as sought after anymore. So I started this business instead. It doesn't attract too much attention, which I like, but it's pricy enough that I don't need a high volume of clientele to keep a growing profit." She stopped. "What's so funny?"

Opute's smile vanished. "You've changed is all. It's strange to see you... business-like."

"I suppose I got bored with the old life. Who knows? I'll probably leave this and start something else in the next couple of years. You can't really keep doing the same thing all the time. It gets stale after a while."

"This time it'll be different."

"Where have I heard that before?"

Opute bit his tongue. He didn't want to argue with her. They'd done enough of that seven years ago when they were involved. He'd already spent three years looking for Exarth. He hemorrhaged away his money, joined up with the wrong crowd, got hooked on twig, and had pretty much destroyed whatever life he had left. Why she ever let him in her life, he couldn't begin to know.

"You still in touch with anyone from the trade?" he asked,

redirecting the conversation.

Zarsa slung her one arm over her shoulder. "Not really. They remind me of that time in my life. I prefer not dwelling on it." She paused. "You seem different now, too."

"I'm off twig, have been for a while. After you sent me packing, it took me about two years to sort myself out."

"I didn't want to, you know."

"You did the right thing. I was a mess."

She paused. "So what changed?"

"Exarth killed someone I knew—a friend."

"I'm sorry to hear that."

"And I'm sorry… for everything."

Zarsa chewed on the bottom of her lip. "Seven years is a long time. We've both changed." She unwound her arm and cleared her throat, her eyes glistening. "Let's just focus on your procedure." She brought up some things on her datapad for Opute to review.

"This should be a fairly simple process. You tell me what you want done, I scan your face and body into my system, we digitally change your image until you are satisfied, and then we move on to the procedure."

"Sounds easy enough."

"Well, we discussed the initial fee; that covers your consultation and assessment. The rest of the payment relies on how much you want changed."

Opute sat back in his chair. He almost toppled over and quickly brought himself back into an upright position. "The face. And the hair. But I'm not sure about the body."

Zarsa smiled, eyeing his muscular physique. "Let's scan you, make a few digital changes to your face and hair, and proceed from there." She motioned for him to follow her into the next room, dimly lit by a single green bulb.

Zarsa pointed where Opute needed to stand. "I'll need you

to undress, so we can get an accurate scan. You'll also need these." Zarsa handed him a pair of darkened glasses. "Trust me."

Opute removed his clothes, put on the glasses, and stood on the mark. The room felt nice and warm. He heard a humming noise somewhere near his feet, which got louder as it rose toward his head. Without warning, a bright light splashed across his face, causing him to involuntarily squeeze his eyes closed.

"Relax your eyes or the image will be distorted!"

Opute obeyed Zarsa's order. Still uncomfortably bright, Opute felt thankful for the darkened glasses. Then, as abruptly as it began, the light disappeared, although the humming continued from his head down to the floor.

After a few more moments, the noise stopped.

"You can remove the glasses now."

He took them off slowly, letting his eyes adjust to the green light before looking over at Zarsa.

"Am I done?"

Zarsa smiled and handed him a robe. "Yes. We can go back into my office and start changing your image digitally."

Opute slid on the robe and followed her, but when he walked into the room, his vision blurred.

"What's wrong with my eyes?" he asked, rubbing them roughly.

"Ah," Zarsa replied as she sat on her stool. "I wondered what effect the light system would have on you. I've only ever used this process on Grassuwerians. Our eyes are designed to withstand drastic light changes. I had those darkened glasses designed especially for your eyes after you contacted me. The blurriness should only be temporary." Zarsa gestured toward a holographic screen projected in front of them. A perfect three-dimensional image of Opute appeared at one-sixth his normal size. Zarsa zoomed in on his face.

"What would you like to change about your face?"

Opute stared, his eyesight clearing. He examined every line, every curve, and surprisingly, every wrinkle. By no means old at thirty-one standard years of age, the wear and tear of his lifestyle still left their mark.

Opute studied himself, wondering where to start. Short dark hair, only a few centimeters long, which he'd kept the same way most of his life. His gray eyes appeared flat and cold, giving off no emotion, which he'd trained himself to do. Average eyebrows, neither bushy nor thin, and a large nose. Thin lips, round mouth, and a strong chin. His ears stuck out, and although not shown here, he knew he had dimples when he smiled.

"How do I start?" he asked.

"Start giving off modifications and the program will show you what that will look like."

"Okay. Let's change the hair to blond."

Instantly the image of Opute had blond hair.

"Not bad. Make it longer."

"Please specify length," the program responded.

"Oh. Umm ... increase length by five centimeters."

The image of Opute now had blonde hair to his ears. Already the difference amazed him.

Opute spent the next hour modifying the image before him, changing hair, eyes, nose, chin, ears, and eyebrows. He finally settled on a nondescript image that looked nothing like him, but one he thought he wouldn't hate to see in a reflector unit.

"I think that will work," he said, satisfied.

Zarsa's blue teeth glistened as she smiled. "Now on to body modifications." She pulled up the screen of Opute's entire body.

They went through the same process, though he found

himself less willing to change his large and muscular physique.

Finally satisfied, Opute signed the form for the procedure to begin, specifying the modifications he wanted. He'd assumed he would have to wait a few days or be prepped beforehand and felt surprised when Zarsa lead him into the operating room.

"Remember," Zarsa said, "it will take several days to fully heal, but everything is non-reversible. I have an eighty percent payment return guarantee if you are not satisfied, or I will remodify you for free. If you do decide to change your appearance again, either to something else or back closer to the original way you looked, I will only charge you fifty percent of the original payment, as a token for being a return customer." Zarsa paused from what sounded like a well-rehearsed speech. "Is anything unclear or do you have any questions?"

"No."

"Do you wish to change your mind or would you like more time to think things over?"

"No."

"Very well, then. Please deliver your payment in the small black box, remove your clothing, and lay face up." Zarsa turned and left.

Opute charged the payment on his card, slipped out of the robe, and climbed onto the table. As he lay there, he wondered for a brief moment at the recklessness of his decision, when he started to feel lightheaded. His hands and feet tingled. Then his whole body felt compressed under a great weight. Opute's eyelids started to close against his will and he could feel the panic rising inside him. However, much to his dismay, his arms and legs wouldn't listen to his orders and he simply lay there, paralyzed. Unable to move or call out, Opute's eyelids closed. Though he tried to fight it, he felt himself being pulled into darkness.

CHAPTER 5

SHE WAS BEAUTIFUL.
His love.
His wife.
Mahri.
He ran through the underground streets of C-9 toward their home after hearing the news of her death. The authorities were already there, combing for clues.
He turned and fled.

Opute awoke, groggy and dizzy. He winced under the room's lights, even though they shone soft and dim. He felt stiff all over. And heavy.

He sat up and cursed as his head hit one of the hanging lamps above him. The light swung back and forth, bathing the rest of the room, which consisted of soothing, earthy colors. He raised his hand to rub his tender head and found both parts bandaged in gauze. In fact, wrappings encircled his entire body.

"Good morning," a voice called out.

Opute looked up to see Zarsa walking toward him. She

began to unwind the bandages from his feet, making her way up his body. "How are you feeling?"

"Stiff," he answered. Opute started at the voice from his tender throat. It sounded higher, a tenor compared to his normal deep bass, and the quality came off flat. "I sound so different."

"That's not the only thing you'll have to get used to," Zarsa said, helping him to his feet.

"How did the procedure turn out?"

Zarsa finished unwinding the bandages around his hands and handed him a loose-fitting pair of slacks. "You tell me," she said, motioning with her head toward a large body-length reflector unit near the door.

He slid the pants on and stared at his hands. He nearly gasped at the change. His skin color, which before had been pale and creamy, now appeared a coppery-caramel color. It shone in the light as if oiled.

Opute gulped and raised his gaze to the reflector unit. He didn't recognize the man before him.

Leaning closer, Opute inspected every detail of his new appearance. His hair, which had been short and black, now appeared blonde with gold and red streaks running through it, and it hung straight to his ears. His eyes, once gray, now shimmered amber with flecks of gold. His nose had been reduced in size and his lips enlarged.

Mesmerized by the new color of his skin, he noticed the little changes to his body. Bone fragments had been added to his shoulders to build them up and broaden his back while the tendons in his neck had been reduced, giving him a smoother neckline.

"It's the best work I've ever done," Zarsa whispered, running her fingers across his back. Their tips tickled his skin. "I would never have recognized you if you walked in the door this way." Zarsa faced him, her slender, lavender fingers sliding along his eyelids, cheeks, and lips. Her eyes glowed with emotion as her hand moved to his chest. "Although, there are some parts of you that didn't need improvement." She smiled and tugged playfully at the tie of his waistband.

Opute swallowed and grasped her hand, flattered by her insinuation, but feeling a bit nervous about it as well. Not only did his body ache from the procedure, but his dream stayed prominent in his mind and guilt bled into his thoughts. He knew he had nothing to be ashamed of. He'd been with Zarsa long after Mahri's death….

But now that he'd started his quest again, being intimate with her didn't feel right.

"Zarsa…" he started.

Zarsa's eyes rolled away from his gaze. "It's okay," she murmured, dropping her hand. "It's just…it's still difficult to be around you without thinking about…us."

Opute wasn't sure what to say. Looking at her now, he realized how much she had cared about him, perhaps even loved him. He felt embarrassed and selfish.

Opute cleared his throat. "I never thanked you for everything you did for me. I mean, before. I wish I could have been better for you."

"And now?"

He thought of his nightmares. About how much culpability he felt about his wife's death. "Now I need to finish what I started."

Zarsa took a step back. She shook her head, almost unnoticeably, and motioned back to the reflector unit. "Everything will be fully healed in a few days. There's an empty room down the hall if you need a place to stay."

Opute nodded, knowing she felt hurt, but also fully aware that whatever he said right now would be wrong. He never fared well when it came to members of the opposite sex.

"I'll be back tomorrow to check on you," Zarsa continued. "Until then, keep out of direct sunlight. You can travel, but you must remain underground in the city."

"No problem." They left the operating area and arrived at the room where Opute would stay.

"See you tomorrow. Goodnight," she said shortly.

"Night." Opute shut the door behind him and cursed under his breath. He wished he knew what to say to her.

Opute checked out his room. A long, padded blanket lay on one side, a refrigeration unit for food storage to his right, a washroom to his left, and a cramped storage space directly next to that. A small table and single chair sat against the wall across from him.

Opute laid himself out on the blanket to fall asleep.

But sleep took a long time to come.

* * *

Opute awoke the next morning gritting his teeth. His whole body felt on fire. Gingerly he stood, aware of the dry, stretched feeling of his skin every time he moved. Slowly, carefully, he made his way down the corridor to Zarsa's office. He knocked softly, wincing at the pain on his knuckles, until the door slid open. Zarsa glanced up, her widened eyes quickly changed by a look of concern.

"What's wrong?"

"My skin is burning ... *everywhere*."

Zarsa rose from behind her desk and walked over to him. She pressed the end of her long arm against the side of his. Opute clamped his mouth closed against the pain. He'd experienced many forms of pain in the past, from accidental to torture, but he'd never felt anything like this. Every centimeter of his skin stung, burned, and ached. It felt like being roasted alive. The mere effort of getting to Zarsa's office had been enough for him to break into a sweat and he could feel the pressure from the small drops running down his face.

Zarsa pulled her arm away, watching his skin turn from his new copper tone to a brownish bronze. She looked up at him with sympathetic, but slightly amused eyes.

"You have an F-light burn," she told him.

"A *what* burn?"

"F-light. It's from the scanner I used on your body. It's similar to a UV light burn, but more painful and less noticeable in color change."

"How do I make it *stop* burning?" Opute asked through clenched teeth.

"I can give you a topical solution to help with the dryness. It also has a painkiller in it. Other than that, it's like a regular sunburn. You'll just have to wait it out."

Opute grumbled under his breath.

"It's my fault, really," Zarsa went on as she rummaged through a drawer looking for the topical solution. "I should have realized your skin would be much more sensitive than ours." She pulled the solution out of the drawer, encased in a long, white tube. "I'm sorry. I'll refund some of your money, if you'd like." Zarsa approached him and squeezed the tube. A dark green cream came out and she quickly spread in over his shoulders and back.

Opute, feeling the immediate relief, allowed his temper to cool.

"Don't worry about it." His entire focus revolved around waiting for her to reach the next spot on his body. It reminded him of getting an itch that started in the middle of your back, and when someone started to scratch it, it began to travel and you needed them to move to reach the next spot.

After Zarsa got the parts he couldn't reach, Opute took the tube from her and started applying the cream to his arms and chest.

"Any other side effects that might pop up?" he asked her.

Zarsa sat back down. "That's the problem; I don't know for sure. With your body chemistry being so different from ours, you could have any number of reactions." She sighed, propping her head up with her arm. "Maybe this was a bad idea."

Opute raised his head and stopped in the middle of applying the cream to his right thigh.

"It wasn't a bad idea." Opute felt the skin on his thigh stretch and went back to applying the cream. "I'm sure everything will be fine."

"When did you become such an optimist?"

Opute looked up at her with mild surprise. "An optimist? I don't think I'd go that far. I just don't think it's going to be as bad as you think."

"And if it is?"

"Then we'll deal with it." Opute finished applying the cream to his other leg and stood straight, putting the finishing touches on his face and ears.

"Well, how funny do I look?"

Zarsa smiled. "You look like you fell into a vat of gooey mold."

"I can handle that." Opute smiled back. "Will I be gooey all day?"

"No. It'll harden after a few minutes. I have another tube if you run out, but you should be fine in a day or two. Which works out okay, because that's about when your new body will have finished healing." Zarsa stood up and walked over to the door panel, which she pressed, and the door slid open in front of them. "I'll check up on you later today."

Opute had just stepped through the doors when an overwhelming urge to thank Zarsa washed over him. He had put her through so much, and now, years later, she'd helped him again, without pressuring him, without asking questions. He paused for a moment, unsure of what to say.

Zarsa's eyes sparkled. "You're welcome."

Opute opened his mouth and shook his head before closing it. Instead, he reached out, wrapping his newly changed arms around her curvy body, pulling it closely to his chest.

"Thanks for not making me try to say it. You know how bad I am with words."

Zarsa made a noise somewhat like a whimper and Opute pulled away quickly. Zarsa's face and chest were now covered with the dark green gooey substance.

Opute's eyes widened in horror. "I forgot!"

Zarsa took her hand and slowly wiped grime from each eye.

"It's okay. I suppose I deserved it, since I was the one to give you the burn in the first place." She grinned. "Just, try to wait until it's dry next time, okay?"

Opute promised, backing away. Once out of sight, he heaved a sigh of relief. He still never figured out how he'd managed to hang on to Mahri. Luck had apparently been on his side, a lot of it.

Opute walked back into his temporary sleeping quarters thinking about his wife. She should never have taken that last job, even though she'd thought it a sure thing. But how could she have known? Thlin, an old associate, set up the deal for her. Neither of them had a reason not to trust him.

And the only thing Opute ever learned was Thlin had taken orders from Exarth to lead Mahri into a trap and blow up her ship.

Anger flared inside him, anger at himself for giving up on hunting Exarth down, anger at Thlin for setting up his wife, even anger at Mahri for dying, but his rage had nowhere to go. He simply felt too exhausted. With his whole body still healing, not to mention the new F-light burn he had just acquired, he didn't have any reserves.

Opute plopped himself down on the chair and sat. Since he wasn't too much of a reader and his room had a beautiful underground view of a wall of dirt, Opute simply sat there, staring at nothing, waiting for the green goo to dry.

CHAPTER 6

"**YOU TOLD ME** he was dead!" Exarth's body trembled with fury as she threw a datapad across her office desk at the man standing there. The datapad stated Ness Opute had stolen six of her battle cruisers and interfered with her business dealings the previous year with the Aleet Army. "He stole from me, ruined my plans, and even though he's still alive, he has mysteriously fallen off the radar. And you knew he wasn't dead!"

The man stood across from her, calm, his white eyes unblinking. He'd wondered if this day would come. He *hoped* it wouldn't, but he never doubted it might. He let out a sigh.

"Yes, he's alive. I never killed him. I misled you."

Exarth's nails dug into the desk's metallic surface. "You've got one chance, Iry, to explain why that is. And I better *like* your explanation."

He crossed his bleach-white hands in front of him. "I realized after I'd told you how he helped perpetuate our horrific childhoods, you would want revenge. And I didn't want you to waste years of your life in pursuit of a hopeless situation. Opute is a wisp of smoke, not unlike how you are a phantom," Iry said, resisting the urge to lean against her desk. It bothered him to no end she didn't have an extra chair in her office. Just because he appeared as ice-white as Coresque, didn't mean he had her abnormal rock-hard skin and inability to bend.

"Don't show off with riddles and metaphors," Exarth spat.

Iry let out a whispered sigh of disappointment. "He is untouchable, my dear, like you are. Follow a lead to his whereabouts and he's already two planets away. Ask for him by name and cold silence fills your ears. Whether out of loyalty or fear makes no difference, the result is the same: he cannot be located."

"Cor said she found him."

He felt a throb in his temple. "Coresque said she *tracked* him. Tracking is simple; finding is a completely different game."

"I would've found him…" Exarth grumbled.

"Most likely," Iry consented, "but what would've been the expense of his inevitable demise? Your life remained divided at the time. You were teetering, unsure of which direction to take. Finding him may have pushed you beyond the point of redemption."

"You had no problem with me crossing that line when we returned to the hospital and I slit everyone's throats."

"That needed to be done for cleansing purposes. But think of the thousands who helped those doctors continue with their experiments. Would you have found them all and murdered them just to slake your own thirst for vengeance?"

"Yes!" Exarth hissed fiercely.

"Precisely. And after your reaction to the news Opute helped them, I knew I had to step in and control the situation."

Exarth barked a laugh as she leaned back in her chair. "Always dictating my life, aren't you? I sometimes wonder if I've made any decisions on my own or if you are always nudging me toward the path you want me to take."

Iry paused, hesitant to respond. Exarth may only be ranting, but if she knew the accuracy of her statement...

"At that moment in your life, yes, you needed guidance. Can you honestly deny that? You were at a crossroads and I...I deceived you to push you along a certain path. I said I'd done the deed for you. I believed I could bear the brunt of your anger over not killing him yourself more than seeing you lose your life to a perilous route. I couldn't watch you do that."

"It wasn't your decision to make!"

"Yes, it was!" Iry said, his temper flaring. Exarth pursed her lips, but did not reply.

"We were a team," he continued, his anger subdued. "You, me, and Coresque. We were the only ones left from the hospital. We balanced each other. Coresque dreamed, I thought, and you did. Take one of us away and the other two perish. Without Coresque, you and I are socially inept, realists without dreams. Without me, you and Coresque cannot see beyond the next step, and are victims of your own emotions. And without you, Coresque and I cannot implement our ideas into action, nor can we find ourselves outside of our own minds.

"We were too spread out, thinned and flung bare to the cosmos. I couldn't lose you to a murderous spree of revenge when the three of us together had the power to achieve anything. And look what we've accomplished," he exclaimed. "We've established a hold in the galaxy that surpasses any other government, corporation, or crime lord. That is no small feat."

Exarth said nothing at first, merely tapping her fingernail on her desk. "We are a team. But I need to trust in you both and I feel like lately..." she trailed off. "I am not a child anymore. You will not keep me from finding him this time."

Iry shook his head. "No, I won't. He caused you personal insult by stealing your ships and interfering with our plans, especially with the Aleet Army. Our alliance with Commander Xiven would have been quite beneficial to the organization. Opute must be stopped."

"Cor said she would inform me if she heard anything more about his whereabouts. I expect you to do the same. I have, however, hired a few searchers of my own to seek him out."

"Assassins?"

"More like bounty hunters. They are instructed to bring him in alive. I will deal with him personally."

It took every bit of will power Iry had not to show his apprehension at this news. "I understand your desire to do this yourself, but wouldn't it be better if you just let them handle things? You do have quite a few projects in the works right now."

"I made the mistake once of believing someone when they told me he was dead," she snapped. "I will not make that mistake again. I will kill him myself."

Iry accepted the sting from her comment and lied, nodding to indicate he would not interfere.

Leaving the room, Iry started calculating ways to locate Opute before Exarth, Coresque, or any of the bounty hunters did. If any of them captured Opute alive and Exarth discovered the truth about what happened so many years ago…

Iry ground his teeth so hard his jaw ached.

She got married. How could that be? He'd been so careful, tracked her as best as possible, but this past year, he had to admit he'd been too busy to keep up all the protocols.

The three of them, him, Exarth, and Coresque, had been split apart for too long. Each on their own planet, each attempting to spread their soon-to-be empire. But reports from Coresque showed she didn't know how to implement her plans. And he found the workers he oversaw beginning to resist his leadership.

They worked the best together, and he needed them to join up again.

Now Exarth had gone and got married. Planned to start a new life, away from the one Iry had worked so hard to achieve.

He hated that he couldn't do it without her.

So what to do about her husband, Ness Opute?

Iry planned for weeks, calculating every outcome, and could only come up with one solution.

Opute must become a villain and die so Exarth would not be persuaded to choose the path of love again and Exarth must appear to die to the outside world so no one would ever go looking for her.

He hired his associate, Thlin, to help him with his plan. Thlin would set up a smuggling run with Exarth. Once on board, he would flood her room with a sedative gas, land and remove her from the ship, then remote detonate it, as if it had crash landed. Thlin would then bring Exarth to Iry so he could explain everything.

When Opute returned home that night to an empty house, Iry would be waiting.

There had only been one problem: the exploding ship caused a public spectacle. Authorities surrounded Opute and Exarth's residence and Iry knew, as he watched from down the street, that Opute would never risk returning home again. His own life as a smuggler would prevent him from ever getting involved with law enforcement.

No matter, Iry believed he'd find Opute eventually to finish the task. In the meantime, he prepared himself for Exarth's reaction.

She blinked a few times, emerging from her sedated sleep. Her green contacts slid around in her eyes and she cringed. She'd cut her hair and dyed it one color. Iry didn't like it.

"Iry? What's going on? Where am I?"

He sat next to her on the bed.

"I have some unsettling news about your husband, Ness Opute." He wove the intricate tale he'd concocted about seeing Opute speaking with the administrators at the hospital they'd all escaped from and how Opute supplied this hospital so they could continue their experiments on the children.

Her reaction did not surprise him.

"This can't be. I know him. He wouldn't...he couldn't..." She paced the floor, her short, brown hair swinging underneath the lights.

Iry solidified the lie. "We have all been split up. I was unaware of your involvement with him and who he was. I came to visit, to congratulate you on your wedding, and I saw him through the window. I recognized him immediately. You know I have an eidetic memory. I do not forget."

Her hands trembled and she sat down in a chair. "That was long ago. He's changed." The words came out soft and Iry knew she doubted, knew he could convince her otherwise.

"We may have been children when I saw him, but he was not. He neared manhood. And can you honestly say he has never done anything questionable since your involvement? Or that you can account for all his time, all his dealings, his shipments?"

Iry saw her shoulders droop. He knew he'd won.

The next morning, she came demanding more.

"I want to find him. I need to talk to him, to have him explain why he, how he..."

Iry braced himself. "You can't. He's dead."

Her face froze for a moment with shock. "What? How?"

"I didn't trust him and with good reason. Before I could come to you I needed to have proof. And I had it. I arranged for your smuggling run with Thlin, to secure you. I had to know you'd be safe. I went that night to confront him, to ask him the questions we both needed answers to. He surprised me. He didn't deny any of it. He laughed at how much credit he'd made during those transactions and said he was sorry the hospital shut down, as it had been his largest source of income.

"I realized then and there he only told me this because he had no intention of letting me live. He didn't realize though I contained a recording device on my body. I ran. I'm not proud, but I did. I knew I wouldn't be any match for him in a one-on-one fight."

"But you didn't get away, did you?" she asked, her hands balled in fists, wetness rimming her eyes.

"No. Rain had slicked the pavement that night and I slipped next to the riverbank. He bowled into me and we tumbled over the river rocks into the water. I prepared for a watery struggle, but none came. He lay there, head bashed open on a rock, dead. I pushed him down the river and exited the scene. My only regret is the recording became damaged in the fall so I cannot produce it for you."

He watched her carefully, gauging the expressions on her face, searching for any flaws in his own story.

"And his body?" she asked.

"Found the next day by the authorities. I sent Thlin to the morgue to destroy the remains, lest they somehow trace back to you." He paused, the following words dry on his lips. "I'm truly sorry, Exarth."

The tale sated her. Iry stood by her through her grief, her rage, her resolution never to be separated from him and Coresque again. They traveled to Belxa and set up headquarters there. They reached out, slowly gaining control of corporations, governments, religious affiliations.

But Exarth rarely left. She became a ghost, never confiding in anyone else again.

And Iry controlled her.

CHAPTER 7

AFTER ENDURING THE fiery sensation from his F-light burn, itching from his healing skin, and being covered in goop, Opute couldn't wait to leave the closed quarters of his room. It had been two days since his surgery and he fidgeted inside his new body to get outdoors, see the sky again, and get back on his ship.

Opute grabbed a small bag, which contained two sets of clothes to fit his altered frame, his money card, and new sets of identification, then headed to Zarsa's office to say goodbye. The door slid open after he pressed the buzzer. Opute entered and stood in front of her desk.

"Guess you're taking off, huh?"

"Yeah."

Zarsa, who hadn't looked up from her desk, fiddled with a stack of datacards in front of her. Opute had never seen Zarsa so ill at ease.

"Is something wrong?" he asked.

"No, nothing's wrong."

Opute cleared his throat, unsure of what to do. The tension

in the room mounted and he couldn't pinpoint why.

"Well ..." he started. "I guess I should get going."

"I guess so."

"So ... see you sometime?"

Zarsa finally raised her head. "Do you want to stay?" she blurted out.

Opute, caught off guard by the comment, paused before saying, "Is there something else wrong with me?"

Zarsa shook her head. "No, nothing like that. I just thought, well, maybe you ..." she sighed. "Maybe you would want to stay because you ... because you want to stay." She hesitated. "With me," she added.

Opute stood there, uncertain of what to say, but knowing whatever it was, it would be wrong.

"I mean," she continued in a rushed tone, "now that you have this new body, you could start a new life. Stop running and chasing ghosts."

Opute took the seat across from her. He thought for a moment, trying to phrase what he wanted to say correctly, trying to put everything into the right words. He forced himself to think about the future, about how this decision would affect their life together.

He gazed at her and felt a longing he hadn't felt for anyone in years. Part of him really did want to stay with her. He knew he could adopt a new persona and be happy with Zarsa.

But a stronger part of him knew giving up again would hang over that new life, poisoning it until it leeched away any shred of joy he might find. Eventually he would resent Zarsa for it, blaming her for being the reason he gave up.

He cared for her too much to do that to her.

"Zarsa, I can't. Don't get me wrong, being around you again has been great, it's just…this is something I have to do. The first time, I simply felt angry. I wanted to create pain, as much as I felt."

"But things seem so different now," she told him. "*You* seem different. You aren't the same man I knew back then—literally and figuratively. Ness Opute doesn't exist anymore. So why do you need to fight his battles?"

"He may not exist to everyone else, but he's still me." He thumped his new fist against his sternum. "And now I'm getting a second chance to make things right. Except this time I *know* I can do it. I can't pass that up." Opute looked across the desk with a terrible sense he hadn't conveyed his feelings very well at all, and waited for Zarsa to get upset or kick him out of the room. To his surprise, she didn't.

"As much as I don't want to, I understand. And I wish you the best of luck," she told him. "Please be careful, and remember, if you ever need me, for anything, I'll be here."

Opute let out the breath he'd been holding and stood. He walked around the table and kissed her gently.

"You're incredible."

She smiled. "And you're an idiot."

"Probably." Opute smiled back. "Thanks. For everything."

With one last stroke of her cheek, he left her room, headed out of the building, and hopped onto the underground shuttle, which would take him back to his docked ship.

Opute traveled two days to Rea, a small, industrial planet, and reformatted his cruiser so it didn't appear like one of Exarth's ships anymore. The technician rounded the cruiser's blunt wingtips, added extra compartments to the ship's belly, and doubled the size of the cockpit's viewport. He then adapted the weapons to be retractable, so they weren't visible on the ship itself, slapped on a new coat of blue and gray paint, and added the final touch, a new name: the *Resolution*. Opute figured a peaceful name would keep him off the charts longer. At least he *hoped* it would.

Opute flew just out of orbit, ready to begin his plan, but although prepared, his stomach wouldn't unclench. On his way to Rea, Opute had time to think about everything he planned on doing and weighed its worth. His thoughts flitted back and forth between Zarsa and his desire to make things right with what happened to Mahri and Lang.

He believed turning down Zarsa's proposal would be best for everyone, but as he neared his destination and the first step of his plan, he couldn't deny the appeal of her offer. His journey toward Exarth would be long and arduous, and may take years. A life with Zarsa could begin right now. He even, for a moment, reached out to plot a course back.

But then the faces of his dead wife and friend flooded his mind.

And for the first time, he thought about how he'd feel if Zarsa ended up in the crossfire, if she somehow made a deal in the future with Exarth or one of her companies and it got her killed, too.

He knew what he had to do.

Opute set the coordinates to his next destination, Belxa, a planet about a day away. On Belxa, he would meet with his contact about starting work for a small weapons company, which Opute knew also had illegal dealings run indirectly by Exarth. By beginning there, Opute hoped to work for a while, and then wiggle his way upwards until he got the attention of someone higher up.

A risky plan, and quite time-consuming, but Opute figured a year or two's wait would be worth it. After all, he'd already spent several years of his life on the path of revenge; would a couple more matter?

As he settled back in his pilot seat to take a nap, he ran through everything in his head one more time: his identity, his background, his goals, and the eventual satisfaction of killing Exarth.

He drifted off to sleep with a smile on his lips.

CHAPTER 8

WHITE.

White everywhere.

White lights, white eyes, white clothes, white skin.

White walls, beds, blankets and machines. Toys, floors, and ceilings. Needles, fans, vents, doors, doorknobs, and locks.

How she hated the color white.

She couldn't get away from it. The sterile, bright room filled with white beds that lined white walls. Nurses and physicians scuttling to and fro, white machines beeping as they tracked heartbeats, blood pressure, and respiration. A sealed, white door that led out, wherever "out" was, and a panel of glass that separated the children from the viewers, who were dressed meticulously in their white lab coats or uniforms. Even the other kids looked exactly the same: white robe, white skin, white eyes, white hair.

Exarth hated white because she knew other colors existed. She remembered when they brought her to the hospital, they shaved her head. She could still picture the dark, multi-colored locks drifting to the floor.

At least, she'd been *told* it was a hospital. It took her less than a standard year after they brought her to the facility for her to realize the ruse. The building and its surroundings looked, smelled, and felt like a hospital, but she figured out the truth at six years of age.

Some of the indications were small, like strange phrases she overheard such as 'congenital defects' and 'military applications.' With some context, Exarth soon realized she and the other children were definitely different, but not necessarily sick.

Exarth also understood she didn't act the same as most of the other children in the facility. She cried less, she didn't really want to play with the provided toys—they bored her, but she often mimicked playing with them to appease the staff, and she had no desire to interact with others. She spent most of her time studying those around her, curious why they behaved the way they did, and wondering about their surroundings.

The physicians had been the biggest tip-off. They claimed they wanted to cure her and the other children, but never told them from what. Exarth remembered asking several times why they kept her here, where her family was, and when she could leave. She got replies, but they were never actually answers.

"Your family knows you are sick, but they cannot see you yet. Not until you recover."

"We told you. You and the others have to stay in the cleanroom until we can make you better."

"You are highly contagious. Do you know what that big word means? It means you can get others sick. You don't want that, do you?"

Exarth knew what contagious meant. She also knew there were too many inconsistencies for the doctors to be telling the truth. Like how her family were instructed not to contact her. They said her family could get sick, too, but she knew a vidlink message wouldn't break quarantine. Or they could stand outside the room behind the thick glass walls in the white suits, just like the other "doctors" in white uniforms would do when they watched the children play.

She also noticed none of the "doctors" ever wore anything to prevent them from breathing the same air as the children. If they could catch the disease, why weren't the "doctors" afraid of getting it, too? If the staff were immune, why not produce something so that others, like the children's families, would stay healthy?

At that point, whenever she saw any of the physicians, she couldn't think of them as real physicians. They were always "doctors" from then on, pretenders masquerading around until she could determine their real purpose. Other staff members, like nurses and attendants helped in between, but Exarth could always tell the difference. The "doctors" came in quickly with an air of arrogance and hostility, like they had better things to do than deal with children.

The biggest reveal of all? None of the children had the same symptoms.

Two standard years after her arrival, at 8 years old, she sat on her bed, getting another weekly blood sample drawn from her pale, thin arm, when one of the other children, two beds down, began to cough. There wasn't anything remarkable about it; it started as a rasp, like when someone swallowed something down the wrong pipe, but then it changed. The cough became guttural, coming from the child's diaphragm, and it rocked him with every breath he expelled. Exarth turned her gaze toward him, just like the other children, and saw flecks of whitish material fly out of his mouth.

The attendant, focused solely on the blood draw from Exarth's arm, only looked when a collective gasp sprung from the other children's lips. The attendant's eyelids widened and she immediately called out for assistance from the other staff members.

"Liph is early! They're coming early!" She bolted from Exarth's side to the boy's, whose coughs quickly turned into sharp hacks.

Suddenly, he threw up.

The other children were once again collective in their response, but this time in a sound of disgust. Most looked away, but Exarth stared, fixated. White bubble-like structures propelled from the boy rolled onto the bed, covered in a transparent and slimy white substance. Inside each of the bubbles something moved. Exarth strained her eyes to see, but found after a few moments, she didn't have to squint anymore. The objects inside grew larger. She made out hands, feet, and a head.

They were babies!

Exarth watched with bated breath. The attendants, now joined by one of the "doctors," frantically scooped up the white bubbles and placed them into a large bag. The boy kept throwing up, his eyes bleeding white blood, until the "doctor" screamed at the tallest of the attendants to get him out of the room.

"Do you want all these clones to start growing on the floor?" the "doctor" screeched. "Get him out of here, now!"

The attendant swooped Liph under his arm and sprinted away, swiping a card at the door jamb, and shoving through the normally sealed doors. Minutes later he returned, out of breath, and paused for a moment at the continued commotion.

Exarth stared with morbid curiosity, her eyes wide. The bag bulged as the bubbles continued to expand. The attendants had almost gathered them all when Exarth heard a sickening 'pop'. One of the bubbles burst, drenching the bottom of the bag with slimy fluids.

An earthshaking cry rang out from inside.

"For the love of the stars! One hatched." The shorter

attendant dropped her edge of the sack and shrank back in terror. "It's alive. It's actually alive!"

The "doctor" almost spilled the entire contents on the floor. "You imbecile!" she screamed at the shorter attendant over the loud cries. "You almost made me drop this!"

The shorter attendant did not seem to hear this. She wrung her pale hands and backed away toward the door. The bag moved, she screamed, then tore out of the room.

The "doctor" cursed and finished shoving the rest of the bubbles into the bag. She slung the bag over her shoulder, white fluids drenching her lab coat, and headed toward the exit. The doors swished closed behind her and an eerie silence blanketed the room.

One of the children burst into tears, causing most of the others to jump. In a few moments, several more joined in. The only children who remained quiet seemed to be in shock.

Exarth quietly sat back down and thought about what just happened. The boy, Liph, seemed like everyone else. A newer addition to their group, having been brought in only a few months prior, he seemed fairly normal. He ate the same meals they did and got visited by an attendant every week, just like everyone else. So what was distinctive about him?

Exarth wracked her brain, trying to remember if she had seen him treated differently. Then she realized: he got shots in his stomach. The other children got blood drawn from their arms, but he got something extracted from his belly into the syringe.

"The clones," she said under her breath. She did not fully understand what clones were, except they were babies that grew really fast. The "doctors" must have wanted Liph because he had those babies in his stomach and the process went wrong today.

Liph needed to be in the hospital for having babies, but

that did not explain her own presence. They never put needles in her stomach. What made her so different? Even worse, what if something went wrong with her, too?

She glanced around at the other children, some crying, some sitting on their beds. She saw fear in most of their eyes when they turned her way, but not in all. A couple of the children, two girls and one boy, had a different look in their eyes. They were *thinking* just like her.

Exarth mentally noted their bed numbers until she could get to know them better. Maybe if they all thought about it together, they could figure out the truth.

Exarth sat back on her bed, tired from the stimulus of the day. While adjusting herself, she felt a strange poke in her arm. Curious, she looked down and saw a needle embedded under her skin. She realized the attendant left it when she went running toward Liph. Exarth grasped it to pull it out when she noticed something unusual: the skin in her arm had healed *around* the needle.

Exarth had to scratch open her skin to remove it. A small bead of white blood appeared where she broke the skin's surface, but she smeared it away quickly and pulled the needle out. She stared at the small hole in her arm and watched it close.

Amazed, but a little scared, she tried to remember if this ever happened to her before. She never had bad scrapes and cuts like the other kids. In fact, she never had bruises after falling, and when she did fall, it never took her more than a few minutes to start moving again, even if she landed on her ankle or arm in a funny way.

Could she really heal quickly? Faster than everyone else could?

Wanting to test this theory, Exarth grasped the needle in her hand like a dagger. Taking a deep breath, she scratched it down the side of her arm, wincing at the burst of pain. White blood flowed through the wound instantly, but stopped almost as quickly. Exarth licked her fingers and wiped away as much blood as possible, revealing a perfectly intact arm without any scrape or scar. And the pain subsided as well.

I'm different. Just like Liph is different. Except that instead of making babies, I can heal myself. Exarth thought about it a little longer as she made another scratch down her arm with the same results as before. *I don't think I'm sick. I doubt anyone can catch this.*

So why am I here?

CHAPTER 9

THE JOB RECRUITMENT center sat in the middle of a busy city on the northern side of Belxa, a planet that made Opute's skin crawl.

Belxa existed as a ball of dirt, sand, and stone. *Nothing* lived on it. At least, not naturally. Original settlers brought atmospheric shield generators designed to block out much of the light, heat, and ultraviolet rays from Belxa's close sun. Not to mention the methane storms that rolled occasionally throughout the day. Underneath the shields, the cities on the planet developed, importing water and soil to grow plants and support livestock.

But to Opute, the cities looked like bubbles of color surrounded by death; death that pressed in on all sides of the shields, waiting for the moment when their energy depleted enough to fail and the heat would come in like a blast furnace, drying up all the moisture in a matter of hours.

He wasn't blind to the comparison of Belxa to a ship in space surrounded by the nothingness of a vacuum. Yet one big difference separated the two: Opute's ship ran under his control. If something went wrong, he would fix it. Being under an atmospheric generator on a planet run by a complete stranger…he didn't have faith in that.

Opute took a deep breath and entered the building, stepping through a pair of huge wooden doors. He stood just inside the doorway, his copper skin shimmering under the hanging chandelier. Though stoic and professional on the outside, Opute's insides churned with nerves. Intergalactic Transporters were rumored to have dealings with Exarth, so that's where he'd try and get his first job. Taking the first step toward reaching her.

Clenching his jaw, Opute started forward. His eyes flitted back and forth as he scanned his surroundings. Always looking for possible exits or entrances, his gaze spotted the latched windows surrounding the interior balcony above him, and four doors; two to his left about three meters apart, a large, old-fashioned wooden one with a hefty iron bar across it to his right, and the glimpse of the edge of one behind the grand staircase in front of him. His usual job as a smuggler kept him on his toes.

An aged man made his way across the imposing room, shuffling his feet on the dark blue carpeting that ran from the staircase to the front door. Dressed in an iridescent wrap, his sunken eyes and puckered skin made Opute think of someone who had risen from the dead. The man stopped a few meters away, bowed his head slightly, and gestured for him to follow.

Opute complied, finding it unusual the man hadn't spoken at all, and wondering if perhaps he had been instructed not to. Or maybe he couldn't. Imagination running wildly for a moment, he pictured a rotted tongue, lolling useless inside the man's decayed mouth.

Opute shook the disturbing image from his mind. The man continued on with his shuffle and led him through the door located behind the staircase. Again he gestured wordlessly for

Opute to take a seat. The man dragged his feet as he left, his bandaged body shimmering in the soft lights.

After sitting down in a beautifully carved, dark purple wooden chair in front of a huge, curved matching wooden desk, Opute looked around. The ceiling arched above him, a rich cream color, and converged into a point from which another elaborate chandelier hung. The bright amber-colored light splashed the walls, casting shadows against the pale curtains, which had been drawn shut over the single window to the left.

A set of paintings, both framed in the same purple wood, hung behind the desk, depicting landscapes of a place Opute had never seen. Skies of a striking yellow covered the first one, dotted with pale green clouds that sent out bolts of dark green electrical discharges. Dark purple flowers, whose heads bent and sagged from the rain, dotted the countryside. The second painting looked like the same picture, except in different colors—green sky, blue clouds, red flowers.

The colors in both pieces of art began to shift and change. They melted into russets and crimsons, grays and blacks, blues and teals. And then, in the first picture, it stopped raining. The sun peeked out from behind one of the clouds and the flowers raised their heads, spreading their petals toward the shining light.

Opute shifted his gaze from the paintings and turned his attention to the intricate sculpture to the side of the desk. A bust of a woman's head, which looked to be made of white stone. It glistened under the amber lights. Opute found her beautiful, with large eyes, a curvaceous mouth, and hair that hung past her shoulders.

Opute leaned closer, fascinated by the final detail of the piece: a translucent veil hanging over the woman's face. The intricacies of the sculpted veil mesmerized him. He almost felt he could lift it to see the woman's face better.

While staring, Opute's body tensed at the sound of the door opening behind him. Casually, he turned to face the newest addition to the room. To his surprise, two individuals entered, one female and one male. The female he recognized immediately as the woman from the sculpture. Her face appeared as white as the bust itself and her long hair as pale as snow. What struck Opute the most though were her eyes. They had no pigment; they didn't even have pupils.

Opute shifted in his chair, trying not to stare. She seemed to almost glide across the floor, her steps so close together that the upper part of her body barely moved. He realized the other sections of her body weren't really moving at all either—at least, not normally. Her knees didn't bend when she walked, her legs barely separated, and her arms didn't swing. Except for the quick movement of her feet, Opute could have mistaken her for a statue rolling into the room.

Shifting his focus, Opute's gaze drifted over to the male, a sharp contrast to the woman. Short and squat with flushed cheeks, the man looked like he'd been shut up in a steam room for several days. By the time the two of them reached the other side of the desk, the man had already wiped perspiration from his face and neck twice with a dampened cloth.

The man promptly sat and the woman stood behind him, as still as her statue.

"Thank you for coming on such short notice, Mister... uh..."

"Gaaht," Opute filled in, giving the man his new name. "Vor Gaaht."

"Right, right. Mr. Gaaht." The man shuffled through some papers, datapads, and other knick-knacks on his desk before continuing.

"Well, Mr. Gaaht, the reason you are here is because you wish to become an employee of Intergalactic Transporters, is this correct?"

"Yes."

"Good, good," he muttered, wiping his face again. "I'm Paja and this is Coresque," he said with a dismissive wave at the woman behind him.

Opute gave a quick glance at Coresque, but she didn't acknowledge the remark. He wondered if a rule applied to the staff like the doorman, to be seen and not heard.

"A pleasure," Opute said, returning his eyes back to the man.

"Yes, yes. A pleasure." Paja paused from his shuffling and glanced up at Opute. "Hmm..." he said, staring. Opute felt his chest tighten.

"Definitely, definitely," Paja continued. "You seem perfect. You're hired."

Opute's eyebrows arched in surprise. "That's it?"

"Uh-huh, uh-huh," Paja confirmed as he went back to his shuffling. Opute wasn't sure what Paja meant to accomplish with his desk items, but they never seemed to get more organized.

"I'm a superb judge of character," Paja went on, pausing to wipe his head, "and I know you are right for the job." Opute watched as the cloth, now oversaturated with liquid, dripped onto the desk. Paja didn't notice and smeared the droplets with the papers.

"Thank you," Opute said. "You won't regret this, sir." He paused. "Do you have a job specs contract for me?"

Paja slapped his forehead with a wet, smacking sound.

"Of course, of course! How forgetful of me." Paja handed Opute a datapad from under the mess on his desk. "Ah...this is the one. Everything you need is on that datapad. Scan through it and let me know if you have any questions."

Opute glanced down at the datapad. He heard Paja snap

his fingers and he looked up. Coresque tilted toward Paja rigidly, unable to bend at the waist. Paja whispered something that Opute couldn't make out and Coresque left the room, accidentally brushing against his shoulder with her arm. Hard as stone and cold as ice.

Opute brought his full attention back to the datapad.

Everything looked as he expected. The contract lasted for one standard year, once training was finished, with Intergalactic Transporters. Pay would be per assignment, but would always total at least twenty-five percent of a standard week's hours, with an option of up to one hundred percent of a week if traveling. He would be doing manual labor, which included pick-ups and drop-offs, loading and unloading of merchandise, and cleaning of transport vessels.

The next section of the datapad contained a confidentiality contract, in which, once signed, Opute couldn't discuss any clients or merchandise with anyone other than Intergalactic Transport or the clientele involved. Grounds for termination included breaking the confidentiality agreement, not performing duties up to standards set by the company, missing deliveries, or repeated late, mishandled, or damaged property.

Opute could only get out of the contract if promoted inside the company, severely injured and could no longer perform the necessary tasks assigned to him, or killed. In very small print at the bottom, he found the ever-necessary disclaimer which stated the previously mentioned terms were subject to change at any time, without notice, and without reason.

"Looks fine to me," Opute said, signing along the bottom of the datapad, "When do I go in for training?"

Paja looked up from his desk. "Tomorrow, if that is convenient for you, Mister Gaaht."

"That's ... that's fine," Opute said, not expecting such a fast turn-around.

"Very good, very good." Paja handed Opute a second datapad as he took the first one back. "You will go to this address tomorrow morning. Everything you need to know including attire, items to bring, breaks, what to expect, and other frequently asked questions are on that datapad." Paja stood up abruptly and stuck out his hands, palms up.

Opute stood as well. He hesitantly placed his hands on top of Paja's, not sure on the proper procedure. Paja gripped his hands briefly from below.

"Good luck, Mister Gaaht, good luck. If you have any other questions, don't hesitate to call the office."

Opute thanked Paja and left the room, wiping Paja's sweat off his hands. The aged man waiting outside shuffled slowly in front of Opute toward the exit. Opute followed him, nodding a goodbye at the completely white woman who stood at the bottom of the stairs.

* * *

Coresque shook. Could the man have been Ness Opute? He didn't look anything like the description she'd been given. He made no mention of anything that would lead her to believe in an alternate identity. And yet…

Coresque couldn't put her finger on it. She did know he hid something from them. There was a reason she'd been put in charge of hiring—her uncanny ability to sense a lie. Something in their movements and body language. Or their energy didn't match their words. She had never been wrong.

This man, this Mr. Gaaht, held something back. She should have asked Paja to push for a backstory so Coresque could listen to him lie, but Paja's job entailed hiring the first disposable individual to walk through the door. A one-way trip, although the individual would never know that.

But Gaaht...everything about him screamed he felt uncomfortable; not with the situation, but inside his own skin. And the inflection in his voice—no one was *that* eager to sign up without a proper interview. Paja hadn't asked for credentials, references, or even experience. That would have made anyone suspicious, and although Gaaht seemed surprised, he hadn't questioned it.

But when the coppery skin of his shoulder touched against her arm, Coresque knew the man had tremendous pain. She felt it ooze through his pores. His mind did not belong to that body.

She reflected on the universe, her thoughts spreading out into the cosmos, wondering about possibilities. Her mind slowly put things together, details about a man who recently fell off the radar. Ness Opute. No one could find him. What if that meant he'd changed his appearance?

But why? No one would want to stop being a successful smuggler with plenty of clients, a long list of allies, and a formidable reputation. Why apply for a grunt position in a cargo transport company making a third of what he could on his own?

Coresque let the feelings of Opute flow through her.

She envisioned a young man in love with his wife... happy...content...

She saw him torn apart with grief and rage when he learned of his wife's death...

She pictured him desperate with misery, knowing only thoughts of revenge, pursuing a way to end his suffering and never getting it...

She understood how hard that must have been, to let go but never have closure.

And then his enemy resurfaced, murdering someone else close to him...taunting him...always just out of reach...

She became him, thinking of what she would do, how she would continue on.

"I'll never find peace until she is dead," she mumbled, enveloped by his personality. "But I failed before as myself. I must do it as someone else. Someone no one will expect. Someone who can get close to my enemy to take my revenge."

Coresque pulled away from inside her thoughts. She stood in the middle of her temporary quarters, having drifted off into her own mind, completely unaware of her present surroundings. She never noticed such things when her imagination took over. "He would change who he is, what he looks like, and infiltrate his enemy's organization. Even if it took the rest of his life, he would not fail again."

Exarth would never sympathize. She would kill him without a second thought. But that could not happen. No matter the consequence.

Coresque needed to talk to him. But how? He would soon leave for the job…

"Oh, no. Oh, no!" Coresque knew Opute or Gaaht or whatever his name wasn't coming back from this contract. He must be warned, but she couldn't risk anyone finding out she had gone to visit him.

Coresque looked over at her "bed", a mechanical lift that slowly tilted backwards until she lay horizontal. Without the ability to bend, a condition that had worsened throughout the years, Coresque created the device so she could lie down and rise without help.

Staring at the contraption, she knew using her Dream-Access would be her only chance to warn Opute. She had three nights before he arrived at the job's destination. But would he understand her messages in time?

CHAPTER 10

THE FOLLOWING MORNING, Opute left his hotel and headed for a large, domed building to begin training for his new job. The hotel he'd originally wanted to book wasn't available. Apparently a recent explosion blew off a huge portion and repairs were still underway. So he'd settled for something less his style, which may have been a good thing. He needed to alter his normal patterns as much as possible with his new persona.

He arrived at the building with a headache from dreams he could barely remember. They must have been intense though, based on how hard his head pounded. The only parts he recalled were images of a snowy, barren wasteland and a flash of bright light.

Several company names scrolled across the top of the door, all located inside the structure. Opute announced himself into a panel next to the doors and they mechanically swung open. A young attendant at a round, metallic desk smiled as he approached, her green gums toothless, her tongue long and pointed.

"May I halp yew?" the attendant asked. Each word hissed through full lips.

Opute handed over his datapad. "I'm here for training with Intergalactic Transporters. I'm supposed to meet a Mister Swilt."

While the attendant read the datapad, Opute caught a glimpse of his own reflection on the surface of the shiny desk. He still wasn't used to the copper-colored face that stared back at him.

"Evary-theengah sams in ordar, Mistar Gaaht," the attendant replied, giving back the datapad. "Take the stars up one flar to the roomah on yewr laft. Roomah two-sixtan, A."

"Thanks." Opute made his way upstairs to the room and walked through the open door of 216A. He noted the three occupants inside, two in chairs and one standing at the front, speaking. The man talking stopped briefly when Opute walked in and gestured for him to take a seat. He lowered himself down and checked out the other two.

Directly next to him sat a man who looked about ten years younger than Opute with long black hair that hung straight to the middle of his back. His eyes were an intense violet-blue and stood out against his greenish-yellow skin. He sat straight in his chair, seeming to hang onto every word being said.

Opute's gaze flitted over to the other seated occupant, a female. She sat slumped in her chair, her head propped up in her hand, eyelids drooping with boredom. Her hair stuck out, short, spiked, and a vibrant red, as though a sunset had gotten caught in it. She absentmindedly pressed her lips together and then pushed them forward, making a quiet popping sound. She caught Opute looking at her, winked, then turned her attention to the speaker.

Opute followed her eyeline and assessed the man standing at the front of the room as he rattled off safety protocols. Short and balding with dark brown skin, he seemed to have a habit of twisting his fingers together. His voice came through high-pitched and wheezy, but Opute also noticed it trembled. This man seemed nervous, but nervous about what?

Opute focused in on the man's words.

"Now that I've finished with the protocol introduction, I can proceed with your actual assignment." The speaker, Mr. Swilt, pressed a small button on the table and several three-dimensional holographic images popped up in front of them.

"In two days, you will meet back here at 0600 standard hours. You will board a small cargo ship, called the *Century*, and proceed on a two-day trip to here," Swilt paused, indicating a small moon orbiting a large red planet. "This moon is Lahtze. You will circle the moon and set down on the opposite side. Once there, you will unload the cargo, which consists of one hundred boxes, and wait until our contact, Dregor, arrives on his ship, the *Mirrored Compass*. Dregor will take the boxes, give you the payment, and then you will begin your two-day journey back here. Any questions?"

The red-haired woman popped her lips once as she examined her short fingernails. The black-haired man sat calmly, his violet eyes glinting under the bright lights.

Opute cleared his throat.

"Yes, uh ... Mister Gaaht, is it?"

Opute nodded. "What exactly are our roles in this… delivery?"

"My apologies, Mister Gaaht. I forgot this is your first assignment with our company. Lym and Reh'dd have done this before," he said, nodding first in the direction of the man and then the woman. "They are experienced and will be your guides for this trip, which counts as your training."

"You ever done cargo runs 'afore?" Reh'dd asked Opute. Her words came thick and slow, as though she spoke to him through a mouthful of food.

"A few," Opute said, his new tenor voice sounding smooth to his own ears. "I used to work for a couple of different businesses, but my last job fell through when the company went bankrupt."

"Well, this'll be easy for ya then. It's real simple. Lym here flies, I do communications, and you do all the running. Real easy."

Opute looked over at Lym, whose gaze had finally shifted in Opute's direction.

"If you two have done this before, what happened to the old runner?" Opute asked.

"Well—" Reh'dd started.

"She was involved in an unfortunate accident," Swilt chimed in.

Opute saw Reh'dd lift her hands in a defensive motion and then slumped back down into her chair.

"This is why we recruited you so soon, Mister Gaaht, and so hastily. This drop-off has been scheduled for several weeks and we didn't want to lose the account simply because we were short-staffed."

Opute noticed out of the corner of his eye Lym's hands tighten on the arms of his chair.

Something else is definitely going on here, Opute thought to himself. Extracting information about Exarth needed to be quick, but who would tell him anything? A tense individual, like Lym, may not be the most forthcoming. Reh'dd might be his best bet. She seemed friendly enough so far. Though maybe asking about Exarth right away on his first job, a training job at that, wouldn't be the best way to stay below the radar.

Swilt finished his talk and when no one said anything else, he dismissed them. Swilt hustled around the chairs toward the exit.

Opute stood and in the middle of stretching, Lym roughly pushed past him.

"You're excused," Opute said, catching his balance on the back of a chair.

"Sorry about Lym," a voice piped in behind him. Opute turned and saw Reh'dd closing the distance between them.

"What's his deal?"

Red crinkled her nose. "He's had a rough week. He and Xeleyn were pretty close."

"Who's Xeleyn?"

"Oh. Our third, 'afore you came along. She was killed on the job, although these corporate morons are trying to make it her fault so they don't have'ta pay for it."

Opute peered over and saw Lym in a heated discussion with Swilt. Swilt wrung his hands again. Lym moved within a nose-length from Swilt's face, said something, then stormed off. Opute did not fail to notice Swilt's dark complexion paled considerably.

"So what *did* happen to Xeleyn?"

Reh'dd shrugged. "A sharp-shooter. Blew half her face clean off."

Opute found it surprising the casual way Reh'dd described Xeleyn's death. He believed she must either be used to it or wondered if perhaps she had been in on the assassination.

Reh'dd popped her lips before continuing. "Anywho, Lym there thinks it was a set-up."

"Why would anyone want Xeleyn killed?"

Reh'dd narrowed her eyes at him. "Not sure," she said.

Opute held up his hands, mimicking her defensive gesture from earlier, and smiled. "I'm just curious." Opute watched Reh'dd's face relax.

"Sorry."

"I can ask Swilt about it. I mean, if it's painful to talk

about."

Reh'dd smiled with the side of her mouth and crinkled her nose again. Opute couldn't help finding the gesture adorable.

"It's not that." Reh'dd lowered her voice. "We do have a two-day trip in front of us. I could prob'ly fill in the details then."

Opute widened his eyes, feigning worry. "I don't want you to get into trouble with Lym. I plan on having this job for a while and I'm sure we'll all work together again."

Reh'dd rolled her eyes in a playful manner, dismissing his comment. "Don't worry about Lym an' me. We've been through rougher stuff. Trust me."

"Then I'll see you back here in a couple of days."

"Count on it." Reh'dd didn't hide watching him leave, a coy smile tugging at the corners of her lips.

* * *

Two days later, Opute made his way back to the building where the briefing took place. During his time off, he felt an excitement build inside him he hadn't felt in years. It might be a foolish feeling, since he'd merely taken the first step down a road that, for all he knew, could be a dead end. But the fact he'd already lined up his first job, when he figured it would've taken weeks to be placed somewhere, fueled his excitement.

As he approached the building, Opute took a deep breath, forcing his roiling stomach to settle. He felt a bit childish, letting his emotions get the best of him, but couldn't help it. For the first time since he began looking for Exarth over ten years ago, he felt on the right track. Like he would finally get what had been missing since the day he heard about Mahri's death: justice for her and peace of mind for himself.

Opute pinpointed his group and saw Reh'dd wave him

over.

"Am I late?" he asked.

"Naw. Lym likes to get here early to check on er'vything and since he's my ride, I had to come, too." He wondered where Reh'dd came from. Her accent wasn't familiar to him and she randomly changed the way she spoke. It intrigued him.

"Oh." Opute looked over to see Lym poring over the cargo boxes.

An enormous dark green truck pulled up next to them. It settled down to the ground off its gravity-repulsion lifters and a tall, lanky female climbed out of the driver's seat. She arched her back to stretch, her large breasts prominent to say the least.

"I'm here to transport cargo to Pad three-one-four. Is that all this?"

"Yuh-huh," Reh'dd answered, bringing over the datapad with the contract on it. The driver signed it and the four of them loaded the truck.

Opute nearly bit his tongue when the driver pulled away from the driveway. The edges of gravity-repulsion field caused the truck to bounce sloppily off light posts and sidewalk edges without ever touching them.

Opute closed his eyes and clenched his stomach when they hit a particularly nasty turn and he prayed his breakfast would remain in his gut. Finally, the truck came to a jolted stop, and the three of them tumbled out. They unloaded the truck and reloaded their cargo onto the *Century*.

A small and lean ship, with a pointed prow and a bubble-shaped aft, the *Century* was clean, but well-used, as indicated by the scratches and dents along its hull. A standard shield emitter sat mounted on its underbelly, but there were no visible weapons. Opute knew, since the job entailed only one flight with three passengers and a minimum amount of cargo that they didn't need a big vessel, but he missed his old cargo cruiser, the

Arrival. Quite a beautiful ship, even though he hadn't flown her in years. He wondered if she lived or if she'd been scrapped for parts by now.

Reh'dd caught his far-off expression and nudged him.

"Ready?"

"Whenever you are." The two of them boarded the ship, finding Lym already comfortable in the cockpit. Reh'dd took her place next to him, placing a thin, metallic strip behind one ear and at the base of her throat to communicate with the ground crew. She nodded to Lym, who lit up a few panel buttons and told Opute to take a seat.

Opute strapped himself in and felt the ship shudder underneath him during liftoff. His gaze drifted toward the viewport and watched as the ship turned to face the sky. With a small lurch, the ship took off, leaving the ground below them.

As the planet's yellowish atmosphere gave way to the black vacuum of space, Opute saw Lym make a few small adjustments, felt the ship turn slightly, and knew they were on their way.

Waiting until Lym gave the all-clear, Opute unstrapped his harness and stretched his legs out in front of him. The gravity stabilizers worked a little too well, pulling much harder against his body mass. Adjusting to this quickly, Opute rose and headed back toward his quarters. An unusually small and cramped space, but livable for the following four days. He threw his bag onto his bunk, not bothering to unpack. Stretching out on his bed, he shut his eyes for what he believed would be just a moment.

About a half hour later, a hesitant knock on his door woke him. Opute got up and hit the door-release button, and the door to slid open.

Reh'dd stood before him

"Didn't know if you wanted to be let alone."

"Just getting a feel for the place," Opute answered, inviting her in. Reh'dd took two steps.

"Roomy, huh?"

Reh'dd smiled. "You get used to it."

Opute sat on the bed and Reh'dd sat next to him. "So what do you two usually do on these trips?

Reh'dd shrugged. "Lym and Xeleyn were pretty close, so they spent most of their time together." She dropped a quick wink.

Opute nodded. "What about you?"

"Most of the trips were day trips, so I never really had to worry about it 'afore. I just kind of hung out."

A silence filled the room in those next few minutes, impregnating the space until it felt as though the walls might bulge outward.

Opute sat there, trying to think of something, *anything* to say. But he could only think that he couldn't think of anything.

Reh'dd licked her lips and scooted closer. "Gaaht—"

"Hey, Gaaht?" Lym's loud voice rang through the communications panel next to the door. The two of them jumped and Reh'dd let out a giggle.

Opute cleared his throat and pressed a button so he could answer Lym.

"Yes?"

"Have you seen Reh'dd? She's not answering in her room."

"Uh, yeah. She's right here."

"Hey, Lym."

A pause. "Oh. Hey. Um ... could you come up front when ... when you've got a second?"

Reh'dd grinned at the awkwardness in Lym's voice.

"No problem. I'll be right there." She turned off the speaker and stood. "Well, nice chattin' with ya. Guess I'll see ya later."

"Right. See you."

Reh'dd bit her bottom lip before smiling out of the corner of her mouth. She turned and left Opute sitting on his bed.

As soon as she'd left, Opute let out a sigh of relief.

This was going to be a long four days.

CHAPTER 11

A FEW MONTHS after the "Liph clone incident," eight-year-old Exarth felt determined to reveal the hospital's secrets. She thought if she got to know the other kids and how they were different, especially the three she picked out, they might uncover the truth. And to see if they could avoid any future danger, similar to what occurred with Liph.

During one of the children's designated eating times, Exarth formed a plan. She pushed around the food on her plate—some sort of protein-carbohydrate mixture that reminded her of mashed pio root, except liquidy instead of stringy—and strategized. She didn't want to alert the "doctors" and appear to do anything out of the ordinary. She'd always been what they called "anti-social," keeping to herself and not really talking to anyone else. So if she suddenly took an interest in others around her, she knew the "doctors" would notice.

An accidental friendship that wasn't really accidental might be her best bet. If she set it up, she could become friends with one of the other kids, in what would seem like a completely innocent way.

She would make something happen to create a bond between herself and someone else.

But what?

She spooned some of the mixture into her mouth and watched the other kids. They all looked fairly mundane, sitting in rows along the white tables, eating their food, chatting with each other, but Exarth knew they weren't. After a week of watching, she hadn't managed to see a single difference in any of the other kids. Her three top choices, the two girls and a boy, were extremely hard to monitor. They mostly kept to themselves, like she did, but were polite to other kids around them, unlike herself.

Exarth procured a little information from one of the newer attendants, since the short one who had dropped the bag of clones and run out of the room no longer worked there. He had a very expressive face and, despite her attempts not to, Exarth found she liked him. Sometimes he told her funny little stories about himself and his childhood. He would say things to some of the "doctors" that they wouldn't understand and then wink at Exarth because she always got the joke. He never talked down to her like the other attendants did and she picked things up quickly, like large vocabulary words and difficult concepts.

He went by Arew, and he became the closest thing to a friend Exarth could remember.

Arew came and took blood samples from Exarth once a week and she felt happiest on those days. Medium height with the same whitened features as everyone else, the only real difference could be found in his long, white hair, which he left hanging loose over his shoulders. Exarth thought he did it to rebel a little against the "higher-ups" and liked him even more for it.

Once Exarth finished her lunch, she decided her best bet would be to use Arew. Not in a bad way, she reassured herself, but he seemed like the only one who could get her an "in" with the other children. In a couple days he would be back to take blood from her and at that point she would have everything planned to find out about the other children and to somehow become friends with them.

Two days later, Arew arrived right on schedule, just after breakfast. He blinked his large white eyes at her and sat forward in the chair next to her bed, humming a tune while he attached the needle to the tube which would draw her blood.

"Good morning, Exarth! How are we feeling today?"

"Same as always," she answered. "Not sick at all."

Arew's eyebrows raised. "That's an interesting thing to say. What do you mean by that?"

Exarth licked her full lips. "I mean I never feel sick, Arew. *Never.* How can the staff tell if I'm sick or not when I don't have any symptoms?"

Arew smiled. "Why do you think we test your blood every week?"

"So it's something in my blood?"

Half of Arew's smile fell away. "Not exactly."

"Well, what then?"

"You know you're not supposed to ask about these things. We've talked about this before."

Exarth blew a stream of air upwards across her face. "I know I'm not supposed to ask about it," she said, "but I'm not a baby anymore. A lot of the kids here aren't. I think we should know what's going on with us. I think we're old enough to handle it."

Arew laughed gently. "At eight standard years old, most would disagree with you. But not me. I've talked to you. I know you could handle it, but it's not up to me to decide. You know that. You've seen how things work here. And as for the other children, there are two, maybe three that could handle the things you can."

Exarth felt a sting of guilt at using Arew as she asked her next set-up question. "Is that why none of the other kids like me? Because I catch on to things faster than they do?"

"What do you mean they don't like you? Of course they like you."

Exarth slowly shook her head, letting her gaze drop for a few moments, half to fake sadness, half because she couldn't bear to look at him while he had such concern for her in his voice. *These are honest questions. Just because I'm asking them on purpose, doesn't mean they aren't true,* she told herself. Why did she feel guilty anyway? Arew belonged to the staff. Just another one of the "doctors'" grunts. He still kept things from her and helped hold all the children here. She needed to consider him one of the bad guys, no matter how much she liked him.

"No, they don't," she said, referring to the other children. "They never talk to me and they look at me funny. Like I'm different. Why would they do that? Do I have some kind of weird ab-uh-abnormality from my illness that makes me look different?"

Arew hesitated. Exarth noticed.

"Have they been saying things to you? Teasing you?"

"No…" she said slowly, stalling for time. This conversation had taken a different turn. She thought he would reassure her she didn't differ from the others, but Arew's response made her wonder. *Did* she look different? Could that be what set her apart from everyone else?

Exarth needed to make a quick decision. Should she push the subject or get back on track to put her plan into action?

She decided to choose the latter. If she had some hideous deformity, she would worry about that after she discovered the truth.

"No," she repeated. "They don't say anything mean. They don't say anything at all. That's the problem."

Arew's tightened shoulders dropped and his jaw unclenched. "Maybe they're scared to talk to you, too."

"Scared? Why would they be scared?"

"You are a little intimidating sometimes. You ask a lot of questions, you get into trouble with the staff... maybe they're afraid if they are friends with you they'll get into trouble, too."

Exarth almost felt saddened by how easily Arew said what she wanted him to say. "I never thought of it like that," she mumbled, dropping back into character. She decided to ask the question she knew would seal the deal.

"Do they really hate me?"

Arew's smile vanished as he reached toward her.

"Who said anything about them hating you? They don't *hate* you. They just don't know you. Trust me," he said, his smile returning, "once someone gets to know you, they could never hate you."

Exarth wondered if Arew would still like her if he found out she was using him.

"How can they get to know me if they won't talk to me?"

"Why don't you talk to them first?"

Exarth feigned surprise. "I didn't think of that." She smiled. "Maybe they think I don't like them because I won't talk to them."

Arew's smile widened. "Maybe," he said with a wink.

* * *

An older man with wrinkles that shadowed his otherwise white face looked up as someone entered his office. "Ah, Attendant Arew Nend. Please, come in."

The young attendant with long hair that flowed loosely

over his shoulders came into the room and sat down across from the older man.

"You wanted to see me, sir?"

"I'd like an update on patient three-four-four-eight."

Arew leaned back in the chair. "The blood work is still coming back inconclusive. We have no idea how her regenerative properties work, but I think we are searching in the wrong place. We should be studying her skin, nerves, and brain patterns while she's regenerating, not her blood."

"Yes, I've read your reports. You've come up with some interesting theories about her. Most of our staff have pretty much given up on her secrets. They've focused instead on some of the more cooperative patients with positive and promising results. And yet you have only been here a couple of months and feel more time and resources should be put into her case."

"Yes, sir. I feel it would be worthwhile. Regenerative properties would be extremely beneficial."

"Hmm...I will review your reports, go over the figures, and let you know shortly what I decide."

"Thank you, sir." Arew started to rise when the older man stopped him.

"Yes, sir?" Arew asked.

"I wondered what your personal opinion is about the girl. You seem to be the only one who has created a bond with her."

Arew took a moment before answering. "Did any of your staff ever test her intelligence levels?"

"Of course. It's standard procedure. The only children who ranked genius levels were patients...uh..." he stopped for a moment as he looked up a file. "Ah, here it is. Patients three-four-three-two, three-four-one-seven, and three-four-five-eight. All children brought in within the past six years. Two girls, one boy. Your girl, three-four-four-eight, only showed medium to slightly high intelligence. Nothing too impressive." He paused.

"Why do you ask?"

"Because at eight years old, she is smarter than most adults I've met."

"What makes you say that?"

Arew ran his fingers through his long hair. "Some of it is the way she talks. She picks up vocabulary words that no eight-year-old should understand; she can decipher difficult problems and come up with solutions that were not presented as options. She gets my jokes, she—"

"She gets your jokes?"

"Yes, sir. To create a bond with her, I had to make myself stand out from the rest of the staff. I tease them in front of her, but they don't realize I'm doing it."

"You tease them?"

"Right to their faces. And they don't get it, but she *does*."

The older man thought for a moment. "You said that was only part of it. What's the other part?"

"Her eyes."

"Ah yes. Shades of non-white. And her hair, too." The older man shivered. "It's just not right."

"Agreed, sir. Any shade but white is an abomination. It is the purest form of shades," he recited. "But this girl's eyes, they also *change* shade. Depending on her mood."

"Ugh. Bad enough they aren't white, but to fluctuate between multiple shadings? Sometimes I still believe letting her continue to exist was a mistake."

"Her regenerative properties are something we have never seen before."

"Yes, I know. It's just…so unnatural." The older man cleared his throat. "But you were saying you believe her changing eyes will be helpful?"

"Yes, sir. I have studied her during our conversations. The first time I noticed was when her eyes turned almost void of white. They appeared extremely dark while I quizzed her. So I began charting her eye shade changes and noticed a correlation based on her moods and have a pretty good idea about what shades mean which emotions—deeper and darker mean she's happy, brighter means she's interested or curious, muted brightness means she's focused or determined, intense happens when she's angry or frustrated, and the darkest pops up when she's thinking about something."

"What does this have to do with her intelligence level?"

"Because she is contemplating, *thinking* almost all the time." Arew leaned forward, his hands fluttering with excitement.

"Once again, I'm afraid I don't follow you."

"Her eyes are almost always tinged or rimmed with the darkest of the intensities. Even when she's sad or frustrated, she's still thinking her way through the situation. She's constantly thinking. All the time." Arew sat back in the chair. "And if she didn't have the anomalies she does, I would have suggested enrolling her in our Strategy and Planning Program."

"You would have enrolled her in the SPP at eight years old?"

"Yes, sir."

"But the age of recruitment is usually fourteen."

"I know, sir. She is that smart."

The older man rubbed his white fingers across his white chin. "Then why didn't she score well on those intelligence tests?"

Arew paused. "I think she might have scored lower on purpose. I believe she pretended not to know all the answers."

The senior officer exhaled forcibly and sagged in his chair. "Do you see this as being a problem?"

"Not yet. She seems to be like most normal eight-year-olds, just with a genius level of intelligence. For example, today she worried the other children didn't seem to like her. She seemed interested in making friends."

"But she's never shown an interest in that before. She seems to always keep to herself or remove herself from a situation that would involve her and the other patients working together."

"I know, sir. I think it's because of her intelligence level. I would guess she doesn't know how she could connect to the other children because she isn't like the other children."

"What do you suggest?"

"I recommend we encourage it. The more she feels included, the less she'll worry about why she's here."

The older officer rose to dismiss Arew. "Thank you for your suggestions, Attendant Nend. I will give serious thought to the proposal you mentioned earlier. As for encouraging her to make friends, I agree with you. Proceed as you see fit."

"Thank you, sir." Arew turned to leave.

"Attendant Nend?"

"Yes, sir?"

"Are you sure she won't be a problem?"

Arew smiled. "She's still only an eight-year-old girl."

* * *

Exarth sighed as she stared at the fourth bounty hunter who had entered her office.

Well, as she stared at the *body* of the fourth bounty hunter who now lay dead on the floor of her office.

The Vorr, the most hopeful on Exarth's list, came back with the same news as the rest: she couldn't find anything on the man who'd stolen her ships except that he went by the name Ness Opute, helped in the Aleet Army incident the year before, and had seemingly disappeared.

And since she provided the same news, she suffered the

same fate as the others.

Exarth wasn't sighing because of the assassin's bad news, but because killing didn't make her feel any better. It didn't help her get closer to Opute, it didn't slake her thirst for revenge, and it didn't do anything except make a mess on the floor which she would need to have cleaned.

She took a seat. Exarth tapped her long fingernails on her metallic desk and watched as the Vorr's yellow bodily fluids seeped from her neck wound onto the black floor. It looked like a punctured sun oozing through starless space.

It looked beautiful.

A feeling welled inside her chest at the thought, aching and twisting at the same time. She hated sometimes how cold she felt, pierced only by moments of rage.

She'd known from a young age about how different she was. She knew she'd never have any semblance of a normal, stable life.

But Ness Opute made her believe she could.

She hadn't meant to fall in love with him. She only thought about him as another smuggler to do business with, well, an attractive smuggler.

However, when she ended up on a second job with him, whatever feeling she denied the first time hit her, hard. She found herself trying to find ways to have a job that would involve him.

He made her smile. A genuine smile. No fear or anger or contempt.

She'd never realized what happy meant until that moment. Powerful, controlling, even satisfied, but never happy.

Her life shattered the day Iry told her Opute betrayed her.

But even worse, when he told her Opute was dead.

Because even through her anger at his betrayal, some part of her still loved him.

She hated herself for that.

Especially because now, when she could easily just have someone else kill him, she wanted him brought to her, alive. She claimed it was because she wanted to do the deed herself, but a tiny spot inside her burned bright with hope. If she could talk to him, maybe…maybe….

CHAPTER 12

REH'DD POPPED HER head into the cockpit. "What's goin' on, L? Why'd you want me up here?"

Lym pursed his thin lips. He sat rigid in the pilot's seat, his gaze locked on the viewport. Streaks of stars filled the screen. "You know I hate it when you call me that."

"A course. That's why I do it." She chuckled and slapped him on the shoulder. "Come on Lym, I'm just trying to get a laugh outta you. I haven't seen you happy since—"

"Since before they murdered Xeleyn," Lym interrupted. His eyes clouded over as though thunder wanted to roll from his sockets.

"She was killed," Reh'dd reminded him. "She wasn't necessarily murdered. Why can't you just accept it wasn't some sort'a conspiracy against you?"

Frustrated, Lym leaned back into the chair, its worn gray covering squeaking in protest. "I know it wasn't a conspiracy against me. It was a conspiracy against *her*. She knew something, Reh'dd. Something she wasn't supposed to know. And they killed her for it!"

"What could'a been so important to kill a goods-n-trade shipper for? We ain't anybody, Lym. We don't know no one, we couldn't tell no one nothin', and even if we could, who would believe us?"

"It doesn't matter. Whatever she knew, they didn't want to take the chance it would get out." Lym's eyes returned to their pools of deep violet. "I just wish she would have told me what she knew. Maybe it could have led me to her killers."

Reh'dd sat down next to him and put her hand on his shoulder.

"Am I interrupting?"

Reh'dd and Lym both jumped at the sound of Opute's voice. He stood there, halfway in the cockpit, his coppery-golden skin shimmering softly under the overhead lights.

Lym's eyes darkened once more. "Not at all," he lied. "What's the problem?"

"No problem. Forgot one of my bags in here." Opute quickly grabbed a small bag off the floor, smiled briefly at Reh'dd, and left.

"I don't trust him," Lym said.

"You don't trust no one," she teased.

"I'm serious, Reh'dd. Think about it. Xeleyn gets killed two weeks ago and her spot opens up. They hire this guy right away and stick him on our ship. We could have done this run by ourselves."

"Three is standard procedure and you know it. Plus it's easier with a third. Gaaht happened to be in the right place at the right time and it worked out. It ain't his fault. Just a convenience."

"I think you mean coincidence."

"Ugh, I hate speaking Universal. Anyway," Reh'dd went on. "The point is, maybe things did just happen to work out this way. No conspiracies."

"I don't know. What about all those questions he asked you about Xeleyn?"

"Wouldn't you be interested if you found out the third you were replacing died, or maybe was murdered on the job? I'd prob'ly want to know, too."

Lym sighed. "Maybe you're right. Maybe I'm starting to see shadows in the dark."

Reh'dd furrowed her eyebrows in confusion.

Lym's lips curved up into a scant smile. "Never mind."

* * *

Opute spent the rest of the day in his quarters, mostly avoiding Lym.

Reh'dd stopped in earlier, but seemed more distant. Opute wondered if Lym said something to put her off.

Opute shook his head. *I don't need to impress these two.* He reminded himself this job only represented the first rung on the ladder toward Exarth. He couldn't form a bond with anyone because when the time came, it might be harder to leave, which would only delay him.

Whatever the problem with those two wasn't his concern. It didn't involve him and soon enough they would be two more individuals he passed while climbing to the top.

* * *

Eight-year-old Exarth wanted to start on her plan right away, but she made herself wait the whole week until she saw Arew again. It had been difficult. Now that she began her plan, she wanted it to keep going, but she needed the delay.

Exarth kept herself busy by testing her regenerative abilities. She started small, with scrapes and blunt force, eventually breaking a finger. She worried about experimenting too far, like chopping off an arm and seeing if it would regrow, just in case it couldn't, but broken bones mended quite nicely in just a few minutes. Even the pain stayed minimal. However after a while, even that got boring.

She hated waiting almost as much as she hated the color white.

A week finally passed and Exarth's stomach boiled with impatience until Arew entered the room. She made herself relax, breathing slowly as her small feet dangled over the side of the bed.

"You're late," she joked as he approached her.

"I know, I know," he answered. Then, with a swift movement, he fell to his knees, clasping his hands together.

"Can you ever forgive me, oh Queen of the Time?" he begged. "I am but your humble servant and know you should take my life as punishment. But it's not my fault I'm late. My time-reader broke, I got dizzy in the hall and had to sit down, my vehicle broke down, a quake shook the building, the turbolift broke three levels up, biting insects attacked me, my eyes fell out and I had to find them, I put my feet on backwards and went home instead of to work, I—"

"Stop!" Exarth shrieked through her giggles. She hadn't planned to laugh, but it felt really good. Tears rimmed the edges of her eyes until she caught her breath.

"You're forgiven," she told him in her most authoritative voice. "But only because you are my only slave and your replacement hasn't arrived yet."

"Words cannot express my gratitude, oh Queen." His white eyes shined. "Ready for your weekly blood loss?"

She put out her arm and rolled up her white sleeve.

While Arew got everything ready and began, Exarth waited. She knew he would ask about their previous conversation sooner or later. She hoped for sooner.

As if he read her thoughts, he brought it up.

"Made any progress with the other children?"

She stayed quiet for a moment before answering. "No."

"No? Why not?"

She let out a fake sigh. "What am I supposed to say to them? 'Hi. I'm not mean. Let's be friends.' They would laugh at me."

Arew tapped the side of the syringe to start the blood flow and sat down in a chair next to her. "They would not."

Exarth scowled, which made him laugh.

"All right. Maybe if you said it with that face they would. But trust me, you'll be fine. Some of the children don't talk a lot either. Maybe they're just as nervous as you are."

"Like who?"

Arew turned and nodded in the direction of four girls; three played together while the fourth sat on the side pretending not to watch.

"That girl, over by the side, her name is Nyma. She's a year younger than you and pretty quiet. Smart, but quiet. You could probably talk to her."

Arew had pointed out one of the three kids Exarth hoped to get to know. One of the three she picked when Liph vomited up those clones. Since Arew knew her so well, she assumed he would point out the other two children also.

Arew didn't disappoint.

"Who else?" he asked rhetorically as he scanned the room. A boy sat on his bed across from them and to their left, reading a datapad.

"There's him as well. He's ten, but I don't think the two years between you two will make a difference to him. He's probably the smartest child here, besides yourself, and an avid reader. He reads anything we throw at him and no matter the length or difficulty, it never takes him more than two days to read it. And he remembers everything he reads, word for word."

"What did you say his name was?"

"His name is Iry." Arew removed the needle and placed a bandage over the wound. Exarth had to refrain from snorting in disgust at his show. She knew the small puncture would heal in a matter of seconds.

"I would start with them," he finished, placing the syringe full of her white blood into a sterile bag.

The other girl, the last of the three, remained unknown and she really piqued Exarth's interest.

The stiff-moving one.

"Anyone else in case I screw up the first two?"

"You won't screw it up."

"Okay." Exarth heard the disappointment in her voice. It would sound like self-doubt, instead of the frustration at not finding out more. Perhaps she could get the information from the other two kids, although they didn't seem to talk to anyone else either.

"You could always try to talk to Coresque, too."

Exarth's eyes snapped upward. "Who?"

"Coresque. She's sitting…over there." Arew pointed across the room at a girl taking a nap in the far corner. The one Exarth had the most interest in.

"But she may be the toughest out of the three to talk to."

"Why is that?"

Arew cocked his head before answering. "She really likes being quiet. Even when one of the staff tries to make conversation, she only responds when she has to and won't say anything more than what they need. She refrains from asking any questions or showing any real interest in anyone. In fact, she doesn't show much interest in her surroundings at all."

"Then why did you suggest I talk to her?"

"Because I think if anyone could get through to her, you could."

Exarth felt honestly surprised. "Really? How come?"

"You two are complete opposites in so many ways, and yet you are both extremely intelligent and curious. The difference is you have a hard time keeping your curiosity to yourself while she goes to the other extreme and never wants to be involved with anything. I think if you talked to her, she would eventually open up. Your strong personality would rub off on her."

Arew sat back in his chair instead of standing to leave. "Will you be honest with me if I ask you something?"

She paused at the question. Her first instinct told her to lie and say 'yes' and then decide after the question whether she would be truthful. But that thought made her cringe internally. Why must her first instinct always be to lie?

"I can't make that promise. But, if you ask a question, I'll either answer it truthfully or tell you I don't want to answer it."

Arew chewed on his lower lip before responding. "Fair enough." He sighed and leaned closer to her, his voice barely above a murmur.

"Why do you really want to get to know these other children?"

Exarth had to resist any physical movement that would give away her surprise. Did he know her plan? How could he? She had never spoken about it to anyone. Did she talk in her sleep? Could he read her thoughts? Or was he just reaching in the dark?

Exarth decided to play it safe. "When Liph got sick, I noticed a few of the other children weren't panicked or grossed out. I always thought of the other children as just…children." She paused. "But at that point, I realized some of them might be as smart as me. They might think like me. And for the first time I realized I wanted to talk to someone else."

Arew peered directly at her eyes and Exarth stared back, holding her ground. It was the truth, although she left out the reason *why* she wanted to talk to them. She could only hope Arew wouldn't ask about it.

"Thanks," he said. "I know it must have been a weird question, but we are supposed to look out for any unusual behavior. They may be symptoms of a progression in your sickness. My boss wanted to make sure your personality wasn't doing flips or anything like that."

Arew stood up to leave. "Well, when I see you next week, I expect a full report on how things went with the other children."

A smiled blossomed across her face. "Hey! Who's the queen here?"

Arew did an elaborate bow and left the room with a wink.

CHAPTER 13

OPUTE'S RESTLESS NIGHT contained nothing but intense dreams. In one he watched himself telling Mahri to be careful on her trip and that he would see her when she got back. He tried to scream at himself to stop her from going, but she went anyhow.

She always went.

In another he stood on the surface of a planet, barren and cold. At a distance a woman hovered, dressed all in white, as pale as the ice-crusted surface around her. She approached him slowly, hands out, eyes completely white. She whispered his name.

His real name.

Opute awoke from that dream in a cold sweat, his hands tingling from lack of blood. While he shook them through the prickly-stinging stage, he glanced over at his time-reader, set to go off in less than a standard hour. Knowing he probably wouldn't fall asleep again, Opute rose and began to exercise, working the muscles in his new body.

An hour later he felt fully awake and, after washing up, headed toward a small room in the center of the ship used as a kitchen, dining room, recreational area, and conference space all in one. Octagonal in shape, with entry points on three sides—one led to the cockpit, one to the sleeping cabins, and one toward the engine room in the bowels of the ship. It contained a roughly circular metallic table in the center with four chairs around it, all bolted to the floor. A blue film lined the doorways—a pressure-proof seal in case of a hull breach.

Opute rummaged through the ship's food supplies and felt excited to see fresh fruit. He grabbed a handful of yemet and took a seat. While peeling back the yemet skin, he heard a light shuffling coming from the corridor next to him. Reh'dd entered the room, her feet dragging on the floor.

"Good morning," Opute said, keeping his smile to himself. One half of her bright red hair stuck straight up, while the other side lay plastered to her head. She wore her shirt inside out, her pants, unbuttoned, hung loosely off the side of one hip, and she absentmindedly scratched her stomach.

Reh'dd responded with a noise between a grunt and a sigh. She plopped into the chair across from him, her eyes half open.

Opute ripped off a piece of his fruit, yellow juice dribbling down his fingers. He shoved it into his mouth, failing to catch the trickle sliding down his sleeve.

One of Reh'dd's eyes had closed completely and the other glazed over.

"Why don't you go back to bed?" Opute suggested.

Reh'dd perked up. "Huh?"

"You look tired."

"Wannnacan't cuz ...light sleepinger ..." Reh'dd's eyelids fell back to the half-closed position.

Opute's brow crinkled as he sucked a piece of rind from between his teeth. "What in space did you just say?"

Reh'dd's eyes fluttered back open again as she yawned.

"I said," she drawled, "I'm a light sleeper."

Opute stared back at her in silence.

"You woke me up with your thumping an hour ago," she explained.

"I couldn't sleep so I exercised."

"No worries. I'll just catch some sleep later on todaaaaaa..." she said, her last word turning into another yawn.

"Sorry."

Reh'dd grinned. "It's not your fault. You didn't know."

Opute managed to ungracefully wipe the remaining juice from his chin with his sleeve and offered Reh'dd some of the fruit.

"No thanks," she muttered, "I don't eat."

Opute hesitantly pulled the fruit back.

"Like ... not at all?" he asked.

"Nope," she replied, stifling a yawn.

Opute waited for her to continue. A few minutes of silence passed and his gaze wandered aimlessly around the room. He wondered if this was the time when a woman would want him to ask questions so he seemed interested or if he should let her tell him.

Lym entered the room, interrupting their silence and saving Opute from having to make a decision.

"Reh'dd, since you're up already, I need you to check the communications coordinates and make sure there aren't any changes with our meeting later today. Opute, go and check the cargo to make sure nothing has been damaged and that everything is ready to be shipped out as quickly as possible."

"Good mornin' to you, too," Reh'dd spat.

Lym glared in her direction. "Now I remember why I never woke you up early."

Opute stood, forcing himself to remain calm. He wasn't used to taking orders from anybody, much less someone who gave him no respect, but he needed to remember he wasn't really Opute anymore. Gritting his teeth, he silently walked past Lym.

"Don't forget to scan and log each package to make sure everything is there. We wouldn't want to find out something is missing."

Opute's steps faltered for a moment. Lym knew they checked all the cargo when they boarded, so the only way something would be missing is if someone on the ship stole it, and Opute had a feeling Lym meant him.

He spent the rest of the morning and most of the afternoon sorting through a hundred boxes of cargo. Everything checked out as Opute knew it would, but he double checked all the package numbers against the log just in case.

Finally satisfied, he went back to the kitchen area for lunch.

An empty room greeted him and Opute took a seat after grabbing a standardized food packet from one of the cabinets above the table. Ripping it open, Opute shoved a portion into his mouth, ignoring the bitter aftertaste, and propped his feet up on the table. While he chewed, he let his mind go blank, washing away the tediousness of the day.

Soon Reh'dd entered, looking much more awake and put together.

"Hey," she said.

"Hey yourself. Good to see you with your eyes open."

Reh'dd smiled. "Did I forget to mention that I'm not an early riser?"

"I'll never forget it now."

"I wasn't too rude, was I?"

"You were very polite, just half asleep."

Reh'dd took the seat across from him. "How did the recheck of the cargo go?"

Opute cracked his knuckles. "Splendid."

Reh'dd put her hand on his arm. "Don't take it personal."

"You've been saying that to me a lot these past two days."

"I mean it. Lym can sometimes be ... well ... Lym. It's just the way he is. He's super organized and a real stickler for having things right. That's why he's high up in this business. He's really sought after."

"Maybe I should be taking pointers," Opute grumbled.

Reh'dd pinched Opute in a playful manner. "Maybe you should." She crinkled her nose again which Opute still found adorable. He hadn't felt so relaxed around a member of the opposite sex since...well, he didn't know how long. Even with Zarsa, tension existed because of their past. But with this girl, it felt...easy.

"You sound like an advertisement for Lym," Opute joked back.

"I don't need to. He really is that good. It's just that sometimes he is a little too serious, ya know? He doesn't quite loosen up when he should. That's why Xeleyn did so good for him. She really helped him take breaks every once in a while."

Opute quieted, wanting to ask about what really happened to her, but afraid Reh'dd would pull back again because of Lym. Luckily, Reh'dd seemed either to have forgotten or didn't care anymore because she continued talking.

"Xeleyn was real sweet and pretty, but her best quality? Humor. She put on the best practical jokes I ever seen."

"Sounds like you two were close."

"Us? Not like friends or nothing. But we got along pretty well on these cargo trips of ours."

"How long had you worked together?"

Reh'dd chewed on her upper lip as she thought. "About a standard year or so. Lym and her had been pretty close for a little less than that. They clicked right away."

"He seems to have taken her death pretty hard."

"He thinks she was murdered."

"I think you mentioned that before," Opute said, shoving another bit of food into his mouth. "Why would he think that?"

Reh'dd shrugged. "He thinks she knew something strange went on with our employers."

Opute felt a tightening in his stomach. "What?"

"I don't know. She never told Lym. But whatever it was, if they really did kill her for it, then it must have been something huge."

Opute drummed his fingers on the table. "Do *you* think she was murdered?"

Reh'dd shrugged again. "Maybe. Prob'ly not, but maybe. When we landed, we set down in the middle of some local civil war thing. We hadn't been warned or nothing, so craziness broke out right before we made the exchange. While heading back to our ship, a sniper started shooting at the guys we were dealing with. Two of them went down and Xeleyn got one in the face. I think it could'a been any of us, but Lym thinks they set things up just to kill her."

"I'm not getting into something I shouldn't have, am I?" Opute said with a smile.

Reh'dd grinned back. "Naw. You're just along for the ride. Besides, we're landing on a dead ol' moon. There ain't gonna be anyone around to be fighting."

Or to witness anything. Opute shook away the thought. Reh'dd could be right. Lym just needed a reason for a random act of violence against the woman he loved. He wanted someone to blame.

Opute could relate.

"Speaking of the moon, when are we arriving?"

"Prob'ly less than an hour."

Opute sat back in his chair as he chewed the processed food in his mouth.

"What about you?" Reh'dd asked. "What's your story?"

"Me?"

"Yeah. I've been blabbing to you for almost two days about

Lym and me. What's the deal with you? How'd you get into this line of work?"

Opute recited his made-up backstory. "The cargo business has been a part of my family for years. It's something I've always done, always been involved in. Once old enough, I left home to start finding work for myself. And I've been doing it for about four years, but this is my first job with Intergalactic Transporters."

"Yuh-huh. There's a lot of folks with that kinda story. I'm a bit backwards. My parents were very professional, but I had no interest. Instead I got really into navigation and communications and a couple of governmental companies recruited me. Did that for a few years, but didn't like a lot of the protocol. This line of work is much more relaxing. Less dignitaries and more time off."

Lym popped his head into the room. "We're coming up on Lahtze. Better get to your stations."

"See you later," Reh'dd told Opute. After they both stood, she perched herself onto her tiptoes and gave him a quick kiss on the lips.

As she trotted out of the room, Opute put his hand to his mouth. "Umm… sure," he sputtered. Did 'see you later' mean an invitation for something to happen later? Opute thought about this prospect and found it surprising he wouldn't be opposed to it. Not that he expected anything, but who knows? Maybe she could be just the type of girl he needed in his life.

Opute shook it off and headed for the bridge. She'd only be a distraction. He had a job to do.

He arrived shortly at the cockpit and saw Reh'dd punch through communication lines on her console and speak with the oncoming vessel. Opute took a seat and strapped himself in, waiting for the ship to land.

"This is the *Century* requesting confirmation code. Please

respond." Reh'dd pressed a few more buttons and waited for the oncoming ship to answer. They apparently didn't have the type of communication for her to connect directly to the patches on her throat and jawbone.

A crackly voice came through the ship's communication speakers.

"Confirmation code eight… four… red… three… nine… gray. Repeat. Eight-four-red-three-nine-gray. Please confirm."

"Code accepted. I have sent you our landing coordinates. We look forward to meeting you on Lahtze. End." Reh'dd swiveled around and nodded to Lym.

"Hang on," Lym said. The ship shot through the moon's atmosphere. Gravity pulled at them hard and Opute felt the ship shudder as Lym maneuvered to compensate.

Gray, dusty clouds greeted them during their descent. The moon appeared barren and icy: completely void of visible life.

While landing, Opute stared out the window at the moon's surface. It seemed familiar somehow.

"All right. Now's your time to shine!" Reh'dd told Opute, clapping him on the shoulder.

"Let's go," Lym said coolly.

The three of them headed toward the cargo room to prepare. Reh'dd and Opute were each equipped with an insulated skin suit to protect them from the harsh environment. Each suit contained portable heaters to keep their body temperatures at their optimal levels. Lym's species had either adapted to the cold weather or didn't register it because he did not wear a suit. He did, however, wear a portable respirator, strapped to an air filtration unit on his back, which matched the ones Opute and Reh'dd wore. When they opened the cargo hatch to begin unloading, puffs of icy crystallized dust swirled up around them. Their contacts on the *Mirrored Compass* landed about a hundred meters away.

Opute walked off the ship, unconsciously tapping his fingers on the top of the doorframe as he exited. He took several strides to stretch his legs as Lym walked over to talk with Dregor, captain of the *Mirrored Compass*, to complete the transaction. Opute turned to his left and saw Reh'dd going over the cargo manifest. He smiled at her when she looked up, the corners of his mouth wrinkling the part of the suit that covered his face. She wrinkled her nose and winked.

Walking out even further, Opute's mind drifted to the thought of spending more time with Reh'dd. Maybe it wouldn't be such a bad thing to get a bit closer to her. Besides, he didn't know how long he'd be around until he got promoted.

His gaze wandered to the barren wasteland of the moon's surface. While staring across the white horizon, his skin tightened and prickled. Opute shook his head, but the feeling worsened. Dread settled into his gut.

Something seemed wrong here.

Then he remembered why he knew this place. He saw it the night before in his dream. And that pale, statuesque woman, Coresque, had been there. He thought she'd been beckoning him, calling his name. Except he now remembered, her arms weren't out to welcome him; her palms had been facing him, to keep him from coming closer.

"A warning," Opute whispered out loud.

Opute's gaze returned to Lym. Dregor handed him the datapad to confirm payment.

"Wait," Opute said. He watched Lym nod and take back the datapad, turn, and head toward the ship.

"Wait!" Opute cried out louder, his voice sounding metallic through the respirator. He waved a hand at Reh'dd. Panic engulfed him, squeezing his chest.

"What is it?" Reh'dd called out.

Lym passed Reh'dd as he made his way up the ramp to the

cargo bay.

Then Opute saw it. A little flashing red light on the bottom of the datapad Lym carried.

"Drop the—!"

The datapad blew up.

* * *

A bright light exploded in front of Lym's eyes and heat engulfed him. For a split second he felt his whole body fly in several directions at once before his mind stopped transmitting signals.

* * *

Reh'dd gasped at the bright flash. A red-hot pulse flung her backwards and her body slammed into the hatchway behind her. She heard her head crack against metal and felt her suit and skin melting off her body. Slumping forward, she screamed for a moment in agony, her insides exposed to the environment, until blissful darkness silenced her.

* * *

Several meters away, the shockwave from the heat-filled energy burst lifted Opute off his feet. He landed on the moon's icy surface about twenty meters away and slid, his bones cracking as he hit and tumbled across it. Jagged rocks sticking out through the field of ice caught his suit, skin, and face, tearing off pieces of flesh as if stripping paint from the walls of a room. Then suddenly, with a quick flip, his body tumbled downwards. He slammed hard onto a solid, cold surface.

Everything went black.

CHAPTER 14

DREGOR STARTED BACK toward the *Mirrored Compass* as soon as Lym turned around. By the time the bomb detonated, Dregor had already powered up his ship's shields to prevent any damage from residual effects of the explosion. During takeoff, he directed the nose of his ship back toward the surface of the planet and made a quick sweep of the area. He saw the chunked remains of someone around the entrance to the hatch, and saw the female, her head splattered against the cargo door, body charred and blackened. It took him a moment to find the trail of blood left by the third member of the group who had been thrown quite a ways away. Hovering as close as he could, Dregor zoomed in on a dark area of the moon's surface. He saw a deep crack in the glacier, full of protruding jagged crystal formations. Dregor circled around and found where the trail of blood slid over the surface.

Unable to see the body, Dregor wanted to assume the third member had fallen into the crevasse and died, but being a professional assassin, he didn't take chances. Powering up his weapons system, he fired at the chasm, triggering several avalanches down the icy cliffside.

"If he wasn't dead before, he is now." Dregor sneered at the surface, whipped his ship around, and finished his assignment by firing on the other ship, the *Century*. The craft blew up in a spectacular blaze; a large cloud of black smoke billowed into the air.

Dregor smiled and zoomed away from the moon into space. He couldn't wait to report to Iry that all loose ends were taken care of.

* * *

Opute grudgingly returned to consciousness. Cold air rasped in and out through his respirator, a machine-like hiss as he sucked in a breath and sputtered it back out. After he registered he'd survived, his senses kicked in. A numbing coldness spread across the entire front part of his body, contrasted with a burning heat that ran up along his back. Everywhere else seared with pain. He stared at the back of his eyelids as his mind processed the situation. Opute recalled the explosion and knew he was in serious trouble.

Okay. Figure out a plan. What do you need to do first? He needed to determine exactly where the blast had thrown him and the severity of his condition. Opening his eyes, Opute saw darkness.

Oh stars, I'm blind!

Panic clenched his chest. But ever so slowly, shadows and shapes took form. He gingerly moved his right arm and brought his fingers to his face, scraping them against a surface in front of him. He realized he faced the ground. Chunks of debris and fresh snow surrounded him. Hissing in a deep breath, Opute tried to turn over. Pain rocked through the left side of his body. A scream ripped through his breathing apparatus.

Gritting his teeth, he changed tactics. Opute gingerly tested each leg and arm to assess the damage. His right leg hurt when he lifted it, but it swiveled at the knee and ankle without too much pain. He couldn't feel or move his left leg. Right arm moved fine, though a bit of discomfort in the shoulder. The left arm, however, resulted in a blast of pain. Opute guessed something must be broken.

Opute cautiously pushed himself up using his right arm, willing his muscles to cooperate. His hand pressed into the icy surface and he propped himself on his right knee. Pain flared at the pressure, but it didn't feel like a break.

Dim light shone from up above, lighting up the wall next to him. Cracks webbed out from rock protrusions and frozen water. He checked around and saw he had landed less than a meter from the edge of the icy ledge. Opute tilted his head and peered over the side into a dark chasm. Pulling back quickly, he shifted his gaze upwards and saw the twinkling starry sky above the upper crust of the crevasse, about twenty meters overhead. He didn't know the moon's orbiting schedule, but even so, it had been daylight when he fell. Opute felt lucky to be alive.

The heat emanating from his back indicated the heater in his suit still worked, which kept him from freezing to death. So why couldn't he feel his left leg? Opute pushed away the thought of the leg being black with frostbite or even worse, not there at all.

Except if he wanted to get out of here, he needed to know. With a deep breath, he peeked over his shoulder behind him. A huge hunk of ice lay across the limb, which explained the numbness. Opute sighed with relief. At least he still had his leg.

The muscles in Opute's right arm, which supported him, began to tremble with exhaustion, so he lowered himself gently back down, his cheek pressing onto the cold ground. How could he get that block of ice off his leg? Huge, and probably too heavy for him to lift, even at his full strength.

Cursing under his breath, he tried to think of what to do. Easier said than done as every worst-case scenario weaseled into his mind, filling it with all the extremely terrible ways he could, and probably would, die. As he lay, wracking his brain for any semblance of a plan, he heard an odd noise. Opute lay very still and listened. The noise came again; a strange, repetitive "ch" sound. It grew louder. Closer. Opute strained in the dim light to make out what it was, or at least where it came from.

When it sounded almost on top of him, Opute finally saw it: a long, dark shape slithering toward him down the side of the cliff wall. The creature expanded about two meters long, and first stretched itself out, then contracted its back end to move forward. It crept its way closer, stretching and contracting, getting closer and closer, making the "ch" noise every time it moved. It had several sucker-like appendages that allowed it to cling to the icy surface. He couldn't make out any visible eyes, ears, or mouth.

Staring so intensely, he didn't notice the one come up behind him, the three crawling up beneath the ledge, or the two slinking through one of the cracks in the wall next to him. It wasn't until they all simultaneously pulsated a rich, amber light that he realized they surrounded him.

Opute's breathing quickened. By this point, they completely encircled him. He forced slow breaths, grimacing at the noise it made through the respirator, and waited. Should he try to scare them off? Should he remain still? Should he throw himself off the ledge before they had a chance to eat him?

Opute was plunged back into darkness as the creatures stopped signaling with their pulses of light. Terrified, he peered through the inky blackness, eyes trying to readjust again to the lack of light, trying to make out the shapes. He heard the hissing sound again as they began to move and nearly screamed when he felt one touch his good leg. He kicked out instinctively. His leg swung out, coming in contact with nothing but air. Creeping his way back up onto his knee, Opute noticed the creature hadn't reacted. In fact, several of them touched him briefly and then moved away.

Maybe I don't taste very good?

The creatures lit up again, this time with a dimmer red light, and congregated on top of the large chunk of ice on his left leg. He watched them, wondering what they were doing, when he heard the faint sounds of dripping.

"You're melting it," he murmured out loud.

The creatures paid him no attention and continued with their project. Opute watched in fascination, wondering exactly how they did it. He figured they must have some sort of internal heating system to melt the ice. As he stared, he saw them swell, and realized they must be collecting and storing the water. He could feel heat on his leg and took that as a positive sign; at least all his nerves weren't completely dead.

Once the ice melted and the creatures realized only his leg remained, everything went dark again. The creatures slithered off Opute's leg and he heard them move about a meter away before stopping. After a moment, the amber pulses lit up the canyon once more. They all began to shuffle off in the same direction, heading upwards toward the surface.

Without thinking, Opute flung himself toward the closest one and dug his fingers into its engorged side. To his surprise, the side wasn't slimy, but instead rough and ridged, covered with tiny hairs. Opute fit his fingers into one of the ridges and hung on with all his might. The creature either didn't notice or didn't care that it now had a hitchhiker and continued straight up the vertical wall.

Opute bit straight through his lip to keep himself from screaming at the pain in his body while dragged. He tried to put all his thoughts and strength into his fingers, willing them to hold on as tightly as possible, but worry crept in at the thought that the creature may not go all the way to the surface. What if it stopped halfway up to melt some piece of ice sticking out of the side of the wall, leaving him dangling ten meters above the ledge?

Sweat poured down Opute's face. His fingers ached. His left arm throbbed. After what felt like an eternity, the creature pulled itself, and Opute, over the cliff's edge and onto the moon's surface. Opute's fingers released in a spasm and he rolled off the creature onto the hard terrain. Unfortunately, he landed on his left side, which caused such an influx of pain that he blacked out.

* * *

Iry smiled. He disconnected the vidlink communication from Dregor. Death had officially consumed everyone who could possibly know about his plans, with the exception of himself and Thlin. Even if that cargo crew hadn't known anything, it was always better to silence them, just in case. And as for the third casualty Dregor mentioned, a late addition to the group called Gaaht, well, he'd been expendable anyway.

Iry sat back in his chair behind his large white desk. Drumming his fingers on his armrest, he began to feel restless, waiting for some test results.

He hated to wait.

He always had to be the patient one. The one with all the ideas, but never any of the credit. The one who sat back and watched as Exarth's name flitted on across the lips of the fearful as his own brought about nothing.

Even as children he'd been passed over for Exarth. The others in the hospital always looked to *her* for solutions, though he came up with the answers. He simply didn't get along with others, so to get the children to do his bidding, he fed Exarth his ideas and observed how the other children followed her.

She didn't even seem to try. That infuriated him the most! They followed her plans, without questioning, without thinking.

So Iry had bided his time, watching, studying, calculating. He learned how to pull strings, what wheels to grease. And finally, he got to a point where he knew how to manipulate others, bring them under his control. He would have her Empire because he'd done all the work.

But he needed to eliminate her from the equation first. Since he didn't know how to do that yet, due to her regenerative mutation, he could attack her through her finances, her business, and her reputation. Then he would collect the remains and build his own Empire.

But he'd been experimenting with some new weaponry....

During that thought, the chimes to his office rang.

"Come," he called out.

The doors slid open.

"Good afternoon, Iry."

"It's about time, Thlin," Iry snapped. Iry's first point of business on his own was to corner the twig drug market. With his knowledge, he'd been able to increase potency and reduce side effects. He couldn't make the stuff fast enough. But increasing the amounts would become problematic, so he'd assigned Thlin to oversee the project.

Thlin smirked. "Data gathering takes time." He extended his muscular arm and handed Iry a datapad. He leaned against the other chair in the room, his stance casual.

"How is the testing going?" Iry asked.

"Most of the patients are responding well. The addiction rate has been increased thirty percent and the extension of the high has increased twenty. There have been some casualties due to potency issues, but the numbers have been acceptable. We also need to find a different way to get the drug into their systems. Injection is an option, but then our targets would also have to worry about purchasing extra items, such as a syringe and needle, and it's harder to hide puncture marks on the skin.

"There are plastic-coated slips that dissolve in one's oral digestive cavity," Thlin continued, "but those can be detected more easily by authorities and are harder to hide in large amounts." He sighed and ran his fingers through his ear-length auburn hair. "I'll think of something."

Iry looked up from the datapad. "I know you will, Thlin."

Thlin smiled slowly.

"Keep me informed," Iry told him, dismissing him at the same time.

"Of course."

CHAPTER 15

DR. LUDD GLANCED out of the small spaceship's viewport as the ship pulled out of infinlight. The stars condensed into little points of light from the streaked, blurred versions they were moments before. Debris from the moon's thin atmosphere struck the ship, causing small dents in the vessel's rusted hull. They had pulled out late again and emerged too close to the surface.

The moon appeared white and flat, but the doctor knew rock formations, ice-encrusted crevasses, and shallow impressions from fallen meteorites covered the surface. Although medicine was his life, he loved to study geology, and read all the charts of the moon before their arrival.

Dr. Ludd strained his bulbous pink eyes to make out Krysh, their destination, on the other side of the moon. The sphere appeared brown and green in color, but they weren't close enough to see any city outlines. He only hoped the medical supplies they carried would be enough for the world, trapped in the middle of a planetary civil war between the western and eastern continents.

At least you're doing something worthwhile, the doctor thought. Although his heavy-set shape and jelly-like consistency gave a different impression, Dr. Ludd was a highly skilled surgeon and physician. Transporting medical supplies wasn't exactly the best use of his time or talents and he couldn't even *help* any injured on the planet for liability reasons, but it was better than nothing. He'd been hired to make sure the supplies were protected in their individual cooling compartments and to monitor any issues that arose with the misa serum, which helped to speed up the body's healing abilities.

After the things I've done in my past, I'm lucky to even have a job in the medical field. When I think of what I've done in the name of "medicine" just so I could be a healer, what I did last year for the Aleet Army….

The doctor didn't want to remember.

A disgrace, he could never return to his home or his family. His past tainted him, so much so he'd even changed his name to continue working.

As they orbited around and passed the sunlit side of the moon, Dr. Ludd leaned his jelly-like body toward the viewport. His round eyes blinked slowly.

A large black spot marred the moon's white surface.

"Well that shouldn't be there," he said under his breath.

"What shouldn't be there, Doctor Mianlo?" A voice popped in behind him.

Dr. Ludd tilted his right flippered hand forward, moving a small switch near his hip that connected to his repulsorlift, which supported his massive jelly-like body. The mechanism wasn't usually necessary because Dr. Ludd's species could lift their own body mass off the floor and move about using an electromagnetic field, but sometimes on smaller vessels it interfered with the ship's working capabilities. In these instances he opted for a repulsorlift that used fuel-powered jets to lift him off the ground. The device moved slowly and awkwardly, as demonstrated by the shaky way it swiveled to face the newest addition to the room.

"Ah, Captain Goljo, you caught me in my thoughts, which I suppose weren't actually thoughts, since they were spoken out loud, but they were, I suppose, an inner monologue instead because they were meant to be heard only by me, which didn't really work, since I both spoke out loud and you also heard me."

Captain Goljo, a short, muscular man with blond hair trimmed neatly to his ears, waited until the doctor finished his rambling speech. "What shouldn't be there, Doctor Mianlo?" Goljo asked again.

Dr. Ludd knew his tendency to carry on in dialogue was often a sore spot for other species. He did his best now to limit his conversation, but sometimes, especially when excited, he found it quite difficult.

He turned back to the viewport. "There seems to be a discrepancy on the moon's surface, or at least something that caught my attention. I'm not sure if it should be there or not, but it seemed unusual considering the nature of the moon's topical appearance."

The captain leaned over to look out of the viewport in the same direction as the doctor.

Dr. Ludd continued. "There is a large black ... well *smudge* is the first word that comes to mind. Just to the north of the moon's equator. Can you see it?"

Captain Goljo stared, his eyes narrow. "Yes, I see it." He paused. "Strange. It almost seems like an impact of some sort—space debris or a meteorite perhaps?—but the spread pattern is all wrong."

"That is precisely what I thought, except as you may well remember, I thought it out loud, which is to say I said it."

The captain moved to his left and hit the communications

panel on the room's wall.

"Lieutenant Payb?"

"Yes sir?" A voice answered over the communications circuit.

"Change our heading to fly over the northern section of the moon. Once you see the blackened area on the surface, head toward it. Do not fly below the moon's atmosphere until I say."

"Yes sir."

* * *

Opute heard voices. No. Not voices. *One* voice. A very bubbly, light-sounding voice speaking fast. It came from above him. It sounded like hearing someone at the end of a tunnel.

"Amazing…truly a work…sophistica…detail…ohnoheswakingup…"

Opute heard a hiss and the voice faded away.

* * *

Opute swam into consciousness. He stared at the back of his eyelids for several moments, assessing his present condition, careful to appear asleep and not change his breathing, which he'd trained himself to do in an unfamiliar situation. No indication of anyone in the near vicinity, so he focused on his body.

A warmth covered him. His skin tingled and he felt sticky—quite unusual sensations since he expected the coldness of the moon's surface. Someone must have picked him up, but who?

Opute opened his eyes. Dark gray lines of a metallic surface stretched overhead. Pinpoints of soft, yellow light dotted the ceiling. He turned his head, cradled in a pillow, and internally tensed in surprise: two dark pink eyes blinked at him mere centimeters from his face.

"Good morning!" the being cried out.

Opute stared at the massive, globular being. He didn't recognize the species, with translucent pink skin, a hairless scalp, and lipless smile, but so far, it seemed friendly enough.

"Well, technically it's afternoon," the being continued, "but most creatures feel as though the term 'morning' is more appropriate when they first wake up—although, since you've been in and out of consciousness for the past couple days, you probably have no time reference whatsoever."

Opute tried to respond, but his mouth wouldn't open.

"Oh, sorry. I should have told you not to try to speak, as your head is bandaged tightly under your chin and your jaw is being reset. You're pretty banged up—to use a non-medical term—and you'd been lying on the moon's surface for what I've estimated to be about two days with several severe cuts and bruises, fractures, a concussion, and hypothermia. We picked you up yesterday, you are on a ship called the *Nuadu* by the way, which is a medical freighter headed toward the planet Krysh, which the moon you were on orbits—and we, well *I* to be honest, saw a strange black mark on the surface of the moon, which you probably know, since you were there for several days, is very odd indeed, since the moon's surface is an icy white color. We landed, that is Captain Goljo ordered his pilot, Lieutenant Payb, to land on the surface and saw the remains of a vessel, which I assume was how you got there, and after searching the area and not finding any survivors—well there were *parts* of them—we assumed...I beg your pardon!" The creature finally stopped in exclamation. "I in no way meant to comment on the dead with any disrespect and if I insulted, offended, or upset you in any way with regards to your fellow crewmates, I whole-heartedly apologize and sincerely hope you'll forgive me."

Opute had no idea what to do. He'd just been bombarded with more words at once than he could sort through, his location put him on a strange ship instead of dying on a frozen moon, and he couldn't open his mouth to say anything to the odd, but pleasant being that hovered over him. Instead, he lay there, blinking slowly, doing his best to shake off his grogginess.

"Well, I guess I'll go now, since I've probably stuck my appendage in my mouth, as the old saying goes, and because you can't answer me—not for lack of wanting, I'm sure—I'll check back in later when you've healed up a bit and fill you in on everything else that's going on with you and the ship you are now on headed to Krysh, which I think I told you about before, and by the time we get there, which should be a couple of standard hours, and deliver the medical supplies we need to, you should be much better and then we can finish our little chat, as long as you are feeling up to it that is because the last thing I would want to do is push you too hard too fast—I've had that happen in the past with a patient and believe me that ended in an almost atrocious manner, although I've forgiven myself for my part, though it took me quite some time to do so—so we'll see how things are when we get there, Krysh that is, and see how things are when we leave and go from there." The being splayed his mouth open in a large half-crescent shape. He pressed a tube against Opute's arm. A quick pinch, then a hiss.

"If you need anything once you wake, just press the button to the left—no *your* left—and I'll come and help you out." The being swiveled around on its repulsorlift and headed out of the room. Before it departed, it called out to him over its massive shoulder. "By the way, my name is Doctor Mianlo."

As soon as the doctor left the room, Opute's eyes rolled back into his head and he fell into blissful sleep.

Opute resurfaced after several hours. Once his eyes

adjusted to the light, he determined the doctor wasn't in the room, and moved his head to one side to glance around. His view consisted of the blackness of space, sprinkled with pinpoints of white light. He realized they had left the moon's orbit and the doctor most likely already made his cargo delivery. But their destination? Opute had no idea.

He then remembered the button to his left and pushed it to call the doctor. A few minutes later the physician floated into the room, his repulsorlift humming.

"I see you are up," Dr. Ludd said, his mouth flopping into a large smile. "I figured you'd be coming around soon. Your wounds are nearly healed and you've been responding to stimulus in your left leg quite well. You nearly lost it to frostbite."

Opute nodded.

"You can talk now. Your bottom lip is still a little swollen, but should be fine."

Opute opened his mouth, his lips sticking. A spastic cough emerged when he attempted to thank the doctor.

"You're welcome," Dr. Ludd said.

Opute tried again, this time with more success. "You saved my life. I would have been dead back there if it hadn't been for you, Doctor ... Milo was it?"

"Mianlo," Dr. Ludd said. "And you are?"

"Gaaht. Vor Gaaht." His false name came out on a wheezy breath. "Why is it so difficult for me to talk?"

"At some point, you crushed your larynx, which of course means you damaged your vocal chords, which then leads to the conclusion it would be difficult for you to speak. It isn't permanent, although I had to do some minor surgery to fix it. Interestingly enough, I found this." Dr. Ludd held up a small, slightly curved metallic-colored disc.

Opute's eyes widened. He just realized he'd spoken with

his normal voice, deep and gravelly, instead of his new tenor voice. The doctor held the voice modifier Zarsa installed.

"It is quite an interesting piece of technology, Mister Gaaht, if I do say so myself. Very advanced."

A film of sweat broke out over Opute's body.

"I didn't mean to alarm you," Dr. Ludd said. "Merely admiring it. Don't worry. Whatever the reason, it's yours, not mine. As soon as your throat heals up, I can reinstall this, if you'd like."

Opute swallowed over his sore throat and nodded. "Thanks, Doc."

"Are you feeling up to sitting? I thought I might bring in some food if you'd like to try eating."

Opute, never wanting to seem weak, sat up quickly, gritting his teeth at the pain.

Dr. Ludd gurgled a laugh. "Mister Gaaht, you have no one here to impress but me, and that is something you do not need to worry about. Please take your time."

Opute managed a tight-lipped smile, but his body ached with relief. He continued adjusting himself into an upright posture, although less quickly, and finally felt comfortable, propped up against the spongy surface of the bed, which had risen into a sitting position behind him.

"Where are we?" Opute asked, his voice still shaky.

"We are heading toward Sula, which is where the Sula Prime Medical Base is located and that's where I'm stationed for work. It's about a day's journey from Krysh, although I don't ever plan on going there again."

"Why not?"

"Let's just say their citizens aren't the friendliest creatures I've ever met and I've been in some unpleasant company in my day. They simply took the supplies and ran off without paying us."

"War zone?"

Dr. Ludd blinked his eyes slowly. "As a matter of fact, yes. How did you know?"

Opute shrugged. "I've been in the cargo business a long time. Desperation is the same no matter the planet." Images returned to him from the moon's surface. The explosion. The two lives gone in a flash of light. He thought of Reh'dd's cute, wrinkled nose and a lump caught in his throat. "Be thankful you made it out alive."

CHAPTER 16

EXARTH'S PLAN TO get to know the other children in the hospital went perfectly. She started by getting to know Nyma, who turned out to be smart but flighty, and so she opted not to include the girl in her plan. Next came Iry, a bit arrogant, but insanely intelligent, who couldn't wait to talk about the truth regarding the "doctors," and finally to Coresque, or Cor as Exarth had come to call her, who was the most imaginative being she'd ever met. The three of them convened during designated playtime. During one of those periods, Iry revealed he could read lips.

"They converse about us all the time—about our progress, our results, and our tests. It's like we're animals in some sort of laboratory."

"Maybe we are," Coresque chimed in.

Iry paused, his eyes narrow in thought. "It would make sense. It seems like every child is here for a specific and individual reason. Exarth, you have regenerative abilities, Coresque, your skin is nearly impenetrable, and me, well, my intellectual prowess is probably unmatched, especially for a thirteen-year-old."

"Not to mention your ego," Exarth joked.

Then one night, Iry came to Exarth's bed, a note of fear in his voice.

"Wake up," he said, shaking her awake.

"What is it?"

"We must depart, immediately."

"What?" she mumbled. "It's the middle of the night."

"I am aware of that fact. But I awoke and read the lips of some of the doctors speaking in the corridor through the safety glass. They mentioned something about 'exterminating the test subjects due to inability to access their genetic traits'. And then they read off five sets of numbers. You, me, and Coresque were each listed!"

Exarth threw off her covers. "You know what to do."

Iry nodded and went to wake the others. Exarth jumped out of bed and got dressed. She ran over to the door and barricaded it with the metal bar from the end of a bed they'd worked at unscrewing for the past few weeks. She turned and saw Iry and a few others already stacking the beds so they could climb out the window.

Exarth grabbed a white monitoring device from next to her bed. She climbed up the stack and whipped it at the window. Glass broke. Alarms wailed.

"Let's go!" she screamed over the noise. She took one last look at the doors and saw two nurses pulling desperately on the handles. With a grunt, she pulled herself up onto the ledge, wincing as broken glass cut into her hands. With a push from someone below, she crawled through the opening and landed softly two meters below on white grass.

That's when she saw herself, reflected in a pane of glass. Her eyes were not white. They were dark and something else she didn't have a name for. And her hair—short and dark on her head.

She only had a moment to register the differences before the first child clambered through. One by one they came. Coresque, heavy as rock, landed with a thud on the ground. It took several moments for the others to set her right-side up.

Sixteen children emerged when the screaming started. Exarth stared in horror as one child, a young girl of about seven, got stuck halfway through the window. She shrieked in pain as white hands yanked her back inside, dragging her body along the shards of the window's broken glass.

"We have to flee," Iry said to Exarth, pulling at her arm.

Fury stole through Exarth's body. She trembled with rage, wanting to stay and save all the children. But she knew it'd do no good.

"Follow me," she ordered. They scrambled over the fences and fled into the streets.

The first few nights were the worst. They could not discreetly hide over a dozen children. They decided to split up into smaller groups and were to meet back at a different location every day.

By the fourth day, they'd lost a whole group. Cor found them splattered on the side of the road from an auto-street-washer. At the end of the week, two more children had such severe withdrawal symptoms from drugs the "doctors" had pumped into their systems that they died; one vomited until blood poured from her ears and nose and the other simply fell over, convulsing until his heart stopped.

"We need to find a permanent place to relocate," Iry said. "We will never survive flitting around between places, especially once the cold season commences."

"Where can we go?" one of the children asked, her white eyes large with concern. "And what are we supposed to do about *her*? She'll get us all killed if the DOLP come after us!"

Exarth grit her teeth at the comment. Her color-changing eyes and short, dark hair stuck out on an entirely pigment-free planet. The Department of Lost Property, or DOLP, was a scary story told to all of them at a young age. "If you ever run away, the DOLP will find you and claim you as their own!," but Iry quickly learned through word of mouth on the streets that they were a real organization. If the "doctors" filed a search-and-return policy through DOLP, Exarth, because of her unique coloring, would be an easy target to find. The DOLP had a reputation for not only returning lost property or individuals, but, strictly off the record, would also eliminate or destroy the lost objects, for an extra fee.

"We'll need to acquire an abandoned building," Iry started, ignoring the child's comment about Exarth, "but it mustn't be too dilapidated. It has to have an address, secure and intact windows, adequate siding, preferably with a decent lawn…"

"Right," the child snorted with disbelief, "like most abandoned buildings have well-kept lawns."

Iry turned his head toward the child. "If the DOLP is contacted, they will be searching for a disorganized group of children hiding in any refuge accessible to them. We must have a secure location to bring in bedding, food, and necessities until we can determine our next course of action. The more maintained our new sanctuary is, the lower the probability of investigation by DOLP. I can also doctor and submit falsified papers to the Department of Housing that will verify our shelter as legitimate. However, I don't expect the ruse to last more than a few months, at best. We'd also better have a contingency plan in order to escape in a quick fashion should we be detected."

Exarth watched a few of the children shuffle their feet and look around, confused. Though an eloquent speaker, Iry's vocabulary suited intelligent adults rather than scared children.

"What he means," Coresque explained, picking up on the

same signals as Exarth, "is we need a nice-looking place so the DOLP doesn't think we're hiding there. And we need to be able to leave the building quickly, in case Iry's papers are discovered as fakes."

Exarth had to admit Coresque had a way with the children that both Exarth and Iry appreciated. Iry talked over their heads, whereas Exarth often lost patience. Coresque embodied the perfect balance of softness, without seeming to patronize them.

"As for your other uncouth question concerning Exarth's unique appearance," Iry continued, "that can be remedied with whitened optics and a covering for her head."

"You could've just said hat and sunglasses," one of the children muttered under his breath. The two girls next to him giggled. Exarth knew she had to speak with Iry about the way he talked. They couldn't afford to lose any more children. Safety in numbers.

"Trust me," Exarth reassured the group, "if I cause any problems with the way I look, I will take off on my own."

Iry looked at her sharply, as if wanting to disagree, but said nothing.

The plan worked, giving the group several months of time to decide what to do with their lives. They were all too young to get jobs, Iry being the oldest at 13, and several wanted to return to their families, but Coresque's warning that the doctors would most certainly be waiting for them at their houses made them reject the idea.

Exarth felt impressed with Iry's ability to modify his vocabulary over these past few months. However, even though he usually came up with all the ideas, the children waited until Exarth gave the order to execute any plan. Somehow she became their leader, although she wasn't sure how. One evening, after a successful shoplifting endeavor, she asked Coresque about it.

"I don't understand it, Cor," she said, separating perishables from longer lasting items. "I mean, Iry has all the ideas and you're easy to talk to, so why do they all look to me for the go-ahead?"

Coresque tilted her head to the side in thought. "Iry likes to talk, I like to dream, you like to act. These children need a leader," she said. "Something more than ideas and reassurance. They require someone to take both those things and put them into action. You do that. You can assess a situation and, regardless of how well-planned an idea is, you always know when to execute it. It helps that you are always right. These children see that in you, and so you are able to lead them in a way that Iry and I cannot."

Exarth kept the things Coresque told her in her mind over the next several weeks and realized the truth. More so when she noticed the group became stagnant. Plans needed to be made and those plans needed to be put into effect.

"We all have a decision to make," Exarth said over the low rumblings of the children talking amongst themselves. They were huddled together in a loose circle on the floor of what would have been the lobby of the abandoned warehouse. It remained dimly lit since Iry hadn't managed to steal electricity for this location, but handheld portable light units created enough glow for everyone to see. A few stolen blankets and a large rug made the floor fairly comfortable, and a bag of food passed its way among the children as they quieted, listening to Exarth.

"Since this decision will affect what we do with the rest of our lives," Exarth continued, "it will not be a majority decision, but an individual one. Each of you can choose whatever path you want to take from here on. You can stay in this building, although we don't know how much longer Iry's cover will last. As for myself, Cor, and Iry, we are leaving the day after tomorrow and have decided to return to the hospital and shut it down."

Exarth gave the other children a moment to register this new piece of information. Then they all began talking at once.

"What do you mean 'return to the hospital?'"

"Are you guys *crazy*?"

"No one is going to listen to you there."

"They'll just kill you if you go back!"

"I'll never go back there. Never!"

Exarth waited for the shouts to dull before speaking again. "That hospital is still running. Do you think they've stopped experimenting on children just because we left? No one deserves to go through what we did and we are the only ones who know what's going on." Exarth raised her voice over the new exclamations. "We are not asking you to come with us. We are telling you what our plan is. It is your choice if you want to help."

"Why don't we tell the authorities? Go to them with our story and have them shut the hospital down?"

"You have all witnessed the news broadcasts about the war our planet is fighting. Our government is desperate for solutions, without caring about how those solutions arrive. Do you really think the authorities don't already know about the hospital? That they are not supporting it? Running to them would be a death sentence for us. I know you have all noticed that 'missing children from local hospital' has not been in any of the headlines. We are obviously a well-guarded secret no one wants to expose."

The children all quieted, enraptured by the terrifying concepts.

"None of you have to come," Coresque said, her voice somehow calm and serious at the same time, "but the hospital will never be stopped by anyone but us. The doctors, nurses, administrators, and directors of that hospital are immoral and evil. They subject children to torture, experimentation, and death to serve their own purposes. They will never receive justice from our government, they will never be punished for their crimes. It is up to us to stop them and I choose to do so. I believe if this planet is supposed to win this war, it will have to be without the misuse of its own children."

Iry stepped forward. "We plan to break into the building, steal any incriminating evidence, and do whatever we must if someone tries to stop us. We will then transmit that evidence off planet, in the hopes someone will use it to their advantage and bring down our corrupted government. Finally, we will find passage off this planet and begin our lives elsewhere."

It sounded terrible presented so bluntly, but Exarth believed the other children would never want to be lied to or kept in the dark again. Half the children looked stunned, the others shifted nervously or whispered to their neighbors.

Exarth took over. "We leave the day after tomorrow," she repeated. "You have until then to decide. To those who don't come with, good luck with your lives. Meeting adjourned."

The three of them used the next two days to track down the equipment they would need. Coresque broke into a painting supply warehouse and stole several portable breathing units. Iry met up with some of the contacts he'd made on the streets and obtained a quantity of twig, a hallucinogenic drug, in a gaseous state. Exarth had the hardest job—she needed to acquire some HEDU's, which were hand-held electric discharge units.

As an eleven-year-old girl wearing a white knit hat to hide her colored hair and white sunglasses for her eyes, she had no idea how to get the weapons they needed. Iry's contacts were no help—they didn't want to get involved with artillery. Exarth said she would figure it out, but after the other two disappeared, she was at a complete loss.

She ran through a list of places that might house those sorts of weapons—military installations, authority buildings, high-security shops which carried them for sale. Each seemed as impenetrable as the last.

Then she saw it. A tall building on the horizon, white as everything around it. Tall white letters, seen only by the shadows their imprints made in the structure, showed any difference from those around it. A meat-processing plant.

A large ovule sped by her, stopping outside the front doors. Streams of children piled out of the vehicle, some wrapping their arms around their puffy white coats, others pulling down their white hats to hide their ears from the cold winds.

Exarth crossed the road in a flash and shimmied behind the rest of the students. She soon realized this wouldn't work with her sunglasses making her stand out, so she took them off, and kept her gaze low, peering out only through her eyelashes.

With slow steps they all made their way into the building, the teacher in front blabbering on about safety concerns and staying with the group. For the first time in her life, Exarth felt a pang of loss, knowing this could have been her life, just a student on a class outing, had things turned out differently.

Once inside, the tour began. A tall man in a white coat lectured about the facility, spouting figures concerning animal safety, food preparation requirements, and even pitching a "you can work here someday, too!" speech.

As soon as she saw a break, she quietly slipped away into a cleaner's room, and hid behind a large barrel of chemicals. The smell made her a bit nauseous, but she settled in for a long wait, drifting into and out of sleep, and ignoring her growling stomach.

She awoke with a start, the room pitch black. Hands outstretched, she felt around until she came to the door. With a flip of a switch, the door unlocked, and she found herself right where she left the tour.

Moving quickly, she made her way toward the animal-wrangling area and found a tall cabinet with a locking mechanism on it. Exarth wracked her brain to remember Iry's decoding training, and after several unsuccessful tries, she managed to open the lock. Inside sat several weapons, usually used to either kill or tranquilize the animals before slaughter. Six HEDU's hung in a row, their handheld size a little big in her small hands, but definitely the easiest weapon for them all to use. Plus it could be non-lethal, which worked better after they decided they didn't want to kill any of the hospital staff, only gather enough evidence to expose them.

Exarth ripped three of the HEDU's from inside the cabinet and fled the building, the soft sound of cooing coming from the animals locked in the pens around her.

Two days later, Exarth, Iry, and Coresque stood in the main lobby, alone.

"Fools!" Iry spat. "Don't they understand what we are attempting to do? This coup will only bring peace to our planet."

"You forget they are only children," Coresque said quietly.

"So are we!"

Coresque gave a small smile, which Exarth knew would infuriate Iry even more. "When were the three of us really ever children? We are different than they are. You know that."

"Exactly! They should have listened to us, followed us. They don't know what they're doing. If just one or two of them came with—"

"We'll manage," Exarth said, shifting a backpack onto her other shoulder. She ignored the look of anger on his face at being interrupted. "We designed this to work with only the three of us, just in case. Having extra hands would help, but we will get this done."

They planned to attack that night, when personnel would be minimal. Iry would first release the gaseous twig he had obtained into the building through the air filtration systems. Once saturated with the gas, the staff would be rendered unable to function, and the three of them, with portable breathing circulatory units, would infiltrate the building and render any lingering personnel unconscious with HEDU's. They knew all the access codes, provided by Iry's eidetic memory after watching the "doctors" come in and out, knew where the laboratories were to collect evidence and files, and would help any other children they found escape to a safe house, since they were in a "clean-room" environment and would be sealed off from any of the twig gases.

That evening, everything went as arranged, and the three of them entered the building, using their HEDU's to stun anyone in their way.

"We'll meet back here as planned," Exarth whispered. The three of them split up to collect different types of evidence.

Exarth came around the corner of one of the laboratory rooms and nearly yelped in surprise. Someone stood in the room, working on a patient. The room must be sealed differently, so the twig gas didn't penetrate inside. Holding her breath, she peeked through the window.

Arew.

Dissecting a girl on the table.

No. Not dissecting. *Vivisecting.* The girl still lived. She thrashed around in her restraints, which only tightened the more she struggled. Exarth peered closer at the girl's throat. Incisions had been made across her vocal chords, which explained why she screamed silence into the air. White beads of sweat coated her body, her face streaked with cloudy tears.

She couldn't have been older than five.

Exarth threw open the door. Arew jumped back from the girl at the noise.

"Printz!" Arew exclaimed. "You scared me half to…" The words dropped. "By the white eyes of Sundar," he said. "You're alive."

She stood there, shaking. She didn't know what to do.

Arew stepped away from the laboratory table, blocking Exarth's view of the girl. "What are you doing here?" he asked.

"You were…" she stammered. "You were supposed to be one of the good guys."

"What are you talking about?" He crept his way over to the wall, where Exarth could see an alarm button. She raised the HEDU.

"Don't move."

He froze. "Exarth, you are sick. You need help. You are probably withdrawing from your medication. You aren't thinking clearly."

"I'm not sick."

"Oh yes," he assured her, "you are. You all are. That's why you were here. We were going to make you better. *Normal.*"

"You…you lie."

"Have I ever lied to you?" he asked her. He narrowed his eyes, searching her face. It put her on edge.

"You're helping this place experiment on children."

Arew nodded. "Yes, but for their own good. We take in genetically distorted children and study them, to see if we can help them be like other children. You must know you're different now, with your hair and eye color. We knew you couldn't live in our world like that. We were trying to help you. To make you pure white, like everyone else." His eyes flickered back and forth while he stared at her.

"What are you doing?" she asked, the unease increasing. "Stop looking at me like that!"

"Okay. I can tell you're upset, but I know you're curious, too." He held his hands up. The girl's white blood dripped down the edge of his scalpel.

"Curious? Why would you think…that's not true."

"Of course it is. I can see it in your eyes. They are your weakness, your genetic mistake. I can read you. I *know* you through your eyes, the different shades of non-white they show."

He is babbling, that's all, to stall for time. Exarth thought the words, but the way he stared at her made her feel completely exposed.

"Don't you want to be normal? Don't you want to be like the other children? I can give you that normal life." He slunk forward a bit, still staring at her eyes. She wanted to look away, but feared he'd move toward her or the alarm if she averted her gaze.

"And this girl?" she asked, her voice quivering. "What is so wrong with her that you would cut her open while she's still alive?"

"This girl is in constant pain. She has been for two years. No one knows why. She burst her own vocal chords after months of screaming; that's the reason we removed them. The things I'm doing to her don't hurt her any more than living does. I'm trying to find a way to deaden the nerves so she doesn't feel this pain anymore."

"And you just so happen to study these effects for military applications, too?" she spat, her anger overtaking her fear. "Must be nice to use this nerve affliction as a weapon against your enemies."

"Enemies? What are you talking about? What military applications?"

"I know this hospital is involved with helping the military." Exarth hated that her voice shook with uncertainty.

"I don't know where you got your facts, but they aren't true. We work independently from the government. Most citizens don't understand why we are trying to help these children. They think these genetic anomalies are defects and the children should be destroyed. We rescued them." He lowered his arms. "We rescued you. You were going to be euthanized."

Exarth's head spun. Could it be true? Could Iry have been mistaken by the things he'd heard and seen? Could he have put together his own thoughts and come to the wrong conclusion?

"Exarth please, let me help you. If you stay off your medication, you'll only get worse. Have you noticed excessive mood swings? Do your emotions seem out of control? These are signs your condition is worsening. Please, let me call for help and—"

"Don't let him near that alarm button." Exarth spun around at the voice behind her. Iry stood there, holding a small disk. "You need to see this," he said to Exarth, and loaded the disk into a data reader.

"Iry?" Arew asked, astonished. "Is that you? I'm so glad you are safe and—"

"Save it." Exarth had never heard heat in Iry's voice before and it frightened her. But then the image on the screen captured her attention. Arew, dressed in a surgical gown, facing the vidlink recording device. He began to speak.

"I am proceeding with test number eleven of patient number three-four-four-eight. This test will be a measurement of nerve response to the incisions on non-critical systems. We will be focusing on the right upper arm."

The Arew in the recording stepped away from the vidlink to reveal a long white table with a patient strapped to it—Exarth.

"Turn it off NOW!" Arew lunged toward the portable vidlink player, but Iry snatched it out of his reach and shot off the weapon to his left, an arc of electricity sparking through the air, exploding a tray full of medical instruments next to Arew.

"Do not do that again," Iry said, his voice emotionless.

Exarth returned her attention back to the screen and watched as Arew repeatedly sliced open the sedated version of herself on her right arm while other nurses observed Exarth regenerate, gathering statistical data on how her nerves responded to the process.

"There are dozens of these recordings," Iry continued. "Of *all* the children. Would you like to see the one where you weren't sedated, Exarth? Where you screamed in pain as they examined your reactions? They gave you a drug so you wouldn't remember, but that didn't mean you didn't feel the pain every time. They did it to you, to me, to Coresque. They are monsters."

Exarth shook. She stood there, blinking at the now blank vidlink screen.

"Exarth, please," Arew pleaded, moving toward her. "I can explain."

Exarth turned and looked at Arew, the sorrow in his eyes evident, and then her gaze shifted to the girl strapped down behind him.

The girl suffering the same torture Exarth had been put through.

Exarth didn't even think about it. She reached over and took a scalpel from the barrage of tools lying next to her. In one swift motion, she slashed it across Arew's throat.

White blood poured from the wound, spraying across Exarth's outstretched arm, splashing down Arew's chest. Arew grabbed at his neck and slid to his knees, his eyes open in disbelief. He reached out for her and she stepped back, letting him fall to the floor, his hand slipping in the pool of his own blood.

She still trembled as anger surged through her.

Iry spoke up behind her. "We have to go."

Exarth didn't move. She simply stared at Arew's body.

Iry put his hand on Exarth's shoulder and she jumped. "We have to go," he repeated.

Exarth nodded. But instead of heading for the door she ran over and released the girl who'd been lying on the table, using the knife to cut through the straps.

"You're going to be okay," Exarth told the little girl.

The girl still silently screamed and before Exarth could stop her, she grabbed Exarth's hand that still held the scalpel and plunged it into her own chest.

She fell to the floor, dead.

"No!" Exarth screamed, reaching for the girl.

"Leave her," Iry said, pulling Exarth away. "We have to get out of here, now!"

"No. No! NO!" Exarth sobbed as Iry dragged her from the room. She followed him blindly, stumbling the whole way until they met up with Coresque outside.

"What happened?" Coresque asked, her white eyes wide with concern.

The room spun, a whirl of white, before Exarth fainted.

CHAPTER 17

OPUTE ROCKED BACK and forth on his bare feet. The grooved metallic floor pinched and prodded, but he didn't care. It felt good to stand on his own. After a week of being coddled by the large jelly-bodied doctor and his seemingly endless supply of persistent automated helpers, he loved doing something by himself.

Opute swiveled around at the hiss of the door opening.

"Good morning, Mister Gaaht," Dr. Mianlo said as he hovered into the room. "I see we are up and about today?"

Opute nodded. He took a seat on the bed for his daily inspection. "Ready to get off this ship as usual, Doc."

Dr. Mianlo began his reflex testing. "Any problems with your voice modifier today?"

Opute reached up and touched his throat. "No. I sound just like someone else."

Dr. Mianlo sighed. "Mr. Gaaht, if you are in any type of trouble and need some help..."

Opute waved away the doctor's offer. "Thanks, but no thanks. The less you know, the better."

"I really might be able to assist you."

"I doubt it." Opute snorted at the thought of Dr. Mianlo being involved in anything unethical. With his large grin and bulbous belly, the doctor sooner belonged in a children's story than able to help Opute with his pursuit.

Dr. Mianlo continued with his exam. "Looks can be deceiving, Mister Gaaht. If anyone should know, it's you."

Opute raised an eyebrow. "Really? Got a sordid past of your own, Doc?"

Dr. Mianlo made a motion, like a rippled shrug. "Let's just say I have seen my own dark days. Perhaps helping you may assist me in atoning for some of the mistakes I've made."

"What makes you think the mess I'm in will help you?"

"You talked in your sleep, Mr. Gaaht."

Opute jumped off the table and shoved the doctor against the wall, his fingers pressing into the jelly-like flesh. "What did you hear?"

To Opute's surprise, the doctor did not seem put off by this aggressive move. In fact, he seemed to be holding back a smile.

"I am not a stranger to threats of bodily harm, Mister Gaaht, though I have to admit it's been some time since anyone threatened me so boldly and—"

"Quit rambling and answer my question."

"Very well. But if you don't mind, would you please sit back down so I can finish examining you? I assure you nothing you have said left my mouth or this room."

Opute eased his grip and plopped back down on the bed.

"Thank you. Now...ah yes, the answer to your question. While most of your words were undecipherable, several made quite an impression on me. The main ones dealt with your wife...or I should say your deceased wife." Dr. Mianlo moved around Opute to check his spine. "The emotion in your voice when you spoke her name moved me. It must have been tragic for you to lose her."

"Well why don't we talk about it then?" Opute said sarcastically.

"My apologies. I didn't mean to offend you or to bring up painful memories. I just wanted to show you why I'm so intrigued with your plight. You see, Mister Gaaht, I myself am married, but for certain reasons, can no longer be with my wife."

"This wouldn't have to do with that 'dark past' you were talking about?"

"As a matter of fact, it does. Because of my mistakes, I am an outcast on my homeworld and am a subject of exile. I am never again allowed to see my family or help those who need assistance. On my world, being a doctor, a *healer,* is not a job, it is my life. Without it, I have no purpose. I would be useless."

"Couldn't you just do something else?"

Dr. Mianlo shook his head. "You say that as if I have a choice in the matter. Being a doctor is all that I am. There is nothing else."

"I don't follow."

Dr. Mianlo put down his instruments. "You have lungs, correct? Imagine if someone said you could no longer use them to breathe. You could use an artificial breather for the rest of your life, strapped to a machine that respires for you. You could adapt, no matter how uncomfortable or different the feeling. Now imagine someone said you could only walk if you made your lungs work your legs."

"That's impossible."

"Precisely, Mister Gaaht. Trying to do something else besides being a healer is not something I could adapt to, like artificial lungs. And thinking that your lungs can do anything else but breathe? It's unthinkable."

"You just don't seem like the 'get exiled' type."

Dr. Mianlo gurgled. "And you appear to be about twenty standard years old with copper skin and a tenor voice."

"I see your point."

"The reason I bring all this up, Mister Gaaht, is that I have the pleasure of giving you a clean bill of health. You are fit to return to your life when you were found nearly exploded on that moon, provided you want to return to it, and it is still my hope that perhaps I can assist you in some way. I have done terrible things, Mister Gaaht, and though I have lost my home, my wife, and my family, I hope to not lose myself. I am a healer and I wish to help those in need. You seem to be in need."

"Helping me never works out," Opute grumbled. He pulled on his shoes. "I'm free to go?"

A sigh. "Yes. I've spoken with the Captain and he has agreed to return you to Belxa where you stated your contract had been signed. It is a little out of the way, but the Captain assures me your story will allow him and his family to eat for a whole year, so it's the least he can do."

Opute paused. "My story did what?"

"On Captain Goljo's homeworld, experiences are equivalent to monetary credit; the more adventurous and daring the experience, the more it's worth. Although I've learned faking a story or setting yourself up to instigate a certain type of experience is highly frowned upon, and in some circles—"

"I get the picture," Opute interrupted. "How long until we get to Belxa?"

"A few hours at most."

"Thank the stars. No offense, Doc, but I'm ready to get off this ship."

"Perfectly understandable. Now about my offer of assistance...?"

"You've done enough. You saved my life."

Dr. Mianlo gurgled softly. "So I did, didn't I?"

A disembodied voice rang through the air. "This is Captain Goljo. Will all passengers please prepare for landing?"

"I must go back to my quarters and adjust my repulsorlift chair to compensate for the gravitational changes." Dr. Mianlo nodded at Opute. "Good luck to you, Mister Gaaht. I hope you find what you're looking for."

"Thanks. And Doc?"

"Yes?"

"You're a pretty decent doctor."

Dr. Mianlo smiled. "Thank you. Sometimes I forget that."

* * *

"I know, I know!" Paja hissed into his communications device. He sat in his office on Belxa, terror in his voice. "And I'm telling *you* Vor Gaaht is waiting in my office as we speak." Paja paused as the voice spoke on the other line. "I don't care, I don't care! This was *not* part of the deal. All I needed to do was hire someone expendable. It's not my fault he wasn't… expended!" Paja clicked off the device and tucked it into his pocket. He knew he shouldn't have cut the call, but he didn't care. He couldn't bear the situation much longer. He prided himself as a businessman, pure and simple. He'd worked for this company for years before Exarth and her associates added it to their multitudes. Ever since then, compromise after compromise. He'd even developed an ulcer! And his doctor warned him about his compulsive sweating. "Get a new job," they said. Hah! No one leaves the company unless they've been told they can leave.

Paja opened a set of closet doors behind him, wincing at the rusty screech of the hinges. The sound reminded him of the stone-like woman when she moved around the room. Coresque unnerved him, constantly watching with her white, eyeless stare.

She never raised her voice, never seemed upset, never did anything except make a comment here or there during a hire. She couldn't even sit down. She just stood there, hovering. Hovering, hovering, hovering!

Focusing his thoughts back on the problem at hand, Paja pulled out a new shirt, changed, wiped off his face and neck with a dry towel, and steeled himself against what might happen when he confronted the very much alive Mr. Gaaht.

** * *

Opute stared at the sculpture of the white woman, remembering her in his dream, warning him to stay away from the planet. He hoped she would show up again today. He had some questions for her.

He glanced up when Paja entered the room, unfortunately by himself, and took a seat at the desk. Sweat already ran down the man's face and he seemed at a loss as his fingers searched for something to move around on the empty cherrywood desk.

"Hello, hello, Mister Gaaht!" Paja said, his voice cracking. "I'm surprised to see you. When we didn't hear from any of you, we assumed the worst. I'm glad to see you're all right."

Opute resisted the urge to see how many teeth he could knock out in one punch. He could tell this guy knew he wasn't supposed to return alive. Instead, he fell into his character.

"It's good to see you too, sir. I almost didn't make it back."

Paja swallowed loudly. "What do you mean?"

"Our ship exploded."

"Your...your what?"

"Yes, sir. That's the only thing that seems logical. While I unloaded the cargo in the back, I saw this bright light and a huge blast of heat and I went flying away from the ship. I woke up on a medical freighter." Opute paused. "They said they found no other survivors."

"Oh dear, oh dear. This is tragic." Paja had apparently forgotten to bring a cloth to wipe his sweat. Perspiration completely soaked his shirt around the collar and under his arms. "We will have to notify the next of kin of your crewmates and contact our buyers and let them know what we found out. I'm sure they are concerned about their team as well."

Opute ignored the sick feeling in his stomach. He didn't have time to care that Lym and Reh'dd's families would never know what really happened to them.

He had to stay focused.

"If there's anything I can do to help, sir...."

Paja paused. "Maybe, maybe." He tapped his fingers against each other. "I will have to consult with my superiors, but we will now need someone to take on Lym's next assignment. Perhaps you could assist with that."

"Anything I can do."

"You've shown yourself to be quite...resourceful. I believe you could be an asset to our company. If you are to receive this assignment, it will be a big step up for you."

"I know I'm new, sir, but I believe that if given the chance, I could handle anything you throw at me. Besides, I really need the job." *Come on. Come on! I'm no threat.*

Paja nodded. "I will see, I will see. And then I will contact you. Expect a vidlink call at your hotel within two standard days."

Opute stood. "Thank you, sir." He hesitated. "Sir, if I may, I'm curious about the sculpture. If I'm not mistaken, it's of your associate...uh...Corest, right?"

"What? Oh, yes, yes. It's *Coresque*, actually. I believe she had it commissioned after a likeness of her mother."

"She's not around, is she? I'd love to discuss the piece. It's quite interesting."

"No, no. Coresque has other duties to attend to. Perhaps I can connect you with the being that created this work, if you like?"

Opute shook his head. "It's not a big deal. I'll be looking forward to your call." Opute walked out of the office disappointed.

* * *

"He hung up on me. On *me!*" Iry turned off his viewscreen and pushed the monitor away from him in disgust. "That little sniveling…sweaty… insignificant... How *dare* Paja think he can treat me this way? Doesn't he know who he's dealing with?"

"No," he answered himself. "And why would he? I'm just some underling who licks the crumbs off Exarth's shoes, aren't I?" Iry stopped muttering when the door chimes to his office rang. "What?" he screeched.

The door opened and Coresque glided into the room, her feet hardly making any noise on the white tile floor. "Is this a bad time?"

Iry immediately composed himself. He didn't want to arouse suspicions. "Of course not. Please, come in. I just completed a rather unpleasant conversation. What can I do for you?"

Coresque handed him a datapad across his desk, her arm's image reflected on the shiny white surface. "Here is the official report on the incident involving the crew of the *Century* on Lahtze's moon from Captain Dregor. Quite a tragedy."

Iry leaned back in his plush, white chair, the back molding to his body. He still kept a lot of white in his room, even after everything he'd been through at the hospital. It soothed him, though he wasn't sure why. "Yes, it was. Do we know yet what caused the ship to explode?"

Coresque shook her head slowly, her stone-like skin grinding with the effort. "Pre-flight checks registered in the green. Something must have happened to them on the moon."

"I'll see if I can find anything out." Iry's vidlink blinked with an incoming call. "Excuse me, I should take this."

Coresque left and Iry initiated the call.

"You've got a lot of nerve calling back after—"

"He wants another job," Paja interrupted.

Iry raised an eyebrow. "He wasn't scared off after his crew died?"

Paja shook his head. "No, no. He seems to really need the money." Paja wiped his sweaty head. "I figured with Lym gone, maybe he could sub in. What do you want to do?"

"I'll get back to you. I need to think." Iry disconnected the call. He shuffled through ideas about what to do with Mr. Gaaht. He had become a loose end, something Iry didn't tolerate.

Iry began to scroll through the assignment list when he saw the perfect job...

* * *

Shock slowly trickled away and guilt edged into Coresque's gut.

Xeleyn. Lym. Reh'dd.

All killed.

All because of her.

Coresque glided down the hallway toward her quarters, oblivious to anyone around her.

It is not really *my fault, is it?* Coresque thought. *I mean, I had no idea Iry would kill anyone. And I tried to warn Gaaht, or Opute, or whoever he is.*

But her intentions didn't matter. The outcome still tallied

three deaths.

Murders.

Coresque wasn't squeamish about death. She'd witnessed Iry and Exarth kill and order deaths before, but she always felt disconnected about it, able to dissociate it from reality. These deaths though were a direct result of her actions to expose Iry's plans.

All because of some stupid transmission I overheard, she thought. *I wish I never heard Iry talking to his associate. I wish I did not know the truth. And telling Exarth would not have solved anything. Iry would simply deny it. All it would do is expose that I betrayed him and I no longer believe our childhood bond will protect me.*

I thought transmitting the message to Xeleyn's ship so someone else knew the truth would solve the problem. I believed she could expose Iry. I did not know she would be killed. Or Lym and Reh'dd, too.

Coresque glided into her quarters and leaned against the wall. *The only good news is Opute is still alive. If Gaaht really* is *Opute. And if he is, do I really think he'll be able to stop all this, to help? Or will he suffer the same fate?*

CHAPTER 18

OPUTE COULDN'T BELIEVE he hadn't worn through the dirty yellow carpeting in his hotel room from pacing back and forth while waiting for Paja's phone call. He couldn't wait to leave this lifeless rock and get back onto his ship, which he'd left docked since the beginning of his work-related journey. He thought it best when he first arrived to appear as a desperate man seeking a job, and having a beautiful ship like the *Resolution* wouldn't exactly fit that image.

Opute nearly jumped out of his skin when his vidlink signaled a call.

"Yes, yes. We have another job for you. We'd like you to continue with Lym's next assignment. You are to meet with the pilot of the ship tomorrow at Docking Pad nine-oh-two."

One more day, he thought as he disconnected the call. He flopped down onto the large, soft, squishy foam bed and stared up at the room's beige, domed ceiling. *One more day and I get off this rock.*

One more day closer to Exarth.

The next morning, Opute set out for Docking Pad 902. The artificially maintained weather kept the space under the bubbles at a comfortable 13 degrees Palc, sunny, and cloudless. Opute knew a grayish haze encircled the planet, its only semblance to an atmosphere. It wasn't very appealing, so this particular bubble, the capital city on the planet, used simulation emitters to project a fake sky.

Arriving at the Docking Pad, Opute pulled his gaze away from the sky and watched the pilot approach. Completely opposite from Lym's thin and toned figure, this man appeared built like a square, uniformly wide and thick from his shoulders through his legs. A mop of curly green hair sprouted from the top of his head and hung just below his shoulders. His yellow eyes widened at Opute's approach.

"You Gaaht?" the pilot asked, his deep voice rumbling from the depths of his belly.

"Yes," Opute answered. A sudden pang of longing for his own deep voice swept over him. He hated how the new tenor range sounded young compared to the other man's.

"Well come. Name is Hunsmat. I be the two pilot."

"Pleasure, Hunsmat. What does the delivery look like?"

A voice came from behind Opute. "It looks like boxes."

Opute whirled around. The woman who'd spoken walked forward toward Opute and held out her hand in greeting, a smile spread across her lips. "The name's Lilfor. I'm the primary pilot." She shook Opute's hand and gestured toward the ship. "And this pretty lady is the *Evader*. Best maneuvering in her class."

Opute eyed the ship. "She's definitely something to be proud of."

"And proud I am. Took me three years to pay off my debts on her, but now she's mine. Just signed over the last payment two weeks ago."

"Congrats," Opute responded. "I know that feeling."

Lilfor's grin widened. "Well what are we waiting for?" She walked up and smacked Hunsmat on the back, a move that seemed to hurt her more than him. "Let's get a move on!"

Opute watched her stroll up the walkway and into her ship, wisps of dark green hair hanging out from under her hat. She had broad shoulders and a T-shaped frame, but less square then her copilot. Hunsmat followed behind her, his powerful legs pounding all the way up the ramp.

As soon as Opute had made it up the incline, it began to close slowly behind him. He made his way to the cockpit and strapped himself into the chair behind the pilot's seat. The ship smelled of plant life, though Opute couldn't see any. Circular green consoles dotted the area, having more of a living room feel than that of a cockpit.

Lilfor swiveled around. "I can't say I'm happy you're here," Lilfor said, "since it means Lym really is dead, but I suppose I can't take it out on you. It's not your fault you got assigned in his place."

Opute shrugged. "I barely knew him. Only worked with him for the one job, but it's not like seeing someone die doesn't make an impression."

Hunsmat stopped his safety inspection and turned to listen to the conversation. "Saw Lym is death?" he asked.

Lilfor lifted an eyebrow. "You were there when it happened?"

Opute hesitated. It seemed these two were close to Lym, but he didn't want to risk blowing his cover by telling them something different than what he told Paja. "There was an explosion which threw me from the debris. When I woke up, I was on a medical freighter. The Doc told me they hadn't found any other survivors."

Lilfor let out a low whistle. "What a way to die. Exploded

into a million chunks."

Hunsmat grunted at her.

"Sorry. Didn't mean to sound morbid. I just always wonder what way I'm going to go. Don't know how the habit first started, but it stuck with me."

"*I'm* stuck, too," Hunsmat muttered before turning back to his work.

She gave him another slap on the shoulder and grinned. "I suppose you are, my friend." She turned back to Opute. "Well, make sure you're buckled in tight, because we are all lights to go."

Opute checked his straps. A moment later his stomach dropped as they lifted off the ground. With a take-off that even impressed Opute, Lilfor shot out of Belxa's atmosphere and into the black vacuum of space. Chips of white light peeked through the darkness, winking at them from a vast distance.

Lilfor snapped her fingers. "Oh, stars, I forgot to ask."

"What is it?" Opute said.

"You ever Folded before?"

Opute's gut rolled in protest. "Folding" described a way to travel faster than the speed of light without needing massive amounts of energy or sophisticated engine systems. With specific calculations and the use of a TimeSphere, a ship could create a miniature fold in space to connect two different points in the galaxy. The ship would then pass through this fold to the other side.

The TimeSphere itself proved a tricky piece of equipment. It suspended the ship and its occupants in a separate time frame from space time, otherwise the crew would continually travel into the past. This TimeSphere accelerated the molecules of anything organic or inorganic so that everything arrived at the destination at the same space time as when they left.

A complicated, messy, and dangerous practice.

Opute had tried it as soon as he could fly. He loved doing it, but only when *he* piloted the ship.

"Of course," he said.

"Good. This will make things a lot easier then. On my mark…" Lilfor began.

Opute grabbed hold of the armrests. The ship shook underneath him. Opute looked out of the main viewport and watched the stars disappear, starting from the center and then spreading outwards into a circle of blackness.

Almost…

A pinpoint of light emerged in the middle of the circle, spreading radially outward, until it covered the whole screen.

Just a little more…

The light brightened until Opute couldn't look at it anymore. It burned through his eyelids and straight into his brain. He couldn't escape it, but in some ways he didn't want to. It felt invigorating and intoxicating and filled his entire being.

"MARK!" Lilfor yelled.

Opute's body heated up. All his natural functions increased in speed. His heartbeat, his breath, his thoughts.

With all his concentration, Opute began to sing inside his head.

WHERE ARE YOU NOW?…COME ON BACK HOME…WE NEED YOU HERE…HERO OF OUR WORLD… TRY AS YOU MIGHT… IT'S DESTINY… RETURN FOR US NOW…HERO OF OUR WORLD…

The heat diminished almost as soon as it began. The light dimmed, draining away from Opute's body and skin. When the backs of his eyelids appeared black once more, Opute opened his eyes.

"Welcome to the Trejah system," Lilfor said, her eyes watery. "What do you do during the Fold?"

"Sing," Opute said.

"I recite a story my Fatha used to tell me when I was younger. It's the only thing that keeps me focused."

"Have you ever lost focus?"

Lilfor shook her head. "No, thank goodness. But I saw someone who did once. She'd never Folded before." She shuddered at the memory. "I heard her screaming about the light and then I heard these strange popping noises, like oil that's too hot on a fire. When we finished the Fold, she just…wasn't there."

Opute closed his eyes for a moment at the thought. Keeping your mind focused in the present was essential, otherwise the TimeSphere accelerated your thought processes too fast for you to handle and you went insane. Once that happened, your entire being became unbalanced and you couldn't separate the present, past, and future. Time would pull you apart.

Keeping a song, a story, or even counting in your head kept you focused enough. But if you were prone to panic and couldn't keep your place….

"What about you?" Opute asked Hunsmat. "What do you think about?"

"Lilfor's story," Hunsmat said.

A look of puzzlement crossed Opute's face.

"We are mind-linked," Lilfor explained as she unbuckled her harness. "Hunsmat and I were joined when we were children. We are a pair."

"Like you have the same brain?"

Lilfor plotted a course for the planet in front of them. "Not quite. Several decades ago," she explained, "our species' existence became threatened by our dying sun. Without it, we wouldn't survive. We knew evacuation would be our only hope. However at the time, we were unaware other planets existed where we could live.

"My government devised a desperate plan. They chose one thousand children and enhanced them."

Opute unbuckled his safety harness and stretched his arms over his head. "What do you mean, 'enhanced' them?"

"We were physically, mentally, and emotionally altered. Physically, we were given greater strength, longer endurance, and a greater tolerance to less hospitable environments. Mentally, we were given increased analytical abilities and emotionally our feelings were suppressed. Then they sent us off planet."

"We fly," Hunsmat added.

Opute raised an eyebrow. "*He's* been mentally enhanced?"

Hunsmat grunted.

Lilfor smiled. "Hunsmat is smarter than you can imagine. He just has a poor grasp of languages. That's one reason we were linked."

"Okay. So you left your planet?"

Lilfor skillfully initiated the landing sequence and continued. "Each child became paired with their complimentary partner. I excelled at linguistics. Hunsmat is a mathematical genius, whereas I can't figure things out without a datapad to help me if my life depended on it." Lilfor took a moment to confirm her identification with the planet's defense network before continuing.

"Each set of children got put into a space module and then shuttled off-world. We were given communication devices and food and water for three months of travel. Our government hoped we would find a nearby hospitable planet. We had a very narrow margin since they expected our sun to die in less than a year. So the government figured that even if it took us three months to find a planet, they could successfully evacuate ten percent of our population in time and return for another ten percent before our sun died."

Opute felt a final jolt as Lilfor finished her landing. The three of them stood and made their way back toward the cargo section of the ship.

"Well I'm glad everything went okay."

Lilfor shook her head. "Not exactly. Team number sixty-three located a planet after the first month of travel. Hunsmat and I returned to our planet to aid in the evacuation, but our scientists were wrong. The sun's rate of decay went faster than they'd calculated and our planet ended up completely covered in ice by the time we'd returned. A small percentage of the population made it off in time, but they didn't have a communication system like us. Since the other children and Hunsmat and I only had a month's supply of food and water left, we had to leave for the new planet. We broadcasted our new coordinates out into space just in case, but…" Lilfor shrugged.

Opute couldn't imagine being a child whose whole planet depended on its success only to return and still have it be too late. "That sounds bad." He cringed at his terrible wording.

Lilfor shrugged again before scanning the first set of boxes. "Oddly enough, it wasn't so bad. With Hunsmat here, I never really feel alone, and the inhabitants on our new home planet took us in and raised us as their own. I got to learn so much about other planetary civilizations and the ins and outs of other species; things I never would have known if our planet hadn't been extinguished."

Opute began lugging the boxes down the ramp after Lilfor scanned them. "You ever miss your family?"

"Not really. I barely knew them. I only remember that story from my Fatha. But my family on our new home is very loving and supportive. I've learned a lot from them."

"And now you transport cargo for a living?"

"Fit perfect," Hunsmat chimed in. "See worlds."

Lilfor nodded. "Definitely. Ever since we both discovered there were other worlds, we knew we wanted to see as many of them as we could. And what better way than as a transporter? Low risk and lots of travel. Perfect."

"Talk too much, Lilfor. *All* the time." Hunsmat shook his head, but the grin on his face made Opute think it was a private joke.

"That I do, my friend. That I do."

They finished unpacking the cargo, placing it on the ground outside the ship, when their contact arrived. A thin pair of bipeds approached them, one male, one female. Opute couldn't remember their species' name, but he remembered the large horn-like protrusion sticking out of the female's head indicated her gender.

"Greetings," called out the female, her voice low and husky. "I trust your flight went well?"

"It did indeed," Lilfor said. "Everything arrived safe and sound."

The female nodded to the male, who started loading the boxes into their vehicle. "Glad to hear it. This stuff sure is pricey."

Lilfor handed the female a datapad to sign. "If you say so. I just run it."

The female's ear spouts waggled in surprise. "Really? You've never been tempted to peek inside and see what you're dragging across space?"

"Nope," Lilfor answered, taking back the completed datapad.

Dust swirled around them. A small, metallic-blue spaceship hovered briefly before landing next to the biped's vehicle. Its triangular nose aimed straight at the cargo receivers; the blue and white insignia on its side looked menacing.

"Nijaci! Authorities!" The female ran to the ramp of her

ship, firing wildly at the newcomers. "How did they know we'd be here?"

The male shoved Opute out of the way, frantically ripping at one of the cargo boxes.

"What the…?" Opute said gruffly, regaining his balance. He froze at the weapon pointed at him. The opened box was full of them.

"Someone must have alerted them," the male said, sneering at Opute.

Opute ducked and rolled as the weapon ignited, sending a flash of red light in the space where he'd been standing. With a low leg sweep, Opute knocked the male to the ground and jumped on top of him. He wrestled the weapon out of the male's hand and turned it back on him, firing.

Red light shined on the male's face and Opute watched in disgust as the male's skin began to melt, sliding down his bone structure in large chunks.

"Don't get hit!" he yelled out. "It's a PT Flash!"

"A what?" Lilfor called out.

"Just avoid the red light!"

Protein Trigger Flash device, or PT Flash for short, had originally been designed as a medical apparatus that could target and eliminate specific proteins in a subject, but the technology quickly became converted into a weapon.

The result of having one's protein dissolved lay in a bloody mess at his feet.

Opute whipped his head around, focusing on the female. Four bipeds had exited the blue ship. They boxed in the female, who hunkered down in her vehicle. Dirt and grit swirled through the air, blurring his vision and catching in his throat.

Opute moved for cover behind the remaining cargo boxes.

Think, Opute, THINK! How are you going to get out of this? Opute peeked around one of the boxes when he heard someone yell at the female to surrender. Someone else screamed, but he couldn't tell where they were or what they said.

"I give up! I'm coming out!" the female called out.

The screaming hadn't stopped. High-pitched sobs pierced the chaos.

"Lilfor." Opute tucked the weapon into his waistband and took off toward the sound, only to have several voices telling him at once to halt. Lifting his hands in the air, Opute stopped.

"Place the weapon on the ground, back away slowly."

Opute followed their instructions, all the while listening to the gut-wrenching screeches of Lilfor. She sounded nearby, just behind her ship's loading ramp.

"Please," Opute called out. "My shipmate sounds hurt. Let me see if she's all right."

"DO NOT MOVE!"

"You have me surrounded. We are merely the transporters. Let me check on her!"

After several agonizing moments, one of the authorities gave a nod, his weapon still trained on Opute. A different one of them trotted over and accompanied Opute toward the screaming pilot.

Lilfor sat on the ground, her hands around Hunsmat. The whole upper half of his head had been blown away; green blood drenched Lilfor's arms and the ground around her. His yellow eyes were glazed and lifeless.

"I can't hear him!" she screeched. "I CAN'T HEAR HIM!" She repeated the words over and over, the pitch growing higher in her hysterical state.

With quick steps, Opute walked over to her. "Lilfor," he said softly, crouching down to her level. He pulled away her bloody green hands from Hunsmat's head. "He's gone, Lilfor. That's why you can't hear him." He turned her face and forced her to look at him. "He's dead."

CHAPTER 19

LILFOR'S VIOLET EYES appeared wide and unfocused. Opute feared she'd gone catatonic and had no idea what to do. He opened his mouth to ask the biped behind him if there were any medical facilities nearby when Lilfor grabbed Opute's face. With a quick movement, she slammed her hand against his ear.

A sharp pain pierced through the side of his head. Opute wondered if she'd ruptured his ear drum. Before he could ask anything, a strange feeling swept over him. His head felt submerged underwater, but he could still breathe. The pressure increased against his skin and scalp, pressing in on all sides until it seemed to sink through his skull.

Suddenly he heard a voice.

Gaahl? Can you hear me?

Opute struggled to sort through what he sensed. The liquid-like pressure changed into waves of light and sound. They crashed over Opute's mind and became images—clips of someone else's life.

Someone with greenish skin, standing over him.

Hunsmat laughing at a joke.

Salty tears on his face.

The images came faster, too quick for him to distinguish. Nausea rolled over him.

Gaaht... the voice called out again. *Focus on my voice. The memories will wash through you. Focus on me.*

Opute concentrated on the voice. He still couldn't distinguish one image from another, but he felt less overwhelmed.

What's...happening...to...me.... Opute's words formed solidly in front of his eyes as he thought them. They shot out across a void of blackness and disappeared into a point of light.

Don't panic. I'm here with you. You're doing fine.

Lilfor? he asked. Opute gasped as the last wave broke over him, showering him with remaining bits of light and sound. He opened his eyes and saw Lilfor sitting in front of him, a small smile on her face, but with a frantic sense of fear in her eyes.

"Just keep breathing," she told him. "The sensation will pass soon."

Opute drew in several raspy breaths. "What's going on?" It took him a moment to realize they were alone. The biped ship had disappeared, along with all the cargo they'd delivered. "Where is everyone?" Opute turned toward Lilfor for an answer, but before she said anything, an image flashed through his mind. He saw himself lying on the ground unconscious. He looked up through someone else's eyes and saw the authorities signaling something with their weapons. Suddenly the area filled with a dense fog, like from a smoke bomb. He leaned over his own body, protecting it. Sounds of shouts, weapons discharging. Then the fog cleared. He peeked up and saw the corpses of the authorities on the ground and their vehicle gone.

The image slid away into blackness and Opute came back to the present. "I...I saw what happened," he muttered. "But how? I was unconscious during it all."

Lilfor placed a hand on his arm. "You saw my memories."

Opute shook his head. "I don't understand. Your memories?"

"That's what happens in a mind-link."

The sudden understanding hit Opute like a solid wall. "You and I are mind-linked?"

"Yes. I'm sorry. I should have asked you, but I…" she flushed. "I didn't want to be alone."

Fury raged inside his chest. "You didn't want to be *alone*?" He stormed at her and though she closed her eyes, she didn't scurry away from the blow he wanted to deal. "You…you have no right. What the stars have you done!"

Lilfor opened her eyes, her body trembling. "When he died," she said, motioning toward Hunsmat, "our link broke. We were joined at such a young age. I don't remember ever being alone with my own thoughts. I always had his memories in my head as a buffer. And when I couldn't hear him, I panicked and…"

"…linked with me." Opute finished. The anger mingled with fear. "What were you thinking!" he snapped.

She cringed. "I-I wasn't thinking. I'm sorry! I just…" Tears poured down her face, followed by hiccupped sobs.

Opute didn't have time for this. "Stop crying. Just give me a minute to figure this out." He rubbed his head. "So now I have all your memories in my head. And your thoughts, too?"

Lilfor shook her head. "Yes and no. We can't mentally talk to each other like telepaths can, but everything we experience gets transferred automatically between us as soon as the moment has passed. Once you get used to it, you can choose what memories to see."

"I can access everything you've ever done in your whole life." It came out more of a statement than a question.

"Yes." She paused. "And I have all your memories as well."

That got Opute's attention. "You have…" he gulped, feeling his pulse quicken. All his secrets, everything from his life, she now knew. She was a liability. She could expose him. She *knew* him.

He needed to keep her silent. The idea of killing her ran through his mind, but the thought sickened him. He didn't want another death on his hands.

Lilfor's eyes focused on Opute's as if reading his thoughts. "I won't betray your secret, Ness Opute. I'll continue to call you by your new name and treat you as if I didn't know about your past or your plan for the future. Our mind-link will be temporary until we can return to my homeworld and I can find a more suitable partner."

He felt completely visible, with no control at all. "You have no right to know those things!" He let out a yell, something feral and emotional. He'd barely begun his plan and already three individuals were dead and some young, foolish woman knew his entire past.

Lilfor cringed and wiped her face. "I promise once we get to my homeworld it'll be over quickly. You'll never see me again." The words were rushed and soft, the fear evident in her wide eyes.

Opute turned and punched the side of the ship, again and again, denting its extremely strong hull. His knuckles swelled and turned dark, but he kept punching until some of his fury subsided. He swallowed down as much frustration as he could. "Let's just get this over with." The two of them dragged Hunsmat onto the ship, his massive bulk making it difficult for them to manage without resting. Once they'd stored his body in one of the perishable cargo areas, they made their way to the cockpit.

"Where to?" Opute asked, his words clipped. He didn't trust himself to say too much more for fear he'd just start yelling again.

"Well, at some point we should head back to Belxa and turn in our payment contract. But if you want to go to the planet I grew up on right away to sever our mind-link, that's fine with me. It's up to you."

Opute took a seat and thought about his choices. He didn't really like the prospect of having someone see his memories all the time, but he didn't want to jeopardize his standings with Paja and Exarth's company either and worried a delay in their payment delivery might reflect poorly on him as a worker.

Although bringing back another dead worker couldn't help his standings either.

Which led to the other problem of a corpse in the back of the ship.

Opute sighed. *What a mess,* he thought.

"Tell me about it," Lilfor said.

"Tell you about what?"

"About what a mess this is."

"I didn't say that out loud."

Lilfor's eyebrows furrowed in confusion. "What do you mean?"

"I mean, I *thought* about what a mess this is, I didn't *say* it."

Color drained from Lilfor's face. Her eyes widened in terror. "Are you sure?" she whispered. "Are you *sure* you didn't say it out loud?"

Opute's skin tightened in fear, responding to her reaction. "Yeah, I'm sure. Why?"

Lilfor jumped out of her seat and paced the cockpit. "Can you tell what I'm thinking right now?" she screeched.

"No," he answered, wincing. "But I can hear you perfectly. Why are you screaming?"

Lilfor plopped back into the pilot's seat. "This could be bad," she said.

"How bad?" And then a noise exploded inside his head as if Lilfor had climbed into his skull, shouting.

DON'T SCARE HIM. LIE. TELL HIM IT'S NOTHING. The words were disjointed and echo-y, like rolling waves. Every time they crashed against his skull he could understand them.

"It's nothing. I'm still just upset about Hunsmat."

Opute heard Lilfor speak out loud and the words seemed muted in comparison. "I heard you," he gasped. "In my mind. I heard you tell yourself to lie to me."

OH, NO. OH, NO!

"Stop!" Opute yelled. "It already feels like you're screaming in my head...it's too loud!" The noise ceased and Opute removed his hands from his ears, not that the action had done him any good.

"I'm so sorry," she told him, her breath becoming ragged. "This is all my fault..."

"Just...tell me what happened." *Please don't let her start crying again. I can't deal with crying.*

Lilfor cringed. "No promises."

Opute felt relieved to hear some of the spunk back in her voice. "So, what's going on? You said we wouldn't be able to hear each other's thoughts."

"We're not supposed to. The mind-link is only a connection between the memory portions of the brain. It's not supposed to read any other wavelengths."

"But something went wrong?"

Lilfor nodded. "I think so. When I first became mind-linked with Hunsmat, we had a guide. She led us through the process of what to think and do to secure the correct type of link. When I connected to you, we did not focus solely on our memories, so I think the connection established intersected other wavelengths."

"So now we can read each other's thoughts?"

"Seems like it."

Great. Just great. Just what I need right now.

I'M SORRY.

Opute winced at the words. "I *know* you're sorry."

"Guess we're going to have to watch what we think."

"Not only that, but can you turn down the volume? Your thoughts are really loud."

"I don't know," she said, hesitantly. "I've never had this experience before. I've only met one other pairing connected on a different wavelength than memories."

"Well what did they do about it?"

"They…died."

Opute rubbed his temples at the forming headache. "How long before they died?"

"Three, maybe four standard days."

"And how long would it take to get to your planet to fix this?"

"No time at all, since we can fold space. But…"

"But what?"

"It takes close to two weeks to reverse the process."

Opute groaned. *Two weeks? I'm going to die with some stupid, childish, impatient woman inside my head!*

I'm sorry.

Opute looked up at Lilfor. "It didn't sound like screaming that time."

"Well that's a plus." Lilfor squeezed her hands together tightly. "There may be another way."

Opute's eyebrow rose. "Anything's better than dying."

"We can try distancing ourselves. When Hunsmat and I were linked, the further apart we were, the worse our connection. Perhaps if I return to my home planet alone, there will be enough distance between us to sever the connection. If it doesn't sever completely, I can begin the reversal process to finish the separation."

"Do you think that will work?"

Lilfor shrugged. "It's all I can think of right now."

"All right. We'll head back to Belxa and I'll stay there. You can return home and start fixing this."

"Sounds like a plan." Lilfor turned and faced the cockpit console and began making preparations to jump through folded space. Opute's mind felt so scattered he couldn't concentrate. He knew he needed to focus during the Fold, but his mind jumped around to too many differing thoughts and memories, none of them his own.

As the ship broke through the planet's atmosphere and oriented itself, Opute could hear Lilfor begin the repetition of the childhood story she thought to herself during the jump.

Desperate not to blink out of existence, Opute concentrated on her story.

CHAPTER 20

OPUTE WAVED GOODBYE to Lilfor as he exited the *Evader*. "Good luck."

"To you as well. I hope you find her," she said, in reference to Exarth.

Opute nodded, still finding it unnerving that Lilfor knew so much about him. And how much he knew about her. During the trip back, with Lilfor's help, he tried to sort through the memory images flooding his mind. He now knew everything about her at once. The massive amount of information was overwhelming to say the least.

But Lilfor assured him the images would fade and lessen with distance. He walked toward the street corner to pay for a ride back to his hotel.

"AHHHH!" Opute dropped to his knees and grabbed his head. Stabs of pain sliced through his skull. He couldn't think. He couldn't see. All he felt was blinding pain.

And then it began to ebb. Gradually, the world came back into focus. He stood and peered around. Lilfor's body lay limp at the bottom of the ship's ramp.

Opute sprinted toward her and knelt down. "Lilfor, can you hear me? Are you okay?"

Lilfor's eyes flitted open. "Opute? I mean, Gaaht?"

"Yeah, it's me. Can you sit?"

Lilfor sat up slowly and rubbed her arms, which were covered with dirt from the ship's ramp. "I don't think it's going to work." The two of them stood, with Lilfor leaning against Opute for support.

"What are you talking about?"

"Did you feel it? The pain when we separated?"

He snorted. "Did I feel it?" he asked rhetorically. "So what does this mean? We're stuck with each other?"

Lilfor nodded. "I think so. As soon as the pain hit I collapsed. Luckily I fell at an angle and rolled down the ramp. The closer I got to you, the better I felt."

Opute groaned. "Okay. Before we jump to any conclusions, let's make sure."

Lilfor let out a deep breath. "Okay. Walk away again, but slower."

Opute took a few steps away with no pain. At about four meters, he felt a slight buzzing in the back of his head.

"Do you feel it?" she asked.

"Yeah." He took another step.

The buzzing turned into a light pressure.

One more step.

Like a drill in his temples.

One more...

"Stop!" Lilfor cried out, breathless. Her hands held her head.

Opute walked back toward her and the pain immediately lessened. "Sorry, I just wanted to test our limits."

"Apparently your limits are more than mine," she said, rubbing her forehead.

"It looks like five meters might be our max, although we shouldn't push it much past four."

"Have I told you yet how sorry I am?" Lilfor said.

"Even when you don't say it, I know you're thinking it," Opute said.

Lilfor removed her cap and ran her fingers through her short green hair. "So now what's the plan?"

"Not what I wanted to do," Opute grumbled. He sighed. "I suppose we should head back to your home planet to try and fix this, if we can."

"But what about you? If you don't check in with Paja, you might jeopardize finding Exarth."

"Okay, it's weird that you know my plans."

"I can't help it."

"I know. But I guess I can't find her if I'm dead, so let's try and disconnect ourselves first. I'll…I'll figure something out."

Lilfor shook her head. "No. Let's go check in with Paja. We're already here on the planet anyway. And it will look better with me to back you up."

"Lilfor—"

"I don't want to hear it. I've made up your mind." She smiled at the joke. "Like it or not, we have to do this together, and I'm still hoping we'll live through this. If we do, I'd like a job to come back to as well." She put her hand on his arm. "I know what you've been through to get where you are and you know what I've had to overcome to build a life. Neither one of us wants to lose that."

"So what you're telling me is that you're stubborn, huh?"

"You have no idea. Now, let's get going so we can save our lives."

* * *

The chimes rang to Iry's office. He folded his snow-white hands over each other.

"Come in."

Thlin entered the room and handed over a datapad.

"Finished so soon?" Iry asked. "I thought the ingestion method of the drug would take more time for you to figure out?"

"It's not about that."

Iry read through the contents of the datapad. His white eyebrows raised in surprise. "Someone sent a copy of our transmission about the twig shipments to Xeleyn? So she didn't find out about our plans on her own."

"It seems like she had help."

"Do you know who sent it?"

Thlin whipped his auburn hair from his eyes. "No. It's encrypted, but I should be able to decode it. Give me, say, three or four days?"

Iry handed back the datapad. "This is now top priority. I want to know who sent this message. It seems I have an unknown enemy. I want that remedied as soon as possible."

Thlin's lip curled sourly. "Don't worry. I'll find them."

Thlin left Iry's office just as his vidlink chimed. Iry answered the call.

"Paja?"

"Yes, yes, it's me. Umm...he's back again."

Iry curbed his anger at the sweaty man. "Who's back again?"

"Mister Gaaht."

Iry tapped his lower lip in thought. "He's quite resilient, isn't he?"

"Sure, sure," Paja answered. "What do you want me to do with him? He's not even supposed to be on the employee roster anymore."

Iry thought about it. A risk, to be sure...

"Tell him we will have more work for him soon."

"And the woman with him?"

Iry frowned. "What woman?"

"Let's see, let's see," Paja mumbled, sorting through a stack of datapads. "Ah yes, a Lilfor Bolf, the pilot on their last drop off, which failed and the copilot died. The local authorities intercepted the delivery."

Well at least that portion of his plan worked out. Another one of Exarth's shipments gone astray. Exactly what he needed to discredit her. "And this Mister Gaaht *and* Miss Bolf came back for more work?"

"It's true, it's true. Times being what they are, some individuals can't afford to pass up work, no matter what the cost."

"Include Miss Bolf in the agreement."

"Will do, will do."

Iry disconnected the call and sat back in his chair. It didn't matter that things were getting more complicated. He would figure it out. He could figure out anything.

* * *

Opute and Lilfor left Paja's office and headed toward the *Evader*.

"That went better than I thought," Lilfor muttered.

"You and me both."

"And he's going to have more work for us in the next few weeks? Seems like you might be lucky for me. I haven't had this much work offered to me in months."

"I didn't know work was that hard to come by."

Lilfor skipped ahead of him and turned around so she walked backwards. "See, if I didn't know who you really were, I might be suspicious by that statement. You forget when you were Opute, folks banged down your door to get you to work for them. You gotta remember that now you're one of us lowly cargo transporters who scrounge around hoping we'll get tossed some scraps."

"Hey, I *earned* the right to have companies bang down my door. I've been doing this for over fifteen years. I've put in the time and I'm one of the best smugglers out there."

"No argument from me. It's not like I've never heard of Ness Opute before."

That stopped Opute in his tracks. "You've heard of me?"

Lilfor nodded and motioned for him to keep walking. "Not many in our line of work *haven't* heard of you. You've got quite a reputation." She stopped and turned back around now that they were at her ship.

"As what?"

Lilfor entered her access code and the *Evader's* ramp began to lower. "I don't know. Like you're hard to hire, but worth the money. Your word is pretty good. Plus you'll kill anyone who crosses you—"

"Hold on. I do *what?*"

"Hey, I'm just telling you what I heard. I know you worked mostly out of C-Sector Nine, but it's not like I ranked anywhere near your league, so I never put much stock in our paths ever crossing." Lilfor snorted a laugh. "Who would've known I'd be mind-linked to you after you changed yourself to look like someone else and created a whole new life to get revenge against Exarth for killing your wife. Oh, and for killing your friend Lang, too." They had just reached the cockpit when she swung around, her hands covering her mouth. "Oh Stars, Opute, I didn't mean to…how insensitive of me…"

ME AND MY BIG MOUTH!

"I get it," he told her, gritting his teeth at her loud thoughts in his head.

"It's just that with Hunsmat, we knew each other so well that we'd gotten past the whole 'be careful because you might offend each other' stage. I mean, we were joined as children so we never really had any secrets. We knew everything about each other all the time. Well not thoughts, but memories. And that's kind of the same thing."

Opute sat down in the copilot seat as Lilfor went through the start-up process for her ship. "So you've never really had any privacy?"

"It sounds worse than it is. I mean, your life is made up of one secret after another. Almost no one knows what you've really been through. I mean, maybe your wife, or that Grassuwerian, Zarsa, but…" Lilfor clamped her mouth shut. "I'm doing it again, aren't I?"

A thousand thoughts raced through his mind—every moment he wanted to keep hidden, every embarrassing situation. The more he tried not to think about them the faster the thoughts came. And it didn't matter. She would see everything. All his careful planning, what he'd done to keep himself hidden, would be exposed. He felt angry and raw, filleted open without his consent.

Opute let out a long breath. "I hate this. I don't want you to know these things."

Lilfor started up the engine and began the liftoff sequence. "I really am sorry. And I will try to think more before I speak."

"I'll just hear that, too."

* * *

"I see the truth!" Arew screamed, digging his fingers in Exarth's eye sockets. "This is where you can't hide!"

Pain flared and bright light exploded in front of her. Her

eyes felt on fire.

"I SEE YOU!"

Exarth awoke, gasping for air. She clutched at her eyes, where the pain had not receded. Clawing her way out of bed, she stumbled to the washroom and turned on the light. The pain intensified at the brightness and she shut the light back off. With quick movements she plugged the sink, turned on the faucet, and plunged her face underneath the stream of water.

Relief. Two black lenses popped out and swam in the water below her.

She had fallen asleep with her contacts in.

Cursing herself, she pulled the dripping lenses from the sink. She lifted her head to look in the reflective unit to see how irritated her eyes were. They were reddish yellow, reflecting her curious and angry mood, but other than that they looked fine.

Exarth laid the lenses out in their solution and went back into her bedroom, the silky black sheets shining in the moonlight that streamed through her window. Bypassing the welcoming bed, she began to dress for the day, thinking about the dream.

Death didn't bother Exarth, not anymore. She learned quickly its place in life and killing could be as natural as breathing. Animals did it, plants did it, insects did it, so why not her? She once saw a video clip of a group of Eonkks, a marine animal, gang up on a Nir and pound it to death with their blunted snouts, leaving the Nir to die. Exarth's "teacher" at the time explained to her and the other children it was a territorial display. But Exarth watched the clip again on her own time and saw something different. The Eonkks weren't just protecting their territory. They could have scared the Nir off or pushed it around until it went away. But instead they *pummeled* the Nir, attacking it repeatedly in ways to make sure it *couldn't* get away.

They wanted it to die, to send a big enough message so

other Nirs would not come back.

Is that the message Exarth meant to send? That everyone knew how far she'd go so they would leave her alone?

Everything started with Arew. His betrayal damaged her to a point where she could never live a normal life. She could never trust in anyone again.

You tried once though, remember? You tried to have a normal life.

Exarth quickly silenced those thoughts. She didn't want to think about him right now, his smile, or the way he smelled….

She cleared her throat and called out through her secured communication panel, waiting for the final bounty hunter to answer. The conversation took a quick downturn.

"What do you mean you can't find him?" Exarth glared through the screen.

"Just as I said, ma'am. I can't find him's anywhere. I been tracking all over and it's just as like he has been disappeared."

"Well he's out there," she snapped, "and if you don't find him, I'm going to find *you*!" Exarth disconnected the vidlink call and forced herself to unclench her fists. After a restless sleep full of nightmares from her past, the last thing she needed was news that no one could find Opute.

On top of it, she knew both Coresque and Iry had been avoiding her. She felt sure either they knew something about Opute's whereabouts or they were dodging her wrath ever since she'd found out they *both* knew he still lived.

I want him found. I just want that part of my life to be done with, finally finished, and in the past where it belongs.

I want him to feel the pain he caused me.

I want to see him.

For a brief moment, a feeling of grief so agonizing swept through her, threatening to overwhelm her. But just as quickly, it reformed into rage.

Exarth stared at the information provided by all five

bounty hunters. What didn't she see? Why couldn't she find Opute?

A loud rap at her door brought her out of her reverie.

"Yes, yes. Come in."

The door slid open and Coresque glided into the room. "You wanted to see me?"

"Hmm? Oh, right, Cor." Exarth looked up apologetically. "Sorry. I forgot."

"I forget sometimes, too." Coresque smiled and patted her rock-hard head. "Sometimes I wonder if my brain is hardening as well. Too bad they did not keep me long enough to find out. Perhaps they could have made their enemies dumber by hardening their minds."

"Please don't joke about that."

A pause. "It *was* just a joke."

Exarth sighed. "I know. I'm sorry. I've just been staring at datapads all morning and my findings are getting me nowhere."

"Anything I can help you with?"

"Not unless you know anything more about Opute's whereabouts." Exarth looked up when she didn't answer. "Cor?"

Coresque became as still as the stone she seemed to be made of.

Exarth jumped out of her seat. "What is it?" she demanded, knowing Coresque couldn't lie. "You said you'd tell me if anyone you knew found out about him."

"They…they did not."

She narrowed her eyed. "*They* did not. But *you* did?"

"I…I cannot tell you."

A feeling of shock coursed through Exarth. "What do you mean you can't tell me? What do you know?"

Coresque slowly shook her head. "I cannot and I will not. I am sorry, Exarth."

Exarth practically jumped over the table. She grabbed Coresque by the shoulders and tried to shake her. The gesture did nothing other than rattle Exarth's own teeth and the lack of response from Coresque infuriated her even more.

"What in space is going on? First Iry and now you? I thought we were a team. I thought we were in this together!" Exarth let go of Coresque and kicked the table. "My plans with Commander Xiven were thwarted, my ships were stolen, the man who betrayed us who I *thought* had been killed is still alive, my *friends* are keeping things from me, and on top of it all, this morning I received information that someone has been sabotaging my shipments and deliveries. My employees are getting killed every time they step off their ships, my merchandise is being confiscated by authorities, and…and…!" Exarth let out a piercing scream that reverberated through the room.

She turned and vented her wrath on Coresque. "Get out!" she screeched.

"Please let me explain—" Coresque pleaded.

"Just…get…OUT!"

Coresque left the office and Exarth slammed her fists into the table, breaking her hands. Within minutes, they both healed.

Exarth found herself at a loss. Normally she would turn to Cor or Iry for help, but she couldn't trust them anymore. She couldn't run everything by herself either. She never wanted to be in charge. She never wanted to lead anyone. And yet everyone looked to her to take action. What had it gotten her? Lies, betrayal, and pain.

One individual represented a focused target for her fury.

Ness Opute.

Killing him wouldn't really solve any of her current problems, she knew that…

…but it will feel really good to slit his throat.

CHAPTER 21

OPUTE'S EYES WIDENED in amazement as Lilfor's ship pulled out of folded space and into orbit around the planet she grew up on. His breath caught in his chest at its beauty. A shallow ocean of greenish-turquoise water surrounded the arid reddish-ginger continents while wisps of dark purple clouds swirled rapidly around the planet.

"It looks like a nice place," Opute said as they began descending through the atmosphere.

"Thanks. Although I know you think it's one of the most beautiful places you've ever seen. Not surprising though since your home planet, C-Nine, is a bunch of cities with little water or vegetation."

"It wouldn't even do me any good to tell you to stay out of my thoughts, would it?"

Lilfor sighed as they plummeted through the dense clouds. "No, but you'll be rid of me soon enough. Although I don't know why you won't say what you think. It's much nicer than what you actually say."

Opute grunted. "I say what I want. No one needs to know

what's inside my head."

"And why is that, do you think?"

"Because it's my own personal business, that's why," Opute snapped. He hated having her in his mind. He wanted his privacy and secrets back. They were his secrets anyway, not hers. She shouldn't get to know them.

"I get it," she said. "Your thoughts. Your secrets. Blah blah blah. Don't worry. You'll get to go back to your own small little world soon enough."

The two of them remained silent while the *Evader* landed softly on the sandy platform. Shooting out of her chair, Lilfor stormed from the cockpit.

Women, he thought to himself, shaking his head.

MEN!

Opute couldn't help laughing at Lilfor's thought and hurried to catch up with her. He felt glad to see the smile on her face.

"I'm sorry I snapped at you," she told him.

"Me, too. I shouldn't have thought those things."

"No, Opute, you should. This whole mind-link thing happened to you without your consent. It's not fair for me to invade your thoughts and try to dictate how you should behave after two days. I spent my whole life with someone in my head. There was no point in lying or pretending to be someone I'm not. Staying private has been your way of life for so long, it's inconsiderate of me to barge in and tell you your way isn't as good as mine."

"You talk too much."

Her smile widened, though a sadness touched her eyes. "Well, with someone like Hunsmat around, I got used to doing all the talking."

"Speaking of," Opute said, "what do you want to do about him?"

The *Evader's* exit ramp opened and Lilfor nodded at the welcoming committee. Two women and a child waited patiently for them to step off the ship. The species, Terruens, physically matched their planet. Their skin color ranged between sand and rust, their hair a greenish-blue like the shallow seas.

"Hunsmat will be taken care of," Lilfor said. She looked a bit out of place with her green skin tone. "His body will be processed for recycling into our soil and there will be a memorial service held next week." She paused. "Our Guardians are going to be devastated." With slow steps she made her way off the ship and walked toward the waiting Terruens. Before she got very far, Opute's head began to buzz.

"Oh, right. I'm coming." He tapped his fingers on the crest of the hatchway as he exited.

Lilfor lifted her chin. *You can do this. Stay strong.* Opute felt confused by the thought until he realized she meant it about herself.

Lilfor introduced the three individuals standing next to her. "Vor Gaaht, I'd like you to meet my Guardians, Xana and Xera. And this little rascal," she said, ruffling the head of a young boy hiding behind his parents, "is my Guardians' son, Xutu. Family, this is Vor Gaaht."

"Pleased to meet you," said Xana. Her voice sounded soft and lyrical, more of a song than speaking. She extended her hand and touched it to Opute's forehead. "You are well come to our home. May you have peace for yourself as for others."

DO IT BACK.

Opute tried not to wince at Lilfor's loud thought. He smiled at Xana and repeated the words and gestures. The same process happened with Xera.

Little Xutu seemed terrified of Opute, so he didn't press the ritual greeting on the child.

Not too big on strangers? Opute thought to Lilfor.

You're the first non-Terruen he's ever seen before...I mean besides my race.

Lilfor finished her thoughts and turned to her Guardians with a somber face. "I'm afraid I have come home on unpleasant terms."

"What has happened, Light of Our Eyes?"

Light of their eyes? Opute thought at her.

Lilfor blushed. *It's a nickname.* "There has been a terrible accident," she continued out loud. "Hunsmat has been killed."

The look of sadness that filled Xana and Xera's eyes brought a lump to Opute's throat. He could almost feel their pain, like a wave of tingling across his soul. The breeze around them turned colder and the purple clouds rolled with soft thunder.

"Healer of Our Hearts has died? He is here then?" asked Xera.

Lilfor nodded, tears rimming her eyes. "His body is on my ship, awaiting recycling to become one with the land and sea."

Opute looked away, feeling like an intruder during a private moment. And then a barrage of images flooded his mind; Lilfor's recollection of Hunsmat's memories. Opute saw Hunsmat as a child in classes, the long journey through dark space to find their new home, his trips with Lilfor, and the moment when the stray shot hit him and killed him.

Opute felt like he'd lived Hunsmat's life, seen everything he'd seen.

You are no longer an intruder, Lilfor thought at him.

Embarrassed, Opute realized tears streaked his face. Wiping them away, he cleared his throat. "I'm sorry for your loss," he mumbled.

Xana looked up. The clouds dissipated and warm sunlight hit her face. "There is loss, yes, but new life shall spring from that. It is our custom to give our bodies back to the earth, to strengthen our land, to add our energy, our emotions, and our flesh to that which sustains our living families and friends. Hunsmat's fate will be a loss in life, but a gain in death."

How am I going to tell them about the mind-link?

Opute jerked at Lilfor's thoughts. She sounded terrified.

You can do it, he thought to her.

Right. Easy for you to think.

I'm trying, okay?

Lilfor laughed softly before she spoke. "There is another problem, Guardians."

Xana and Xera looked at her, puzzled. "Yes, Light of Our Eyes?"

"At the time of Hunsmat's death, when our link broke, I...I mind-linked with another." Her gaze dropped to the sandy ground.

Xana raised an eyebrow at Opute. "Are you the one?"

Opute nodded.

"Then you are well come to our family."

"No," Lilfor said, "I didn't do it right. We need to be separated. We can...we can hear each other's thoughts."

"Then you must go to your own brothers and sisters and seek their help." Xana nodded at Xera. "We will take care of Healer of our Hearts. You must take care of yourself." She put her hands on either side of Lilfor's face. "Will you survive, Light?"

Lilfor stammered. "I-I am unsure, Guardian."

Xana touched Lilfor's forehead and then reached out and touched Opute's. "This bond is strong, but not wrong. You will be healed, but not as you wish." Xana gave her head a sharp nod. "We will see you for supper." With that, she, Xera, and Xutu headed toward the *Evader*.

"What did she mean by that?" Opute asked.

Lilfor furrowed her eyebrows. "I don't know. But we'd

better get to the Temple before everyone leaves so they can start the separation process."

The two of them headed eastward toward a large, metallic building about a kilometer away. The structure seemed out-of-place among the earthen buildings around it; all of them built from rust-colored clay and a yellowish woven material. The air smelled of sweet spices and sea water.

Opute felt at peace. Everything around him soothed his senses. He felt safe, happy, and warm. Even his situation seemed less terrible. That somehow, everything would work out exactly how it needed to.

"You really like it here, don't you?" Lilfor asked.

Startled, Opute nodded. "Yeah. It's very…calming."

Lilfor made a noise of agreement. "I know what you mean. When the other children and I arrived on this planet about twenty standard years ago, we all felt the same way. Even though we were only children, we had the mental capacity of adults and recognized the distinctiveness of this place. Hunsmat and I…" she trailed off, swallowing hard.

"I don't mean to pry, but I thought you said you and the other children's emotions were suppressed?"

"They were," she said, "but my Guardians and a few others helped us to remove the blocks our species put upon us. Sometimes I can still hold things back."

Opute thought about how different his life would have been without emotions. *Probably would have been a lot easier.*

"I doubt it," Lilfor responded out loud.

"You don't know what I've…oh yeah, you *do* know what I've been through." Opute shook his head. "Then you must know my life would have been easier if I didn't have emotions. I would *kill* to not feel so much."

"You say that now," she said, "but life wouldn't be right without your emotions." She turned when he didn't respond.

"Opute?"

Stop talking, he told himself. *Stop blabbering on about things you don't really want to talk about. No wait. Stop* thinking *about this stuff. She can still hear you. Think about…um…well think about something!…like rain, or the shield generators on your ship, or killing Exarth or…*

"I get it," he heard Lilfor say. "You don't want to talk about it."

Opute grunted. They reached the doors to the Temple. "And I don't want you to know about it unless I talk about it."

Lilfor flinched at the harshness of his words. "Let's just go inside and not talk to each other anymore. Even if we hear each other think, okay?"

"Lilfor…" he began, but she'd already walked ahead through the doors. He followed and glanced around the room, once again unconsciously looking for any other exits or traps.

Lilfor began to say something, but shook her head instead.

"What?" he asked her.

"Nothing. Was going to make a comment about you being so suspicious…never mind."

The domed ceiling extended ten meters above their heads and shone like polished silver. There were two other doors on both sides of them and a fountain in the center of the room that flowed with green water. The fountain contained a sculpture of some type of bird-like animal, with piercing eyes and a curved beak. Water poured from the tips of its three-meter-long wing span.

Several other individuals roamed around the room, most of them with the same green shade of hair and skin as Lilfor and Hunsmat. The males all stood stocky and squarish, the females a bit less.

One of the females turned away from the fountain and saw the two new arrivals. "Lilfor?" she asked, her eyes lighting up. "Is it really you?"

"Yes," Lilfor said in a subdued voice.

Opute felt confused by her reaction. *What's going on?*

Stay out of it, she thought back at him, a fierceness in her words.

The woman came over and the two of them exchanged the planet's ritual greeting. Then the female wrapped her arms around Lilfor in a huge embrace.

She looks familiar… Opute tried to place the woman. Was she someone he knew? Someone Lilfor knew?

"It's been months," the woman exclaimed. "You've cut your hair short. I like it!" The woman turned her attention to Opute, and then looked around him. "Where's Hunsmat?"

Lilfor paled. "Kytt, Hunsmat died."

Kytt's smile faltered. "He…what?"

"He was killed…on our last cargo shipping assignment."

Kytt's violet eyes darkened like the clouds of the planet. "He's dead? You let him die?"

Opute felt startled by the outburst from this seemingly cheerful young woman. Before he could do anything, Kytt pushed Lilfor, who, not expecting it, tripped and fell to the floor.

"You got him killed!" Kytt screeched. She brought her foot back to kick Lilfor. "You and your stupid desire to get off this planet." With a thud, she struck Lilfor in the ribs. "And now he's dead. My husband is DEAD!"

OH STARS SHE'S GOING TO KILL ME.

"Hey!" Opute yelled.

STAY OUT OF IT! Lilfor yelled the thought at him.

"It's your fault!" Kytt yelled, bringing her foot back for another blow.

OH…I CAN'T BREATHE…. Lilfor lay gasping on the floor.

Without thinking, Opute grabbed Kytt and pulled her away before she could release her kick.

"Get off me!" Kytt screamed, thrashing wildly at Opute.

Lilfor got to her feet. *I told you to stay out of it!* she shouted in his head.

Opute cringed and held on. "Yeah right!" he snapped back at Lilfor. "What do I care if she breaks your ribs. Oh yeah... except I can see what you're going through and hear your pain in my head!"

"She deserves to hurt me. She's right! It's *my* fault that Hunsmat left this planet and his wife and family. It's my fault he was there and got killed."

Please, Opute thought, rolling his eyes. *Like you forced Hunsmat to come with you. He made that choice himself.*

"Right," Lilfor said out loud with a snort. "Just like you don't blame yourself for Mahri's death, right?"

Opute felt a rage flow over him like an animal. "How DARE you talk about her as if this is the same thing," he hollered. "How dare you—"

Opute, let go of Kytt...

The words were filled with fear. Confused, Opute looked at Kytt. He'd been gripping her so hard she couldn't breathe.

"Oh Space," he cursed. He released her. "Sorry..." he mumbled.

Opute looked around to see several others had gathered. As soon as he let go of Kytt, another young woman ran over and grabbed her shaking body.

The woman holding Kytt looked first at Opute then at Lilfor. "Lilfor, what's going on here? I received an image from Kytt of you telling her that Hunsmat is dead. And who is this man hurting her?"

"Brue, it's true...Hunsmat is dead. This man with me is Vor Gaaht. He witnessed Hunsmat's death. I was...unprepared when it happened and in desperation I mind-linked with Gaaht." She paused. "It did not go as it should have."

Brue motioned for someone else to take the crying Kytt into another room. "How bad of a connection is it?"

Lilfor didn't respond, her gaze solely on Kytt leaving the room.

Lilfor? Opute thought softly, bringing her back to the issue.

"Sorry," she muttered. She turned toward Brue. "It's bad. We can hear each other's thoughts and we can't separate farther than about twelve steps without pain."

"How long ago did you connect with Gaaht?"

"Less than a day."

"Have there been any other symptoms? Impaired hearing or vision? Nausea? Fatigue?"

Lilfor looked at Opute and he shook his head.

"Me neither," she answered.

Brue chewed on her lip thoughtfully. "You've put me in an awkward position, Lilfor. You know my place is by Kytt's side during this painful transition."

Lilfor swallowed. "Normally I would forfeit my life immediately for hers, but no blame should be placed on Gaaht. I will take responsibility for Hunsmat's death after—"

"The Stars you will!" Opute interrupted. "Hunsmat's death was not your fault. I saw it, remember?"

Not now...

"Yes, now!" he said. "You're not going to die for something that wasn't your fault."

"You do not know our customs, Visitor Gaaht," Brue said coldly. "It is not your decision to make."

"Right. This coming from the woman connected to that hysterical mess in the other room. If you can sense what she's going through in a fraction of the way I can sense what Lilfor's going through, then I bet your judgment is biased right now."

Opute paused to catch his breath. "I'm not trying to dismiss what happened, but Lilfor is also in pain. And right now if we don't get help, we'll both die."

Opute shut his mouth abruptly, embarrassed by his rant.

You're such an idiot...

Lilfor's insult rang through Opute's head, but when he looked at her, he saw the beginnings of a smile at the corner of her lips.

Opute's gaze returned to Brue. She'd closed her eyes and when she opened them, a look of determination filled them.

"Your bond must already be intense for you to defend her so strongly after only a day's connection." Brue chewed on her lip again. "We will proceed with the separation process. I can't guarantee success—we have never worked with a member of your species—and the irregular symptoms may cause complications with the procedure, but we will try."

"Let's just do it," Opute said.

Lilfor nodded in agreement.

"Very well. The procedure will begin tomorrow morning during first light."

"Any reason we can't start now?" Opute asked.

"We will need to tap into the planet's energy and the sun will be necessary for that."

"Uh...right...." *What does she mean?* He thought to Lilfor.

It's complicated. Don't worry about it.

"Right now I must attend to Kytt," Brue continued. "I believe your Guardians are expecting you for dinner, even though it's late." With a sharp nod, Brue left the room.

Lilfor grabbed Opute and practically dragged him from the Temple. They were halfway to Lilfor's home when she finally let go.

"In a hurry?" Opute asked.

"I've made a huge mess of things." She plopped down on

a large rock along the path. The planet's sun had just set and a dark red light stretched across the horizon, intensifying the land's rusty color. A cool breeze surrounded them, smelling of salt and soil.

"It's not that bad," Opute offered lamely.

Lilfor looked up at him and rolled her eyes. "Nice try."

Opute took a seat next to her. "Look, I know I don't know about your culture, but do you really have to give up your life because Hunsmat died?"

"You don't understand. I'm responsible for Hunsmat. He had a wife and a family and I wanted to leave the planet."

"Then why did he go with you? I thought you said you two could distance yourselves from each other?"

She shrugged. "I don't know. We've just always been together...maybe he felt obligated to stay with me?"

"So you didn't force him to go with you?"

Lilfor looked at him sharply. "Of course not! He had a wife and a family. I would never make him leave if he hadn't wanted...oh. I see what you did there."

Opute kicked a stone and watched it skip across the sand. "Hunsmat may not have ever left the planet if it weren't for you, but it doesn't mean you're the only reason why he did. And if I recall, he seemed pretty excited about seeing other planets. Maybe he *wanted* to go?"

Lilfor shook her head.

"How do you know?"

"I just...I just do! I knew him, inside and out."

"No. You knew his experiences, not him."

"It's the same thing."

Opute raised an eyebrow at her. "Really? Just because you knew his memories, doesn't mean you knew his thoughts. You could only see what he did, not what he thought and felt."

"Do you really think he could have been hiding things from

me?" she asked.

Opute shrugged and stood. "I only know what you showed me of his life. But I also know what I thought when I met him. He seemed happy to be flying on a ship with you and seeing other planets." He held out his hand to help her to her feet. She took the help and stood.

"They won't understand how he might have wanted to leave his family of his own accord."

"There's nothing you can do about that," he said, as they began walking again. "You may have given him the excuse he needed to do something he wanted."

Lilfor narrowed her eyes at him. "When did you become so insightful?"

Opute shook his head. "I don't know. Guess all this 'can't hide my thoughts and feelings anymore' thing has made me better at talking about them. But don't get used to it."

Lilfor smiled in the red glow of the sinking sun.

* * *

Dinner with Xana and Xera had been simple, yet completely satisfying. The combination of their soothing lyrical voices, the fluffy mounds of a salty seaweed dish called *malu*, and the smell of sweet sand lulled Opute into a sense of security he'd never felt before.

"This place is remarkable," Opute told Lilfor as they cleared away the dishes.

She smiled. "It is, isn't it? I've been away for too long."

Opute nodded at her Guardians. "They really care about you, don't they?"

"Yes, they do. I couldn't have asked for a better new home."

The two of them headed toward the guest room. The dark

clay room was small, but comfortable. Two beds lay head to foot against one wall. The beds themselves were large sheets of *malu*, stretched thin and tight, and filled with sand.

Xana entered the room, holding two large blankets made from the fuzzy tips of desert grasses. "The relief room is next door, but I believe it will be close enough that the distance will not cause you pain."

"Thanks," Lilfor replied, taking the blankets and spreading them across the beds.

"You are both reporting to the Temple early then?"

Lilfor nodded. "Before sunrise."

"Your chances are low in this process, correct?"

Blunt, isn't she?

Lilfor scowled at Opute's thought. "Because of Gaaht's heritage, we don't know what will happen."

"That is true," Xana said, looking at Opute. "He has an energy about him that is...not what it's supposed to be. As if his actual self is being blocked by the skin he wears."

Lilfor...?

Don't worry. She is sensing that you don't really belong in that body, but she doesn't know what it means.

She's sensing it? What under the stars does that mean?

Quiet! She just asked you a question. Say 'no'.

"Uh...", Opute stuttered. "Um...no?"

"Very well," Xana said with a smile, her pink teeth shining under the lights. "I hope you sleep well, Vor Gaaht, and may your deeper consciousness explore its life through your dreams."

"You too," Opute said as she left. He whirled toward Lilfor. "Okay, what did I just say 'no' to?"

"She just asked if you needed anything else." Lilfor grinned and crawled onto one of the beds. "What? Don't you trust me?"

"I don't trust anyone, remember?"

"How could I forget?" she grumbled.

Opute lay down on the bed adjacent to hers and closed his eyes. The sound of the water lapping against the land soothed him.

You really like it here, don't you?

Opute flipped onto his stomach and looked at Lilfor. "Yeah. I don't know what it is, but it just feels so...stable."

"I know what you mean. My Guardians and their species live in such a perfect balance with their environment, it's almost scary. I came from a highly industrial and technologically advanced planet. I mean, the genetic achievements they accomplished on myself and the other children are beyond anything I've seen in the galaxy.

"And yet," she continued, "this place, in all its simplicity, is further ahead of anything that technology could ever give a planet. My Guardians are a part of their world, not separate from it. They don't own it, but it doesn't own them either. They are one and the same—a circle that nourishes itself through its own life and death."

"Then why did you want to leave to do cargo runs?"

Opute saw her silhouette shrug. "There is a beauty in balance, but also a beauty in chaos. I wanted to see it all."

Opute rolled over and closed his eyes, thinking about Lilfor's statement. There *was* beauty in chaos, but chaos had to be balanced or it consumed itself.

Deep.

Opute grunted a laugh at Lilfor's thought. *Good night, Lil.*

Night, Opute.

A moment of silence passed.

Opute?

Yeah?

I'm going to miss being inside your head.

Opute smiled. *I won't.*

Opute fell asleep to the sound of Lilfor's soft laughter.

CHAPTER 22

OPUTE'S LEGS PRICKLED with pins and needles as if they were falling asleep. He'd been kneeling for close to a standard hour on the temple floor, waiting for the separation process to begin. So far, it consisted of being dressed in some strange, green flowing gown, having over one hundred tiny electrodes glued to every inch of his face and scalp, and Brue telling him to stop sweating because it made the electrodes slip off. But no matter how hard he willed his body to stop, it wouldn't listen. The temperature in the temple felt well over 85 Palc and Opute's body didn't regulate the heat as well as Lilfor and her species did. But it gave him something to focus on besides the pain in his knees, the tingling in his legs, and the ache starting in his neck and lower back from holding the position for so long.

I feel like an idiot, Opute thought to himself, fighting the urge to once again readjust his garment blowing in the room's hot breeze.

He heard someone snort a laugh.

You look *like an idiot.*

Opute cracked an eye at Lilfor's thought. She knelt across from him on the floor of the Temple, wearing a similar gown; a silhouette against the night's pre-dawn sky. Harsh artificial lights lit the room and Brue stopped next to Opute, once again adjusting the string of lit electrodes around his head. The rest of the room emptied and Opute could hear nothing but the sound of the fountain.

And of course Lilfor's thoughts in his head.

"Eyes closed," Brue repeated.

He quickly shut his eye again.

Ha. Ha. Made you look!

What are you, a child? he thought back.

Figured I'd get one more laugh in, in case things go badly.

"Could you two please stop talking to each other?"

"We're not talking," they both said in unison.

"You know what I mean," Brue scolded. "Your faces twitch when you think to each other. It's moving the electrodes too much." Opute could tell Brue faced the window when she said her next comment because her voice came from a different direction. "The sun is about to rise. It's time to begin."

Opute tried not to feel nervous, but he didn't like his high chance of dying on a strange planet surrounded by strangers and wearing some sort of strange "light wreath" made up of electrodes on his head.

Strange-looking head. Don't break the chain of repeating adjectives now.

Seriously, how old are you? he thought at her.

It's starting, Lilfor thought back.

Opute felt a slight buzz in his head.

Can you feel it? she thought to him. *The lightness? The sense of relief? Like everything is going to be okay?*

Opute wasn't sure what he felt, but it wasn't anything like Lilfor's description. The buzzing got louder and he felt a pressure rather than a sense of lightness.

After placing a hand on Opute's forehead, Brue began to chant, her voice low and guttural. He'd been told to focus on her voice, but each syllable vibrated in his head.

I don't...I don't think I feel... Each word of Opute's thoughts pounded against the inside of his skull. His head felt full of pressure, like it slowly filled with a thick cord winding itself from one corner of his mind to the other, overlapping and filling his head with layer upon layer of material.

Lilfor? He asked, the word deafening. Each syllable drummed against his skull.

We must be separating, he thought. The words pounded against bone. *I didn't think it would be so painful.* The words dug into his brain. *Stop thinking!* He told himself. *Stop...* WHAM!... *thin-*...WHAM!...*king*...WHAM!

Lilfor...help...

* * *

Opute? Opute, can you hear me?
"Gaaht? Can you hear us?"
"I think he's coming around."
"Don't crowd him!"
Oh Stars, if he dies...
"His breathing has become regular again."
Please be all right...

Opute's eyelids flickered open. He blinked in the brightness of the sun and several figures standing over him came into view: Lilfor, Brue, Xana, and Xera.

Why are her guardians here? he thought.

"He's okay!" he heard Lilfor cry out.

Slowly, someone helped him sit up. A wave of dizziness washed over him for a moment, but then his head cleared.

"Lilfor?" he asked, turning toward her. "What happened?"

Lilfor looked at Brue. "We aren't really sure. You started screaming and then you blacked out. My guardians were called out because Xana is a healer."

"I felt drumming," he began, "in my head. My thoughts pounded against my skull and it really hurt and I couldn't hear you anymore. I thought pain meant it was working."

Can you still hear me?

Opute nodded.

Lilfor helped him to his feet. "Brue," she asked, "what's going on? What happened to him?"

Brue shook her head. "I'm not sure. The process isn't supposed to cause pain. Nothing like this has ever happened before. But then again, this kind of connection has never happened with anyone outside our species. I don't know any other way to disconnect you two."

Xana walked over and placed a hand on Opute's forehead. Her touch felt cool on his hot skin, the electrodes now gone. She closed her eyes for a few moments before frowning. "There is something trapped in here. The process echoed in upon itself."

"What does that mean?" Opute asked.

Xana opened her eyes. "You and Lilfor are as one. There can be no separation this way."

"What?" both Lilfor and Opute said at the same time.

"I can't have her tagging around ten steps behind me the rest of my life!" Opute looked over at Lilfor and saw the look of hurt on her face. "I didn't mean it like that."

"Yes, you did," she answered, her face back to neutral. "And you're right. It's one thing to be in someone else's head, but another to be near them all the time. Hunsmat and I were linked, but we were able to live our lives separately when we wanted to. This arrangement won't work."

"Well, what are we going to do?"

Brue started collecting the equipment. "I don't know what else we *can* do. Nothing like this has ever happened before. We could maybe try again...?"

"No," Lilfor said emphatically. "I'm not putting Gaaht's life in danger again to separate. If it were me being in pain, that's one thing, but he could have died."

"You *both* might die if we don't do something."

"That is unlikely," Xana chimed in. "The bond you share is stable. You will not be lost as an outcome."

"We're not going to die if we stay linked?" Opute asked as a translation.

Xana nodded. "That is correct, Vor Gaaht. Your life is not in danger. Neither is our Light's."

Opute turned to face Lilfor. "Now what do we do?"

"I don't know." The exhaustion and guilt were evident in her voice.

I really screwed things up.

Opute put a hand on her shoulder. "We'll figure out something."

"Until you do," Xana chimed in, "you both are well come to stay in our home. As it is, I believe that rest would be the next appropriate step for you both before you decide anything." She paused. "And I will think."

"Rest is probably a good idea," Lilfor mumbled.

"I will return to help Kytt," Brue told them. She put a hand on Lilfor's arm. "I'm sorry the process didn't work."

"Thanks for trying."

Opute, Lilfor, Xana, and Xera made their way back to Lilfor's home.

"I must be getting old," Lilfor muttered, as she crawled into the bed. "I haven't gone to sleep in the middle of the day for years."

Opute lay down in the other bed. "I bet I could sleep for a week. My head feels like it's full of sand." He closed his eyes, grateful for the chance to let oblivion consume him so he didn't have to think about what to do next.

"See you in a week," Lilfor joked.

Opute answered with a gentle snore.

* * *

Coresque lowered herself down to sleep, attached to her bedlike contraption. She had prepared herself the best she could for her Dream-Access to work. Although now that it came down to it, her anxiety threatened to overwhelm her. She would be revealing everything. She couldn't turn back once she did this.

He needs to know the truth—about all of it.

He needs to know the truth about Exarth, who she really is.

It is the only way to save her.

Coresque slowed her breathing, preparing herself for the task at hand.

* * *

Thlin waited impatiently for the last communications message about Iry's plans that had been sent to Xeleyn to decode. He leaned forward in his chair, biting his nails. This would prove to Iry he could be a great second-hand man. And once Iry sabotaged enough of Exarth's operations, her empire would crumble and Iry would step in. There'd been enough time without a man in power. Iry possessed the brains behind it all anyway. Exarth embodied a thug who couldn't control her temper. He couldn't wait for Iry to dispose of her.

Except he didn't know how Iry planned to do that. She

could regenerate. Iry said he had a plan, but how would he be able to kill her?

As for the albino statue woman, Thlin merely waited for the word. Her stone-like skin made her impervious to all weapons, but he was smarter than that mindless woman who walked around all day with her head in the stars and no thought about reality.

What a fool, he thought to himself.

His datapad chimed, signaling completion. From the looks of it, the transmission that betrayed Iry originated from their very building.

Down the hall, in fact.

Three doors away.

It was Coresque. She had leaked the information about Iry's plans to Xeleyn.

Thlin's face lit up and a sneer curled on his lip.

Found you.

* * *

Hunsmat came toward him, his face half-disintegrated from the blast. Vital liquids oozed along his cheeks, matted in his green hair.

"You did this!" he screamed at Opute. "You killed me!"

Hunsmat reached out, his thick fingers gripping tightly around Opute's throat.

"My wife mourns while you live! YOU MUST DIE!"

Opute bolted awake, his skin slick with sweat, pawing at the air around his neck. He looked next to him and saw Lilfor also sitting up in bed, doing the same motion, the moon shining on her through the open window. They'd both slept the entire day.

"Bad dream?" he asked.

She nodded, her eyes wide. "Terrible."

"Me, too. Guess it's another thing I'll have to get used to."

"What's that?" she asked, stretching her arms over her head.

"Sharing each other's dreams."

Lilfor looked at him, confused. "You just had my nightmare?" she asked, throwing back her covers to cool off.

Opute snorted. "Yeah, cuz I'd dream about *that*." He paused. "Wait, am I not *supposed* to be dreaming what you dream?"

"No."

He sighed. "Chalk it up to another unforeseen side-effect?"

"I guess so." Lilfor rubbed her hands across her face. "Ugh," she muttered. "It felt so vivid. Like I was actually there."

"Don't remind me." He paused. "You must still feel a lot of guilt."

"Guilt? What has that got to do with it? I didn't even recognize the two women."

Opute blinked. "Women?"

Lilfor suppressed a yawn. "Yes. A dark-haired one and some kind of albino. Don't you remember?"

Opute's face paled and he gripped the blanket in his fist. "An albino woman?"

"Yeah…why?" she asked.

"I didn't dream about any women. I dreamt about Hunsmat."

Now Lilfor turned pale. "Hunsmat? What about him?"

"I dreamt he accused me of being responsible for his death. I could see him—the way he looked when he'd been killed—and he reached out for me, grabbing my throat, screaming at me…. I just assumed it was your dream. Isn't that what you dreamed?"

"No. Nothing like that. I saw a completely white woman

pointing at something and then a woman with dark, multi-colored hair who laughed and cried…it didn't really make any sense. Then the dark-haired woman looked younger and then the white woman tried to say something, something really important, like the point of the whole story and then she seemed to be suddenly snatched away…like I was in *her* dream and then she woke up. It happened so fast it felt like everything, the sound, the air, all of it disappeared. I couldn't see or breathe." Lilfor shuddered. "Weird, right?"

Opute grabbed Lilfor's arm. "This albino woman, did this mean everything about her appeared white? Her hair and eyes as well?"

"I think so. Why?"

"What did she try to tell you? Could it have been a warning?"

Lilfor scrunched her forehead. "I don't really remember. Like I said, she pointed at the dark-haired woman and then attempted to tell me something and then *whoosh* she disappeared."

Opute gripped her harder. "Think really hard. *Try* to remember."

"I *am* trying," Lilfor snapped, pulling her arm away from him. "What's your problem anyway?"

Opute got up and paced the room, the soft, sandy floor cushioning his feet. The description Lilfor had just given sounded like Coresque. She'd warned him already in a dream about the danger during the shipment drop with Lym and Reh'dd. Was she trying to send him a message again? Only Lilfor had intercepted it because of the mind-link? Maybe this dark-haired woman was a threat?

This is so frustrating! I just want my own life back!

Lilfor shied away from him, cringing at the anger in his thoughts. "I'm just…I'm just going to go get ready for the day."

Opute let out an exasperated breath. "I'm sorry."

"Don't be. I need to be okay with you being angry because you have every right to be. And I'm trying not to be upset about it because I know you don't want me to cry or blame myself or feel bad, but I do and I can't hide that from you because even if I don't say it, you can hear me think it and I don't want this anymore either." She took a breath and bolted into the restroom.

I can't even run away from him because otherwise my head will probably explode!

This is impossible, Opute thought. He knew she could hear him, but how could he not think? *We can't live this way.*

A moment of quiet passed before Lilfor responded. *I know,* she thought back, *but what are we supposed to do? I don't know how to separate us, mentally or physically. We are going to drive each other crazy.*

Opute looked up as she walked back into the room.

"It doesn't do any good to be in another room," she said.

"We're going in circles with this," Opute said. "I have to close my eyes whenever I do anything I don't want you to see and yet all you have to do is read my thoughts to know what I'm doing and I can't be more than a room away either." He growled in frustration.

"Perhaps I can be of some assistance."

Opute looked up as Xana entered. She reached out and touched Lilfor's forehead in greeting. "My Light," she said. "You are so troubled. Although your connection is stable, it causes instability. This link has served its purpose. It must be severed."

"Purpose? What purpose?" Opute asked. "And I thought you said our bond couldn't be broken?"

Xana smiled. "I do not know what purpose. It is your life and therefore your purpose. But I do know it is complete for you and my Light are no longer in harmony. And the bond will not be broken, simply severed."

What in Space is she babbling about? Opute thought.

I'm just as confused as you are.

"We will begin now."

"Now? As in *right* now?"

"Begin what?" Lilfor questioned.

"Begin the end." Xana motioned toward Opute. "Come. Follow me."

Opute looked at Lilfor. "What is going on here?"

Lilfor shrugged. "Beats me. I just know to trust her." She put her hand on his arm.

The two of them walked behind Xana and left the house. They made their way toward a flat, sandy circle of ground where a number of candles created a triangle surrounding Xana. Her gauzy dark nightdress billowed and her cerulean hair fell in long tresses down her back, the wind blowing it softly around her face.

It couldn't have looked or felt more different than the sterile, technology-based ceremony they'd tried earlier.

Xana gestured for them to each stand in a point of the triangle. She closed her eyes, the flames dancing across her face. She held her hands toward each of them.

The wind died.

The clouds stopped rolling through the sky.

Time seemed to stand still and silence blanketed the planet.

And then she spoke, each word sharp like a knife through the silence, crystalline and pure.

"This bond was created. It has existed. It has lived."

A low thunder rumbled in the background. The purple clouds swelled, blotting out the starry sky. Darkness covered the land.

"A connection of the mind between light and darkness may exist," she continued, her face eerie in the candlelight, "but if it is not properly maintained, then balance becomes chaos unleashed upon itself."

Opute felt the wind stir, blowing sand against his face, though the candle flames did not flicker. It smelled of the normal salt and soil, but this time something sweet echoed in it, like fresh fruit juice.

"Unbalance becomes destruction for destruction's sake."

Opute gasped, his arms flapping at his sides as the wind whipped around them in a tornado, lifting them off the ground.

"Death must be for life and not for death."

Xana's words, though quiet, pierced Opute's mind like daggers. Each syllable sliced away a chunk of his mental defenses, exposing his mind and opening it up raw, but the pain felt more like that of a pinpointed massage, digging in just where it needed.

"Life must be for death and not for life."

The candles went out.

The wind screamed in his ears.

Lilfor! He called out with his mind.

Xana's hair flowed around her head, suspended in the air, lit by a single ray of moonlight which punctured the dense clouds.

"Pierce this veil and destroy what is one so that they may once again be separate and whole."

Opute! Opute heard Lilfor's call, but it sounded faint in his head.

"IT IS DONE!"

With these words the clouds cracked apart and the beam of moonlight split into two with a noise like the tearing apart of time, shining on both of their faces.

After the briefest moment of pure light, a shockwave of energy hit him, hurtling him across the sands. He fell against the earth, bashing his head on something hard, and succumbed to the depths of darkness.

CHAPTER 23

OPUTE GROANED. His head felt heavy.

"I think he's awake," he heard someone say.

Blinking several times, Opute's view came into focus.

"Oh Stars, Gaaht, you scared me half to death."

Opute coughed. *I'm okay. My head hurts.* He raised his hands to his head and felt it wrapped in some sort of bandage. As soon as he touched it, his fingertips went numb, he assumed from some sort of chemical painkiller in the material.

Opute remembered falling and cracking his skull on something very hard. But then he noticed Lilfor waiting for a response. She couldn't hear what he thought. And even better, he couldn't hear her either.

"It worked?" he asked, still daring not to hope.

Lilfor nodded. "Watch." She walked out of the room. A few moments later she returned. "See? No pain. And I can't hear what you're thinking."

"It *is* blissfully quiet in here," he replied, touching his head gingerly.

"That's because there wasn't much going on in there to

begin with," she joked. She began to remove the bandage from his head, her gloved hands immune from the numbing effects.

Opute smiled and looked around. The comforting colors and textures of Xana and Xera's house soothed him. He reveled in the quietness of his head. "What happened?"

"The energy used to separate your mind link to our Light knocked you down," Xera explained. "You had a very resistant barrier. The amount of energy needed to separate the two of you was quite considerable."

"I'm just glad it worked and we're not dead." He pushed himself into a sitting position once free of the head wrap. His head tingled a bit. "Where's Xana? I'd like to thank her before I leave."

"Xana became consumed by the process," Xera said.

"What?" Opute demanded, throwing aside the blanket. His head swam at the movement, but he blinked the feeling of dizziness away. "You mean she's dead? For helping save us?"

"Relax, Gaaht," Lilfor said, putting a hand on his arm. "She's not dead."

"Well then what did she mean by 'consumed?'"

Lilfor paused. "It's difficult to explain. Xana has, temporarily, become one with this planet."

"Right," he responded sarcastically. "Because *now* that makes sense." He paused. "What *exactly* does that mean?"

Lilfor gave Opute his shirt and boots and explained. "Remember how I told you my Guardians live in balance with this planet? Well, Terruens have a unique connection with Terrue. They are tied between their own energies and emotions and the world around them. Does that make sense?"

Opute thought back to when he'd first arrived and Lilfor had told Xana about Hunsmat's death. He remembered how sad Xana seemed and how the weather reflected that sadness. "It doesn't really make sense, but I think I know what you're saying."

"In order for Xana to do what she did," Lilfor continued, "she needed to tap into the energies of the world. To do that, she had to...become one with it."

"So she's a bunch of energy now?"

Lilfor nodded. "In a way, yes. Her entire being has been broken down into its molecular form, combining itself with the planet's natural energy."

"Do not concern yourself though," Xera added. "Xana will rematerialize and once again become corporeal."

"Solid like us," Lilfor added.

"I *know* what corporeal means," Opute retorted. He finished lacing up his boots and ran his fingers through his hair. "I'm glad to hear she's going to be all right. Will you please thank her for me when she becomes solid again?"

Xera raised her eyebrows. "You do not wish to stay and thank her yourself?"

"No offense, but I had a timetable before I came here."

"Ah, yes. The fire that consumes you to blackness and yet drives you forward." Xera cocked her head. "Is it not tiresome to spend your life searching for something when you already possess the things around you to make your life whole?"

"Xera," Lilfor warned. "Don't meddle where you don't belong."

Opute growled. "How does she know this stuff?" He turned on Lilfor. "Did you tell her about my wife?"

"I didn't tell her anything," she snapped back.

"Please," Xera said softly, "I did not mean to invade where not invited."

"Xera," Lilfor said, gesturing at the tiny woman, "deals with the realm of the emotional. Xana deals with the physical. That's why she knew about our connection and its unstableness."

"So Xera is an…em…empath?" Opute said, struggling to remember the term. He'd dealt with an individual in the past who read him like an open book. He didn't feel like repeating the experience, especially when he just got rid of Lilfor as a mind-roommate.

"Not quite," Xera said. "I cannot read emotions as a normal empath would. I am unable to sense when you are joyful or saddened. I merely receive images of an individual's emotional life force."

Opute's head started to throb. "I'm kinda tired of all this 'energy' and 'connection' and 'life force' junk. I just want to get out of here and get back to my own life."

"Are you sure?" Xera interjected.

"Guardian!" Lilfor hissed. "Let it go. I've seen inside his head." She turned toward Opute. "This is the path he has chosen and he must see it through. And I can't say I wouldn't do the same in his situation."

"As you wish." Xera touched his forehead. A feeling of warmth exuded from her fingertips. "May you have peace for yourself as for others." She left the room.

Opute felt a tension inside him loosen he hadn't even known existed. "Lilfor, I…"

She shook her head. "You have a lot of individuals who care about you, but they can't see into your soul. Nuis, Zarsa, even myself, we want you to be safe and happy, but the blackness of your thoughts and the veil over your heart can't be erased until you decide to let them go." She moved closer and hugged him. "Whatever happens, whatever you decide, we're here for you. Don't ever forget that though you choose to do this on your own, you aren't ever alone."

Opute walked up the ramp of Lilfor's ship, the *Evader*, waving as he went. Lilfor decided to stay on her homeworld and made him take her ship. She told Opute that her connection with him made her realize she wanted to live for others for a while, instead of herself. She also wanted to live without being mind-linked to anyone, to listen to her own thoughts instead of depending on someone else.

"Good luck. Maybe you'll like it by yourself."

She ran her fingers through her hair, massaging her scalp. "It's still so strange. I keep expecting to see Hunsmat's memories or hear your voice. Aren't you lonely by yourself all the time?"

"Guess I think of it more as privacy then being alone."

She smiled.

Opute cleared his throat. "Uh, if you change your mind and want to get back out there, I know a couple individuals who could maybe help. I'm sure you remember them from my memories, Nuis and Zarsa. They could find you some jobs, and they wouldn't be mixed up with Exarth's companies."

She nodded. "Thanks. I'll keep that in mind."

He handed her a datapad. "Here's where I'll be staying for a while, probably just a couple of weeks. But I'll get back to you if you call."

Her eyes glistened. "Take care."

"You too."

He boarded the ship and made his way to the cockpit. As he began his take-off sequence, he looked across the planet's surface, its red deserts and turquoise seas, and a lump rose in his throat. His homeworld of C-Sector 9 never gave him comfort, with its vast cities and bustling crowds. He'd never really felt home anywhere, but this place appealed to him.

Maybe someday....

He lifted off the ground. The blue-green waters sprayed into the air. The sunlight hit the drops and for a few moments, a glistening shape of a face shined at him.

Xana, saying goodbye.

* * *

Something felt wrong.

Coresque was sending her Dream-Access message, but she felt like Opute wasn't receiving it. Like a river diverting the message away from him.

She didn't have time to try and figure it out. If she postponed any longer, she might lose her nerve. And she didn't have time to waste gathering up courage to try again. She sent her message, depicting Exarth, then herself, and just when she began to say the secret she'd been hiding for so long, a jolt of pain shocked her out of her dream.

Coresque awoke to pressure—tons of it pressing against her chest, her legs, her arms. She couldn't move. Even her face remained fixed in its position to the side, where she could see two feet pacing across her floor.

"Who are you?" she called out, her words distorted by the object pressed against her cheek.

The figure knelt to the ground and tipped his head to the side so she could see him. He flipped his auburn hair out of his face and smiled. He seemed familiar, but she couldn't place him.

"Comfortable?" he asked.

"What is going on? Who are you?" she repeated.

"Figures you don't know me. I'm not surprised since you insist on living with your head in the stars instead of looking at what's right in front of you." His face contorted with anger for a moment. "Let's just say I'm Iry's messenger," he continued, "and this giant one-ton weight lying on top of you is his message."

"I do not understand…" And then she remembered him, Thlin. She'd seen him in Iry's office.

Thlin moved so close to her his hot breath beaded on her

face. "I know you intercepted Iry's transmission and sent it out into the world," Thlin told her. "And I know that because of your impenetrable skin nothing can physically harm you. But I can trap you." He pulled his face away, laughing.

"Please, Thlin," Coresque cried out. "You cannot leave me here like this!"

"So you *do* know who I am? It doesn't matter. I like the way my name sounds attached to someone begging for help. And I've sealed the door so no one will be able to hear you. Beg all you want."

"Why are you doing this?"

"You backed the wrong choice. Exarth will fall and Iry will rise. No one will find you because no one else knows you're here." He let out a guttural laugh.

His feet disappeared from her view and she heard the door close behind him.

* * *

Opute stepped into his hotel room after having spoken with Paja about his next assignment. Paja offered him a permanent contract position, starting in a few days, with some high-up associate. Apparently this higher-up had been extremely impressed with how Opute handled himself during his previous "distressing" situations.

This is what he wanted—to rise in the ranks. Except he hated having to climb over the dead bodies of good individuals.

"It'll be worth it, to see Exarth dead." The words sounded hollow in his ears.

He rubbed his temples, trying to stave off the headache he knew would come. He worried the price of success may be too high. He felt so certain when he started that nothing and no one mattered if he could reach Exarth. But between his experience with Lilfor and the words of her and her Guardians, he didn't know what to think.

Opute laid down on the bed. *Just hang in there,* he told himself. *A little more and you'll find Exarth and all of this will be over.*

* * *

Exarth's fifth and final bounty hunter lay dead at her feet. She'd planned ahead this time, meeting the assassin at an outside location so she wouldn't have to clean up the body. She'd departed Belxa and currently stood on the planet of C-Sector 9, where Opute had grown up and lived for most of his adult life.

Being on C-9 brought back memories for Exarth. She'd done a lot of work here, met a lot of interesting individuals: it seemed like an entirely different lifetime. So much had happened since she, Iry, and Cor had slaughtered the "doctors" and nurses from the hospital and left their forsaken homeworld. It seemed logical for them to find a place where they could live and they knew two things would be essential to that: anonymity and easy access to the essentials. They'd stowed away on a medical frigate headed for C-9 and once they arrived, they did anything necessary to survive.

Eventually, they met other runaways and abandoned children. They brought them together and with their superior intellect, found it easy to keep them in line.

Iry took charge at first, but once again, just like back home, the children depended on Exarth for the final word. Exarth knew it bothered Iry, but he seemed content after a while to simply create the ingenious plans that got them food, lodging, and eventually jobs.

Being a runner seemed the easiest thing to do and so most of the children did that. All earnings were gathered and split equally. The setup worked well, until one of the children, an older boy, stole their saved money and disappeared with it during the night. Furious, Exarth wanted to find him, but Iry held her back. He didn't want to risk exposure, especially if the boy went to the authorities with a tip about their whereabouts.

After that incident, Exarth restricted where she put her trust, leaning more heavily on Iry and Cor. They had been there since the beginning and would be there through the end.

Then she'd met Opute and, try as she might to resist, found herself opening up to him. She spent so many years with the sole focus of survival, she couldn't believe how much she began to enjoy thinking and planning for a future. A future less reliant on staying angry at the galaxy and one more filled with hope.

Or so I thought. Opute lied. Iry lied. Even Cor is holding back. Well this time I'm not relying on anyone. I'm going to find Opute on my own, even if it means I have to kill everyone who has ever seen, heard of, or talked to him. I'm going to make him pay for destroying that hope.

The only good thing from this fifth bounty hunter was a location. It appeared some of Exarth's stolen ships ended up on Sintaur. Wondering if Opute had sold the ships to the government, the bounty hunter tried to trace the sales transaction, but to no avail.

What a fool, Exath thought as she headed toward her transport vessel. *Opute would never make a transaction with someone for those ships and leave a trail. Which means either he sold the ships and destroyed the evidence or...*

...whoever bought the ships covered Opute's tracks.

Exarth powered up her ship and soared out of C-9's atmosphere, plotting a course for Sintaur. A tic in her left eye twitched a few times.

"Let's see who on Sintaur knows Opute."

CHAPTER 24

OPUTE ARRIVED TWO days later at his new job. The large, cylindrical building had sleek lines and the windowed walls reflected the fake sun's rays. Two guards at the door allowed him in after he presented identification and stated his business.

He climbed into an air-propelled ovule, punched in the floor he wanted, and the elevator whisked him throughout the building. The ovule slowed to a stop and the door opened.

Opute exited the transport and walked up to a large, black, circular desk. The receptionist looked up from his datapad.

"Can I help you?"

"My name is Vor Gaaht. Paja's office sent me about a job."

"Of course, Mister Gaaht. Iry is expecting you. Please enter though the second door on the left."

Opute headed toward the door and knocked lightly before it slid open.

His breath caught in his chest. It took him a minute to realize the man behind the desk was, first off, a man, and second, not the white woman who had invaded his dreams. Although aside from the gender distinction, the two could have been twins. This man also appeared completely white, as if skin, hair, and eyes had been soaked in bleach.

As the man stood, Opute noticed another difference. He didn't move in the statue-like manner that Coresque did. His movements were fluid and normal.

"Mister Gaaht," the man said, gesturing for Opute to sit down. "My name is Iry."

"Pleasure," Opute replied, slapping on a phony smile as he fell into his crafted persona. "Have to admit, I'm a little surprised to be here." Glittering white marble sat between him and Iry. In fact, Opute realized the whole room was draped in white, some different shades or accented with metallic flicks, but no other colors seemed to exist.

Iry laughed, the sound light and musical. "Understandable. You did just commence your term of employment with us a few weeks ago. But we inspect and estimate the promise of all our employees, new or old, and are always on the lookout for someone who has…special potential. We believe, Mister Gaaht, you may have that potential."

"I'm flattered," Opute lied. *This guy is so full of it.*

"I'm glad to hear that. Now then, I'd like you to join my personal staff, Mister Gaaht, if you're interested. It consists of myself, my assistant, Mister Aug, and my receptionist, who will deal with the financial elements of this position."

"What does the job entail?"

"It varies, depending on each situation."

That isn't much of an answer. "What does it pay?" he asked, sticking to what his character would ask about.

"Enough," Iry replied.

"My enough may be different than your enough."

Iry laughed again, the timbre getting on Opute's nerves. It sounded too perfect, as if manufactured and played like a recording. "Too true, Mister Gaaht. I assure you, however, that your version of enough is less than mine. In other words, you shall no longer have any financial difficulties. We will supply you with accommodations, transportation, attire, and any other provisions you may need. These benefits will continue as long as you are my employee. The question then becomes, Mister Gaaht, are you the type of individual who is willing to work for someone who will keep you financially sustained for the rest of your life?"

Opute felt stunned. No real employer could ever offer anything like Iry's obscene proposal without some sort of catch.

And yet it represented *exactly* the kind of offer that would entice the character of Vor Gaaht and Iry knew that.

This man was smart. And smart men were dangerous.

Plus Opute had a feeling that if he refused, he wouldn't stay alive very long.

"When do I start?"

* * *

Two days later, Opute received orders to fly a small cargo vessel and transport the materials on board for a drop-off in the next solar system. The exchange would be short and sweet, according to Mister Aug, who told Opute to think of it as a "trial-run."

"I'll contact you once you've entered Yek's atmosphere," Mister Aug's voice continued on the recorded message. "From there I will give you instructions on where in the city the meeting is supposed to take place."

Opute left his hotel to find a transport vessel waiting to take him to the city's main hanger bay. He entered the bay, found the cargo ship, checked over the goods, and warmed up the vessel. After a few minutes, the ship lifted off the surface and headed out into open space.

The trip itself would be short, about two standard hours one-way, so Opute set the controls to auto-pilot, kicked up his feet, and closed his eyes for a short nap.

A brisk, stern voice awoke Opute from his slumber.

"This is Yek's Space Controller—please identify yourself."

Opute shook off his lingering sleep and hit the communications button to open a channel. "This is Vor Gaaht, requesting permission to land. I am a transport vessel making a cargo run." He looked over and cursed the proximity alarm for not going off when he'd arrived near the planet.

"Please identify destination and cargo."

"Uh..." he started, struggling to remember the name of the city. "I'm headed for...Keya," he said, finding his instruction sheet. "My cargo is Trawalian spices."

At the same moment, his personal communications device lit up. The frequency indicated the message came from Mister Aug.

Not now, he thought at the device.

"Mister Gaaht, Trawalian spices are illegal to transport and trade in this region. Please power down your vessel and prepare to be boarded so we may confiscate your cargo." The patrol ship's weapons powered up, aiming at Opute's ship.

"What the...?" he started. "Uh, sure...I, uh-I didn't realize...hang on while I power down." Opute turned off his ship's communications and answered his personal communications call.

"Mister Gaaht," Mr. Aug's voice began. "I take it you have successfully reached Yek?"

"Yeah, except that Trawalian spices are *illegal* on this planet," Opute snapped, his temper flaring. "What kind of game are you playing here?"

"I can assure you that—"

A voice in the background, who Opute recognized as Iry, interrupted Mr. Aug. "Thlin! I need those specs!"

"I'm on it," Mr. Aug replied to Iry. Returning to Opute he continued. "As I was saying, Mister Gaaht, we were unaware of any—"

"Save it," Opute cut him off. "I'm going to...wait, what did he just call you?"

"You aren't going to do anything, Gaaht," Mr. Aug retorted, his voice a whisper, "except die. Iry may like you, but you're too slippery to stay in my boat." The call ended.

"Thlin!" Opute cried out. He couldn't believe it. The name came back full force. Mr. Aug was Thlin, the man who'd blown up his wife's ship! He'd been working for that backstabbing, treacherous, *murderous*... Opute's internal rant got cut short when a loud alarm began to wail. The ship's self-destruct mechanism activated.

The timer read less than a standard minute.

"Stars!" Opute swore. He slapped the communications button. "Attention patrol ship: my self-destruct sequence became accidentally activated. Get out of here, NOW!" Without waiting for a response, Opute raced through the ship to the escape pod. Adrenaline coursed through his body, forcing him to continue, even though his brain told him he'd never make it in time.

Diving into the compartment, he sealed the hatch and reached for the lever to detach from the ship when he felt an enormous pressure fill the escape pod. The hatch door folded inward, towards Opute. Opute's head rattled as the pod rocketed away from the ship.

Through the porthole, he watched the ship explode.

Hysterical laughter barked out of him as the tiny pod tumbled end over end. *They must have put a separate charge at the base of the escape pod door, to prevent me from getting in, but it blew too late and instead pushed me away from the ship. They saved my life by trying to kill me!*

Opute floated away from the remnants of the destroyed cargo vessel and soon saw the patrol ship swing around, weapons pointed at the pod. Opute waved his arms as best he could inside the crumpled shell and prayed they wouldn't immediately fire. He only hoped his warning message had been perceived as a sign of good faith.

Otherwise he'd wasted those seconds for nothing.

Opute breathed out a sigh of relief when the patrol ships flashed their docking lights at him and approached. He continued holding up his unarmed hands through the viewport. The patrol ship pulled up next to him and engulfed his pod into their cargo area.

Opute waited, since he couldn't get through the half-melted door. At last he heard a loud hiss. A blast of bright light and smoke shone through and the damaged door fell off, revealing five individuals pointing their handheld weapons at him.

Coughing, Opute exited slowly, keeping his hands raised.

"Attention Mister Gaaht, you are under arrest for the transportation of illegal substances in the Yek sector, sabotaging and destroying evidence, and attempting to flee the authorities. We also have reason to believe you have been working for the known terrorist, Exarth. We will escort you to our detention facilities where you will await a trial that will occur in two daily rotations. If you have any questions or would like to add anything to the record, now is the only time you may speak."

Opute's shoulders relaxed. If he had a chance to defend himself, he might get out of this in one piece. There were plenty of worlds whose criminal proceedings might have had him thrown into a cell to rot away regardless of his side of the story. Although the fact that the authorities were told he worked for Exarth and that he'd been sent to the system where Trawalian spices just happened to be illegal didn't bode well for the situation.

"I would like to say for the record," Opute began, "that I didn't know Yek sector laws regarding Trawalian spice trade, as noted by my statement of having the cargo on board when I arrived. I'd also like to state my innocence concerning the activation of the self-destruct mechanism. This had been somehow programmed into my ship's computer to take place once I'd entered your system."

"These statements have been noted. Anything else?"

"Yes. I'd like to have the record show that when I discovered the activated self-destruct, I attempted to warn your approaching vessel to move away. And, since I am unfamiliar with your laws, I'd like a copy of any and all policies and procedures dealing with criminal behaviors on your planet."

"We agree to these terms. Please follow us and we'll escort you to the detention cell."

* * *

Nuis looked up from his datapad at the woman who entered his office. A smile bloomed on his face, his white, even teeth dazzlingly bright even with Sintaur's sun pouring through the windows.

"Please," he said, gesturing to the woman, "have a seat."

The woman sat down, a slight smile touching her full lips. Her green eyes were wide and vibrant and she threw her shoulder-length blonde hair over her shoulder.

"Thank you for seeing me on such short notice," she told him, a soft drawl touching the end of each word.

"Not a problem. I'm happy to help, Miss…ah…"

"Caki Yetbay," she filled in. "But please, call me Caki."

"So, Caki, you work for the Sintaur Press, correct?"

Caki nodded. "I'm doing an article on Sintaur's Day of Darkness." She leaned forward. "I did a little digging and discovered you were an instrumental part of Sintaur's success last year. I'd like to ask you a few questions, if you don't mind."

"Not at all," Nuis said, leaning back in his chair. "Fire away."

Caki pulled out a datapad and began entering information. "Is it true Sintaur defended its territory by both ground and aerial assaults?"

"That is correct. They put me in charge of organizing governmental cooperation during the crisis."

"Umhmm." Caki said, her face buried in her datapad. "And who commanded the aerial assault?"

Nuis cleared his throat. He felt reluctant to give Opute's name, as his friend had tried very hard to keep himself out of the limelight. "We had outside help," he said evasively.

Caki looked at him and raised an eyebrow. "Did this 'outside help' have a name?"

"Of course."

"And it is…?"

"Classified," he said with a grin. "You understand."

Caki's own smile turned sour. "Of course. I understand you are covering up for a man who is a notorious smuggler and thief and divulging his identity would reflect poorly on Sintaur and taint the success of that day."

Nuis's grin faded. "Excuse me?"

Caki snorted. "Face it, Nuis, I'm on to you. I know Ness Opute helped you bring in a fleet of ships."

Nuis felt the blood drain from his face. "You need to recheck your facts, Miss Yetbay."

"You need to not tell me what to do, *Mister* Nuis Weri." Caki's sweet-looking face turned bitter with a scowl. "I know Opute stole those ships. I know he helped this pathetic excuse for a planet. And I know the two of you are friends.

"I also know," she went on, "that Sintaur's ship compliment recently increased by six attack cruisers, the same number minus one stolen by Opute."

"Who are you?" Nuis stammered. "How do you know this?"

Caki laughed, the sound low and sultry. The drawling accent disappeared as she spoke. "I want to know where he is."

"I don't know what you're talking about." Nuis reached under his desk to trigger his silent alarm, but a feeling of fire swept through his right side. He looked down; his arm lifeless at his side.

"Nerve disrupter," she said casually, pointing a metallic ball with a pointed end at him. "The damage is permanent, I'm afraid, but it can stop with just your arm. And feel free to scream if it helps. I've paralyzed your assistant outside. We have several hours before she wakes.

"Now," she said, pointing the weapon at his other arm, "where is Opute?"

"I don't—" Nuis cried out as his other arm felt on fire. "Oh stars," he cursed. "You're crazy!"

Caki tapped the weapon against her bottom lip as if considering this statement. "No," she said, shaking her head, "I'm just angry. No more lies. This weapon will kill you and I've heard it's excruciating. I know your arms feel like they are on fire. Eventually they'll go numb. Imagine that throughout your whole body. Until your automated systems stop working and you die, unable to speak, unable to scream.

"One last time," she said, leaning forward with each word. Her eyes widened, as if hungry for his reply. "Where is he?"

Sweat poured down Nuis's face. "He...he," he licked his lips, his eyes darting toward the door, hoping someone would come in, hoping *anything* would happen.

"Yes?" she prompted.

"He's involved in some sort of smuggling ring. Somewhere on the planet C-Nine."

Caki tutted at him, though her body shook. "Lies do not become you," she told him. She lunged forward across the desk and raked her fingernails across his face, ripping through his skin.

Nuis screamed.

"He's *not* on C-Nine. It's the first place I checked!"

"You just..." Nuis huffed, "you just can't find him. He's a ghost. He could be anywhere or anyone."

"Any*one* you say?" she said, a gleam coming into her eyes.

Nuis couldn't be sure, but it seemed like colors swirled underneath the green? As if she wore colored contact lenses.

"Wh-what?" Nuis stammered.

"You said he could be anywhere or *anyone*. That's an interesting statement."

Nuis tried to move his arms, but a fresh burst of pain rewarded him.

Caki turned her chair around and straddled it. "You know," she began, scratching the weapon against her head, "I am really tired."

Nuis remained silent.

"I let myself believe I could have a normal life," she continued, ranting. "Have love, a family, a house, a good job. I don't think those things are too much to ask for. But apparently that is not what's in store for me. Instead, I'm surrounded by individuals who betray me, who help my enemies, who lie and cheat, and all the while they smile in my face and think of me as a fool."

Caki leaned closer. "I'm not a fool."

"I believe you," Nuis answered, sweat dripping into his eyes.

Caki smiled, a ghostly look that frightened Nuis even more. "You just think I'm insane."

Nuis blinked rapidly against the salty sting. "No, you're just angry."

The woman barked a laugh. "You know what? I like you. And I can see why Opute likes you, too."

The anxiety in Nuis' chest loosened for a moment.

Her face fell, crestfallen. He couldn't keep up with the myriad of emotions flitting through her.

"That's why I'm sorry I have to do this." In a flash, Caki dragged a nail across Nuis's throat.

Nuis gurgled as blood poured from the gash, his useless arms unable to reach up to stop the flow of blood. He fell out of his chair and crashed to the floor.

The woman rose and leaned over him. "Opute *must* understand. I will find him. Now...let's see who you've been talking to...."

Nuis gasped one more breath, watching the woman lean over his vidlink, before the pain disappeared and blissful darkness swallowed him.

CHAPTER 25

OPUTE SAT IN a detention cell staring at a datapad in front of him. It held a copy of the legal system on Yek and all its policies, procedures, and penalties for the criminal element.

He meant to read through it, but all his focus centered on the fact that Thlin had been within his grasp and he never realized it. Venting his anger, Opute kicked his bed, popping off part of its rusted metal frame.

You need to focus, he told himself. *You won't be able to kill Thlin until you can get out of here, so concentrate, read this stuff, and find a loophole.*

With a new resolve, Opute set to work.

Several hours later, Opute finished skimming Yek's laws. The good news stated he could contact someone as a personal reference, which apparently held a lot of sway if said reference happened to be prominent, wholesome, ethical, and a lot of other things that made them "good" in the eyes of the judge.

The bad news explained the Yek used death as the punishment for *any* crime.

At first Opute considered contacting Nuis, since Dignitary of Off-world Affairs on Sintaur and basically a war hero would hold a lot of sway, but Nuis didn't know of Opute's new look and identity as Gaaht and might not accept the call. He also thought about Lilfor, but as a lowly cargo transporter and barely an adult, he figured the court wouldn't take her seriously. The only other individual who could vouch for him in his new identity and had a credible business standing was Zarsa. He hated to get her involved, but he knew she wouldn't hesitate to help if she could.

With a yawn, Opute called out to the guard. A tiny metal slot opened.

"What?" the guard snapped.

"I'd like to vidlink my personal representative."

"Should have asked earlier. No calls until the morning." The slot slammed closed and locked with a clink.

Opute cracked his knuckles. He laid down on the squeaky bed and fumed until he fell asleep.

He was swimming.
No, floating.
Or maybe flying?
Either way, his feet didn't touch the ground.
A greenish ether surrounded him, suspending him in time.
The ether darkened into the vacuum of space and tiny pricks of light shone through the velvety blackness.
The stars neared. Their brightness enveloped him and covered him with shimmery light.
He felt at peace; calm and safe.
And then the brightness died away into complete nothingness. No stars, no sun, no light at all. Completely alone with no one around him and no one to talk to. Just himself and his own thoughts.
Completely and utterly alone.

Opute woke up in his holding cell with a crick in his neck and a terrible feeling of loneliness. It had been the fourth dream in a row he'd had in which he felt alone.

At least I'm not having dreams about death, which could quickly become a reality, he thought while he stretched. His breakfast already sat in his room. Hunger consumed him and he shoveled half the food into his mouth in one bite. Forcing himself to slow down, he planned his defense, which according to the procedural manual, he had to do himself. He also planned what to ask from Zarsa.

A sudden knock startled Opute. He tried to swallow back down the food he coughed up.

The door opened. "It's time for you to call your reference," the guard told him, motioning for him to follow. Opute put down the rest of his breakfast and complied. They made their way through a labyrinth of corridors before they reached a small enclosure with a vidlink monitor inside it.

"You have one thirtieth of a rotation to call your reference. You are being monitored." The guard left abruptly, closing and latching the door behind him.

Opute quickly did the mental calculations in his head and determined he had about one standard hour to talk to Zarsa. He sat down in front of the vidlink, inputted her access code, and waited for her to answer.

* * *

Zarsa heard the soft beep of her vidlink.

"Hello?" she murmured, not really looking at the caller as she answered.

"Zarsa?" a light tenor voice asked. "It's me."

Zarsa turned her attention to the screen and felt her heart

jump. A man with copper-colored skin, light auburn hair, and amber eyes stared back at her. "Op...I mean, Gaaht. What a surprise."

Opute smiled. "For you and me both." He paused. "I need your—"

"Gaaht," Zarsa interrupted, "I'm glad you called. There's been an accident."

"What do you mean? What happened?"

Zarsa shook her head. "I tried to find you, but you know you, you're pretty unfindable."

"What *happened*?"

"It's Nuis. He's...he's dead. Been killed, actually."

Opute's eyes widened. "He's what? When? Who did it?"

"I don't know. I found out yesterday. He and I have been keeping in touch since your procedure."

Opute's jaw tightened and his words came out guttural. "Who...did...it?"

"I told you, I don't know. Nuis's secretary said some blonde woman from the Sintaur Press came in to interview him. Then she remembered waking up. Apparently the interviewer drugged her. She called into Nuis' office to ask what happened, but he didn't answer, so she entered and found him on the floor. His throat had been slit. And now Sintaur Central Authority is on their way here to talk to me about it."

"Why is someone coming to talk to you?"

"They traced his calls. I was the last one he contacted."

At that moment, Zarsa's door chimes rang.

"Stars," she cursed, "the officer is here already."

"Zarsa, wait! Don't disconnect. I won't be able to call you—"

"Then just stay on the line," she interrupted him. Her door chimes rang again. "I can't keep the officer waiting. I'll put you on silent. You'll still be able to hear everything. Maybe you can pick up on something to help find out who Nuis's murderer is." Zarsa quickly muted the call, over Opute's protests, and blacked out the screen before remotely unlocking the door to her office.

"Come in, Officer," Zarsa said with a smile. "Sorry to keep you waiting."

A young, female entered. "No problem," she said, her words crisp and precise. "I appreciate you seeing me. I understand this must be a difficult time for you."

The officer took a seat after flashing a set of credentials. "My name is Officer Chele, and I just have a few quick questions for you." Officer Chele took a moment to tuck a stray strand of reddish hair under her cap. "I promise to make this as painless as possible." A look of sympathy crossed the officer's bright blue eyes. "Now then," she said, checking her datapad. "it says in my report that you were the last individual to contact Nuis Weri, about two standard days before the incident occurred, is that correct?"

"That sounds right."

"Did Mister Weri seem nervous to you at all?"

Zarsa shook her head and then remembered Opute could hear, but not see. "No," she answered out loud. "He seemed fine."

"Did he mention anything unusual to you, any worries or comments about someone coming after him?"

"Not that I can think of."

"Did he mention any current work plans or deals that may have gone sour?"

"No."

"Did he mention anything about a recent influx of attack cruisers he acquired for the Sintaurian government?"

Zarsa furrowed her eyebrows. "Attack cruisers? I don't think so."

"Hmm," she remarked, scrolling down on her datapad.

"And how about any mention of an individual named...oh yes, here it is, Ness Opute?" Officer Chele looked up at this question.

"Who?" Zarsa asked, feigning ignorance.

"Ness Opute."

Zarsa shook her head slowly. "Doesn't sound familiar," she lied. "Why?"

"We have reason to believe he may be responsible for Mister Weri's death."

Zarsa snorted. "Doubtful."

Officer Chele raised an eyebrow. "Really? Why is that?"

Zarsa's eyes widened and she mentally cursed herself. "I just meant that Ness Opute is a known smuggler. Nuis wouldn't have had any dealings with him."

"I thought you said you weren't familiar with the name."

The officer's words hung in the air.

"Uh..." Zarsa stammered. "I just meant I'd never heard Nuis talk about him. But, I mean, I've *heard* of the man before. I mean, you know, you hear stories."

"I see," she responded. "You run a business that deals with changing physical appearances, correct?"

Zarsa felt surprised by the abrupt subject change. "It's a medical facility, but yes, we've done some facial and body reconstructions."

"I would like to see your files."

"I'm sorry. Those are confidential."

"Of course they are. I would like to see them."

Zarsa blinked. "I'm sorry," she repeated. "I'm not at liberty to disclose personal information."

Officer Chele sighed. "You know, this would be much easier if you'd just cooperate."

Zarsa's irritation grew. "Come back with Galactic Invasion Permits from Sintaur and Grassuwer and then we'll talk. You may leave now."

The woman didn't move. "Did you know, Zarsa, that you can find out pretty much anything you want, if you just know where to look?"

"I asked you to leave," Zarsa said, reaching for the com link to her secretary.

"I wouldn't," the officer snapped, her clipped accent gone. She lifted a weapon and leveled it at Zarsa's head. "It's a nerve disrupter. And Mister Weri could tell you how painful it is to have it fired upon you. If he were still alive, that is."

Zarsa pulled her hand away. "You? You killed Nuis?"

"Yes."

"But why?"

"Information, my dear, is easy to come by if you know who to ask. Would it surprise you to hear that I know Nuis *did* have dealings with Ness Opute? In fact, he recently purchased six attack cruisers from the man mere weeks before his death. And they had been colleagues for years.

"Would it also surprise you," she went on, "to know I'm aware of your own past *intimate* relationship with Ness Opute?" A sneer graced her full lips. "That would have been, what, five years ago now? I assume he *claimed* he loved you and left you high and dry." The woman paused and closed her eyes, as if regaining control over herself. "But it doesn't really matter. What *does* matter is Opute's contact with Nuis and Nuis's contact with you, so I have a feeling you were in contact with Opute."

"I don't know what you're talking about."

"More lies," Officer Chele snapped. "I am so *SICK* of lies! First Nuis, now you.... I really thought you'd be different. Why are you protecting Opute? He's no different than anyone else. He's not special."

Zarsa's blood raced through her body. What was this

woman ranting about? Why would the authorities talk like this? They wouldn't. She must be after Opute. "What do you want?"

"I want to know what he looks like, now that you've altered him."

"I didn't—" Zarsa screamed. Her left arm blazed like it was on fire.

"Excruciating, isn't it?"

"It doesn't matter," Zarsa wheezed. "I erased the files. You'll never find him. You're just some pathetic bounty hunter who made it all this way for nothing."

Officer Chele laughed, the sound soft and sinister. "You think I'm a bounty hunter? How quaint. No, my dear. I am the woman Opute betrayed. He stole my ships and has interfered with my life for the last time. I will have my vengeance."

In a flash, the officer leaned over the table and slit Zarsa's throat with her long fingernail. Blue blood gushed from the open wound.

"And if I can't find him, then perhaps when he hears of his loved ones' deaths, he will come to me."

CHAPTER 26

"ZARSA! *ZARSA*!" THE ROOM exploded into a sea of bright lights and harsh smells. Opute grabbed the vidlink so tightly he broke it, slicing into three fingers, but he didn't register the pain.

"NO! Zarsa, please! Exarth I'm going to KILL you!" With a deafening howl, Opute whipped the vidlink across the room.

Everything hazed into a red blur. Guards came at him, restraining him. A hard, sickening pain across his head. Woozy steps out of the cell. A prick in his neck. Then dizziness and darkness.

Opute came to, laying in his holding cell, his wrists bound behind his back. He looked around. Nothing remained in his room, not even his bed.

Once alert, he almost cried out to the guard to tell him what happened, but the words died on his lips. Hours had most likely passed since the call and someone must have already found Zarsa's body. It would only connect him to her death.

Her *murder*.

The problem was, authorities may have already checked the

call logs or Exarth may have, since she did the same with Nuis's. Because Opute wasn't aware of how long he'd been sedated, Exarth may already be on her way. Or perhaps she would just send someone to kill him.

He had to get out of this place. Locked up, restrained, and under guard, he wouldn't stand a chance.

Not to mention the uncontrollable urge to rip Exarth's heart out urging him on.

Opute assessed his situation. He shifted his view to examine his restraints, craning his neck to see the edges of his hands. The wrist binders were a simple design: metal, with a locking mechanism. He would not be able to break them, but his arms were just a bit longer than normal for his height and he'd be able to slide his cuffed arms around his back and pull his legs through. A trick that had helped him a couple times in the past.

Next, the guards.

He assumed that since his outburst there would be one, maybe two extra guards put outside his door. He may be able to take them, but if they were armed, he might die in the process. Opute frantically peered around his windowless cell with solid walls, floor, and...

Opute looked up. It *wasn't* solid. A panel sat in the ceiling above him. It appeared to be some sort of light metalwork, like ductwork for a ventilation system.

He groaned. Climbing through a maze of cramped ducts without lights while shackled at the wrists did *not* meet with his idea of a good time. Especially since he didn't really like tight, dark, enclosed spaces. But he had to choose either the ventilation system or a confrontation with the guards that may likely lead to his death.

He grunted and shimmied his hands around his backside and under his legs. He stood, blinking away the rest of the sedative, and glanced upward.

The shaft opening sat directly above him: an arm's length out of reach.

"Stars," he cursed rubbing his face. He jumped a few times even though he knew he couldn't reach it.

Well there goes that idea. Opute started to wonder if he could somehow climb the walls or wedge himself between two of them for leverage when he heard the door to his cell unlock.

In a flash he hid behind it. The door came toward him and he wrenched it open, grabbed the tray of food from the guard, and bashed him in the face with it. The guard went down and the one next to him only had time to drop his jaw in surprise before Opute cracked him in the head with the backside of the tray.

Grabbing the guard's keys, he unlocked his cuffs and took off at a sprint, keeping his eyes open for anyone else on watch. He made his way through the corridors in a hurry, stopping only once when he heard footsteps in a passage nearby. Luckily for Opute, and for the individuals themselves, they were headed in the opposite direction.

Alarms blared. He reached the door to the hangar bay, opened it with the correct key, and made a dash for the nearest ship. Opute made a split-second decision, figuring a patrol vessel would be quickest and would arouse less suspicion than a cargo vessel or freighter.

Finding one with an already open hatch, Opute entered quietly. He caught a technician from behind and cut off his air flow until he fell unconscious. Opute dragged the body to the hatch ramp and unceremoniously rolled it down to the hangar floor. He then raced back inside, closed the hatch, and hurried to the cockpit.

After a cursory glance at fuel, shields, and weapons, Opute lifted off and sped toward the planet's atmosphere.

He thought he'd made it until a voice came in through his com unit.

"Cap'in Chaar," the voice called out. "Din' know you'se was up on our route t'day. We work'n some sor'ta spesh drill?"

"No," Opute answered, having no idea how Captain Chaar would reply. "Just testing some repairs. Carry on." Opute cringed as he waited for the inevitable.

"Please identify yo'self."

Opute said nothing and he silently urged the ship to go faster.

"This is Patrol Ship three-six-four. Stop where you are an' prep to be boarded."

"Great," Opute muttered. He shot forward and barrel-rolled away from the approaching vessel. With a quick flick of the controls, he fired a few shots into the pursuer's underbelly. A massive amount of sparks spewed from the ship and they veered away.

Opute pushed the patrol ship to its maximum velocity and plotted the fastest course for Belxa, Zarsa's screams of pain echoing in his mind.

* * *

Iry paced back and forth, a bit of froth forming in the corner of his mouth. Thlin had reported back about Coresque's betrayal and that he'd contained her for the time being. Impressed by Thlin's thinking, he sent him to trail Exarth. His initial report of the dead bounty hunter confirmed what Iry feared: she wanted to find Opute.

But when Thlin reported that Exarth killed Nuis Weri and a Grassuwerian named Zarsa, Iry put his genius brain to use. The executions were messy and publicized. She wanted them to be reported, for word to spread about the killings.

She wanted to enrage Opute to find her instead.

Iry couldn't let that happen. The two of them could *not* meet.

Iry ordered Thlin to return to Belxa. Once back, he inserted a communications device inside his associate's wrist.

"If you get a whiff of Opute in the building, press this. It contains a homing beacon so I'll know where you are and I'll come find you."

Thlin nodded and left the office, rubbing his wrist.

Iry went to the closet toward the back of the room and pulled out a strange device—long handled with a circularly jagged blade attached to the end.

His fingers tingled with anticipation as he held the weapon. His dreams were about to come true.

With a push on the back of his closet door, a panel opened. Iry looked into a single, individual ovule—he'd had it installed two years prior. He'd connected it to two rooms—Exarth's office and Coresque's room, in case he ever needed to sneak in. It could bring him to either room, where he'd installed secret panels in their closets for access.

Iry closed the panel, laying the weapon right next to the door, and shut the closet. He resumed his work at his desk, the remnants of a maniacal smile touching the corners of his mouth.

* * *

Opute slammed the door open to his hotel room. He'd arrived on the planet minutes earlier and wanted to stock up on some of his...less conventional weapons before heading back to confront Thlin.

He couldn't believe he'd been on the same planet this whole time as the man who murdered his wife.

He finished pocketing a poison dart shooter when he

noticed his vidlink's message button flashing, telling him he had multiple messages. Tempted to ignore it and just continue, a nagging feeling in the back of his head told him he should listen. Besides, who would be leaving messages for him? No one knew he was here except…

He hit the button and watched the screen hum to life.

Lilfor's face looked back at him.

He turned up the volume.

"Gaaht," she began, "I hope you're receiving this. I had a dream last night. I think it may have been *your* dream. I can't say any more. Please return my call as soon as you can."

The message date read four days ago. Two more messages, pretty much the same as the first, urging him to return her call. Then the fourth and final message began.

"Gaaht, I need to tell you about my dreams. I don't know if you are receiving these or not, but you need to know what's going on. It's not safe to leave a message so I'm coming to Belxa. I will be there at 0900 hours on Third Day. I will meet you where we first met. I don't know if it's safe to meet at your hotel. I'll wait three hours. If you don't show, I'll assume the worst."

Opute glanced over at the time reader on his wall. It read 1128 hours, Third Day.

Torn, Opute took a moment to think.

Okay. Thlin will still be there. He thinks I'm dead, remember? Besides, if Lilfor is coming all the way here, it must be important. Maybe that Coresque woman tried to send me another dream? But Lilfor and I were separated, so how could that be?

Either way, a dream about Coresque could be a warning. Opute needed to know, just in case.

Opute finished the rest of his weapons inventory by palming a retractable knife that attached to a bracelet and fit under his jacket sleeve, then headed toward Docking Pad 902.

He arrived with ten minutes to spare and saw Lilfor pacing in front of a small cruiser.

"Oh I'm so glad you got my message," she told him, after enveloping him in a hug. "I almost left."

Opute awkwardly patted her on the back until they divided. "It's good to see you," he said. "What's going on?"

"I've been having dreams about the albino woman."

"Coresque? What happened?"

"The first couple dreams were about that dark, long-haired woman, but then they abruptly changed. Coresque was trapped somehow underneath something. I think she may have been on the floor because someone kept walking by in front of her, all I saw were shoes. But I could see the layout of the room—a table and two chairs and a picture...and a corridor...it's hard to describe. And then I saw someone who looked just like her, all white, but it was a man. I think she wanted to tell me he trapped her there.

"I don't know what any of it means, but I think she needs help," she finished. "I knew I had to tell you and I don't trust vidlink calls. I'm betting you know where the whitened man is and that's where she is. I think I could find the room she's in if I see the inside of wherever she's being kept, but it's hard to describe."

Gut-wrenching rage racked his stomach. "I do know where the whitened man is. I'll find Coresque."

"I'm coming with you."

CHAPTER 27

"NO," OPUTE TOLD her, "you're *not* coming with me."

"Like space I'm not!" Lilfor retorted.

Opute shook his head. "It's too dangerous. I found the man, Thlin, who shot down my wife's ship. In fact, he recently tried to have me arrested for criminal charges and when that plan went astray, tried to kill me. He hired me. And he works for Iry—the albino man."

"I *knew* you would know him!" she exclaimed. "Well what are we waiting for? I have to go help this...Coresque, right? She's going to be where this Iry guy is so let's go. We go in, you kill the man who murdered your Mahri, I save Coresque, and we call the authorities on Iry. Sounds simple enough to me."

In her excitement, Lilfor had not seen Opute cringe at his dead wife's name. He forgot Lilfor knew everything about him. He looked into the eager young woman's violet eyes. He could practically picture them, dull and lifeless—another corpse to add to his ever-growing list. First Mahri, then Lang, now Nuis and Zarsa. Would Lilfor be next?

Anger boiled inside him, this time mingled with grief. She made it sound so easy, like some sort of grand adventure. "This isn't a game," he snapped, grabbing her fiercely by the shoulders. "Everyone in my life *dies*! Do you understand that you selfish, childish, naive—"

TWHACK!

Opute reeled at the blow across his face.

"You don't get it, do you!" she said, shaking her stinging hand. "I know all the pain you went through. I saw it. I *felt* it. I feel like I lived it. I feel like Mahri was my wife and I lost her to a murderous underling who doesn't care who he kills because he's following orders to climb some ugly, fictional ladder. I feel like Lang was my friend who helped me out of some tough scrapes and I found his body with a scorched hole through it in his shop on C-Nine." Tears streamed down her green face, cutting tracks through her dusty skin. "They are still in my head and heart and I can't get them out and now there's this woman who needs my help...your help...whatever, and you just want your revenge because I *know* you!"

"You don't understand," he said, rubbing his face. "More have died. My friends, Nuis and Zarsa, are dead. Exarth killed them to send me a message that she's looking for me. She killed them personally."

Lilfor's breath caught in her throat and her hand went to her chest. "Wh..what? They're both dead?"

"Yeah. They were the only friends I had."

Lilfor let out an exasperated breath. "Hello? I *know* that, remember? What happened to them?"

Opute's words came out fast. He didn't want to talk about this, to share anymore, but they tumbled from his lips like a bubbling brook. "Nuis was killed two days ago and I could hear through a vidlink call when Exarth killed Zarsa. I was calling her from a detention cell on Yek, which I just broke out of recently, and it won't take them long to track me back to my employment here. I'm out of time."

"That's why you need help," she said, her tone fierce. "You can't do this all by yourself."

"I don't want your help," he snarled. He pushed her away harder than he meant to and she stumbled and fell to the ground.

She stood, brushing off her hands. "So this is what it comes down to? I am the only one you have left!"

"I KNOW!" he screamed. A shudder racked his body. "I can't...I can't lose you, too. You're like my family. I never even knew mine and never cared to have one. Except when Mahri came. And now she's gone. They're all gone." Opute swallowed hard against the lump in his throat. He didn't have time to think about everyone he'd lost. He didn't have the strength to lose control right now. He needed to stay focused and finish what he'd started.

"But what you don't realize," Lilfor said, "is that I *can't* sit back and do nothing. Those individuals in your life, they are a part of mine, too. Just like you cared when Hunsmat died and you protected me when Brue wanted to sacrifice my life for his. You *knew* how much I suffered and you wanted to keep any more suffering from happening, even though it may have jeopardized our mind-link being severed.

"We became a part of each other's lives," she continued. "I feel as compelled to do something as you to punish Thlin." She paused. "However, I am realistic. I'm not a killer or a fighter. I can't help you against Thlin or Iry, but I can help save Coresque while you do the stuff you need to do," she said lamely. "You know what I mean."

Opute shook his head. He wanted to tell her to go back home and forget everything that had happened. But how could he? If he were in her position, he would have done everything he possibly could to help her because she was right—they were a part of each other's lives. He knew if Hunsmat had been murdered instead of just caught in the crossfire, he would've wanted to find his killer, because he remembered all of Hunsmat's life through Lilfor and felt a brotherly attachment to Hunsmat.

Opute let out a sigh and a look of determination filled Lilfor's face.

"We need a plan," he said.

CHAPTER 28

ONE OF THE guards in front of Iry's building nudged his fellow sentry. He nodded at a young woman who walked down the street in their direction. She carried a large bag of items and her black skirt ended above her knees, revealing toned, sleek, greenish-colored thighs.

"My wife would *kill* me if she knew I looked at that pretty thing," the second guard muttered.

"That's why single life is the best, Berto," the first guard said. "You can not only look, but if you play your cards right…" He smiled as the woman's bag ripped open and spilled its contents on the ground in front of them. She cursed, squatted down, and began to wrangle in the mess. Her skirt crept upwards a few centimeters more and the guard's smile widened.

"I'll be right back," he said to Berto, smoothing back his frizzy red hair. Rushing over to help the young woman, she rewarded him with a dazzling smile and a look of gratitude in her large, beautiful violet eyes.

"Let me help you, Miss," he said, crouching down next to her.

"You are so thoughtful," she replied. They managed to put everything back into the bag, which she now held with the rip pointing upwards. "However can I thank you?" she asked, a seductive smile playing on her lips.

Too easy! "How about a drink later? When I get off my shift?"

"Tempting," she told him, "but I don't think you'll be awake by then."

The guard had less than a moment to wonder about her comment before someone struck him from behind and he blacked out.

* * *

"Ugh," Lilfor grunted as she helped Opute move the guard's body out of sight. "What a creep." She adjusted her black skirt that had been tucked under and it now hung twice as long. "How much time do you think we have before someone notices these guards aren't at their post?" she asked, nodding at the one at her feet and referencing the other one who Opute knocked out first.

"Probably not long, but we don't need that much time. Let's get going."

As the two of them entered the building, the receptionist looked up and smiled.

"Ah, Mister Gaaht. Welcome back from your assignment. If you wait one moment, I will let Iry know that you are—"

Lilfor cried out in surprise as Opute shoved her to the floor. She heard a *fsst* sound and when she looked up the receptionist was slumped over his desk, a handheld weapon clasped in his grip.

Opute reached over and helped her to her feet.

"What happened to him?"

"Poison dart," he explained, showing her how he rigged them to fire from his wrist.

"How did you know he had a weapon?"

"I didn't."

Lilfor gulped. They walked into Iry's office to find it empty.

"Now what?" Lilfor asked. The words were barely out of her mouth when they heard a surprised shout in the lobby.

Opute rushed back in and found a muscular man with auburn hair checking for a pulse on the receptionist.

"You!" the man hissed.

Opute leapt over the desk and grabbed the man before he could reach for his weapon. He pulled the man's arm up tight behind his back and pressed his own weapon against his neck. He shoved him into Iry's office. Lilfor closed the door behind them, her face sallow with fear.

"Where's Iry?" Opute growled.

"You're supposed to be dead!" the man wheezed. Opute recognized the voice. It was Thlin. The man who murdered his wife.

Opute shook, the knife digging deeper into Thlin's throat. It took every ounce of will power he had not to kill him here and now. But his rage still needed to be satisfied a little.

A crack rang through the air and Thlin howled in pain.

"Oh, I'm sorry," Opute said sarcastically. "Did that hurt?"

"You son of a—"

Opute drove the man's already broken arm higher against his back. "Don't." He snarled over the man's shriek of pain. "I'm barely keeping my temper in check already. Where's Iry? I won't ask again.'"

"I don't know," Thlin spit out, sweat pouring down his face. "He left the building for something and will be back later. I *swear!*"

"Okay, then where's Exarth?" Opute asked, putting his

mouth right next to Thlin's ear.

Thlin sucked in a breath. "You want…" He wiggled slightly in Opute's grip. "Okay, I can…I can take you to her."

Shock hit him. "She's in *this* building?"

"Yes."

"Lead on." Opute nodded to Lilfor. "You coming?"

Lilfor shook her head. Her eyes searched the area. "I think I know how to find Coresque. And Opute," Lilfor said with a pause, "keep an eye on this one," she said, motioning toward Thlin. "He's up to something."

Thlin's eyes widened. "Opute?" He pressed his good hand against his mouth, as if astonished.

"Yeah. I've waited ten years to meet you." Opute shifted the man's arm up a little higher, satisfied when Thlin squealed. "Don't worry, Lil. Just find Coresque and then get out of here. Do *not* wait for me. No arguments."

She nodded with understanding. "Good luck."

"You, too."

Lilfor left in a jog down the corridor.

Opute shoved Thlin through the door. "Let's go."

The two of them made their way to the ovule transport and got in. When they reached the destination Thlin spoke of, the door hissed open and they exited.

"She's in the third office on the left," Thlin told him, his face wracked with pain. "She will most likely be by herself. Now let me go."

Opute snorted. "I don't think so. You're going in with me."

Thlin squirmed even though the broken bones in his arm ground together. "She'll kill us both!" he said.

"Not if I kill her first."

"You don't understand!" he pleaded as Opute dragged him down the hallway. "She can't be killed! She has this strange ability to regenerate or something."

"Everyone can be killed."

Opute kicked open the door and shoved Thlin through first.

* * *

Iry felt the vibration in his pocket. Thlin's emergency communicator sending him a distress call. This could only mean one thing.

Opute was here.

Iry stood from his desk and headed over to the closet. He yanked it open, his eyes bright with anticipation.

* * *

Exarth looked up from her datapad at the sudden intrusion. A muscular man fell through the doorway, one of Iry's pets as she recalled, followed by a young man with coppery skin, reddish-blonde hair, and intense amber-flecked eyes.

"Exarth," the man said.

She rose from her chair. "Who are you?"

Without any hesitation, he lifted his arm. Several *fsst* sounds occurred.

Exarth felt the darts penetrate her flesh. She looked down at the tiny bits of metal sticking out of her chest. Before she could react, the stranger flicked two concealed blades from his wrists and they hit her through each eye. She fell backward into her chair, which toppled over, just as an electric current flooded her body.

Blinded and shocked, she passed out.

* * *

Thlin giggled hysterically, half from pain, half from

happiness. Iry would be so pleased with him. He managed to help someone get to Exarth and kill her. And Iry would be on his way soon. And now with Exarth out of the way, Iry could take over, and Thlin would be the right-hand to the most powerful man in the—

Thlin's delusions of grandeur stopped cold. Terror gripped him as he watched Exarth stand. She pulled the knives from her eyes, along with a pair of black-colored contacts. Her flesh knit back together. The scorch mark on her chest from the electro-volt weapon still sizzled, but her torso began to heal itself. In a moment, she plucked each of the poison darts from her chest and Thlin blinked his eyes in amazement as the poison dripped back out through the tiny pinprick holes.

"Opute," she said, her eyes whirling between shades of red, violet, and gold. "How you've changed."

* * *

Opute hadn't moved a muscle since his last volley of weapons went off. He stood perfectly still as the bane of his existence rose from the floor and dismissed his attack as if he'd pelted her with grains of sand.

None of his weapons worked.

Rage so intense it hurt swelled in his chest. He let out a guttural roar and charged her, directing all his anger, grief, and pain into her face.

A feeling like a metal pole striking him in his chest shocked him and he stumbled backwards. She'd held her arm straight out and it hit squarely. He could see her mangled hand, severely broken from the impact, repairing itself before his eyes.

Weapons wouldn't hurt her. And she could withstand anything he physically did to her.

He puffed out his chest, ready to attack again, knowing

he'd most likely lose, but he didn't care.

Before he could take a step, she spoke. "You won't win. And I knew you'd come," she said, her voice low and sensual, not like the clipped accented words he'd heard when she killed Zarsa. Something about it seemed familiar, edging on the recesses of his mind, but he shoved it aside, He needed to stay in the present.

She turned her datapad screen toward him—a picture of him before and after his total body surgery. Opute recognized the images from Zarsa's files. The thought brought on a fresh bout of rage.

"You look good," she said. "Young, but good. I never would have recognized you."

Opute trembled with fury. He watched as Exarth looked over at Thlin, who cowered in the corner, a sweaty, blubbering mess.

"Iry will be displeased to hear of your betrayal," she said to Thlin. "Or did he plan for this to happen, to test my limits? It wouldn't surprise me. You can't trust anyone," her gaze flitted back toward Opute, "can you, Opute?"

Opute kept his eyes locked on Exarth. Without removing his stare, he gazed past her. The wall behind her moved ever so slowly. A panel swung open, bit by bit.

He was outnumbered. But then Iry did something strange. He made a motion for Opute to keep quiet.

Opute had seen what Exarth could do. He knew Iry couldn't hurt her. But maybe if he and Iry worked together they could?

"Betrayal is a strange thing," Exarth continued. "You expect a certain amount of it from strangers or villains, but usually not from those you consider mentors, friends…"

Exarth's eyes narrowed. "Or husbands."

Iry came closer through the paneled wall, creeping up

behind Exarth. He held something out in front of him.

Suddenly Exarth's words struck Opute and his focus came back to her. "Husbands?"

"I know it's been ten years, but don't tell me you've forgotten your own wife. Maybe I should cut my hair short and dye it again and put in my brown contacts. Would that help?"

Realization dawned on Opute. "Mahri?" It was her. She looked so much thinner and sharper. The softness of her face gone, her black eyes empty. But somehow, he knew it was her. He could feel it.

Exarth sneered. "You didn't know?"

His breath seemed to go out of him. She lived, here, in front of him. His wife. His love. For a decade he'd raged over nothing. All this time lost. A spot in his heart—so many years full of blackness—lit up with hope.

He barely managed a few words. "They told me you were dead." He took a deep breath. "They said Exarth…you…killed my wife, killed you. Mahri." His words failed him. Everything felt slow. Confusion and shock paralyzed him and melted away into one perfect moment: she was alive. Only the two of them existed in that instant.

Exarth's sneer faltered. Her face softened. And he could see her. His wife.

She spoke again, but her voice wavered, unsure. "I don't know what you're talking about. Iry told me you helped the hospital. You betrayed me."

"What hospital?"

A myriad of small movements crossed her face, as if she raced through a thousand thoughts.

Realization won out. She smiled. "Then that means you never—"

The words barely spilled across her lips when Iry's contraption tore through her from behind.

She screamed, arching her back as the whirling blades slashed and ripped.

"No!" Opute cried out. He tried to move forward, but Thlin grabbed onto his ankle and he stumbled, catching himself on the edge of the desk.

"Thank you for being my puppet," Iry jeered into Exarth's ear.

"Mahri, no!" Opute screamed, his vocal chords straining in protest.

With a wicked grin, Iry twisted the object and it burst through the front of her body, continually spinning to keep the wound open. White blood sprayed from the gash and Exarth sunk to the floor, shrieking. She tried to grab the weapon, but it cut through her hands.

"Just DIE!" Iry screamed at her, spittle flying from his lips. He shifted awkwardly as her body slumped to the floor and he let go of the weapon, which continued to whirl. He turned to Opute, his eyes wide with wild glee. "Finally! And thank you for keeping her distracted, Mister Gaaht."

"He isn't Gaaht!" Thlin cried out from behind Opute, holding on with his one good arm. "He's Ness Opute!"

Iry's eyes widened. "No...it can't be..."

Opute kicked Thlin in the chest, making him release his grip. His insides burned with fury. He turned toward Iry and lunged over the table. Iry backed into the wall and held up his hands, but Opute batted them away. He slid his hand under Iry's chin and the other on the back of his head. In a swift motion, Opute snapped his neck.

The albino man fell ungracefully to the floor, a look of pure surprise in his eyes, but Opute had already turned back to Exarth. He pulled out the spinning weapon and threw it at Thlin, where it sliced through his face, spitting pieces of flesh and bone, before it thumped to the floor, followed closely by

Thlin's dead body.

Opute gathered the woman into his arms. His love, his wife. "Mahri?" he asked, tentatively. "Is it really you?"

A white bubble of blood formed at her lips and she nodded. He watched as parts of her body began to knit themselves back together, but they moved so slowly, too slowly. White blood covered him and the carpet, spilling out of her like paint primer.

"I...I...what can I do? HELP!" he cried out. "Oh please... *please* don't die. I love you so much. They told me you were dead. I thought you'd been killed by Exarth...by you? I don't understand. Just please don't die! I've missed you so much."

At that moment Lilfor ran into the room with Coresque closely behind her.

"Opute!" Lilfor exclaimed, seeing Exarth on the floor.

Opute looked up, confusion and fear tightening his chest. "It's my wife," he babbled. "It's Mahri." He turned back to the woman on the floor. His breath came in hiccupped gasps. Terror raced through his veins as white blood began to congeal on his arms. He couldn't do anything to help her.

She blinked and the black contacts popped out of her eyes. Jeweled-toned emeralds, tinged with sapphire, seemed to shine at him from her pale face. They peered into him, into his soul. Then they looked past him, their spark gone.

A rage as hot as a thousand suns burst through his body, the flames licking his insides, his screams echoing into an explosion of pain.

CHAPTER 29

OPUTE?
Go away.
I can't go away. I need you to talk to me.
Leave me alone.
If I leave you alone, you'll die.
Then let me die.

Opute?
What?
I'm not going to go anywhere.
Fine, then can you be there and be quiet?
No. I know my talking irritates you and if you're irritated you will want to fight back.
Show's what you know. I don't want to fight anymore. So talk all you want. I don't care.

Opute? Opute!
WHAT!

Just checking.

Lilfor? Are you there?
Yeah, I'm here.
What's going on? Where am I?
You're unconscious. Kind of.
You always were great at explanations.
Did you just insult me while in a coma?
Opute smiled.
Then he opened his eyes.

He recognized the clay walls and soothing smells. He lay in a room at Lilfor's guardians' house. Lilfor sat in a chair next to the bed, dark circles under her eyes.

"Hey," he croaked.

"Hey yourself. How are you feeling?"

"Great," he said sarcastically. "Thirsty."

Lilfor handed him a glass of water. She helped guide it for him and tipped it against his lips. The water felt cool and clear and his parched mouth absorbed it as soon as it touched his tongue. He sucked in a deep gulp and promptly coughed it all back up.

"Easy," she told him, wiping up the spilled drink.

"I'm on Terrue, right?" he managed.

She nodded. "Yeah. I didn't know where else to take you."

"How long have I been here?"

"Two weeks."

"Two…" Opute struggled to sit up as the memories of Exarth…Mahri…flooded through him. "Where is she?" he said, getting tangled in the blanket. "She needs me!"

Opute felt surprised at how easily Lilfor restrained him.

"She's dead, Opute," Lilfor whispered. "She died when we were on Belxa. You…you went crazy and…and you went catatonic. I thought we'd lost you, too, but then I realized I could hear your thoughts again so I knew you were alive. Coresque and I brought you here and we've waited to see if you would recover. Now that you're awake, I can't hear your thoughts anymore. I guess it only worked while you were unconscious."

His head throbbed as the terrible scene battered at his mind. Guilt crept in, chewing at his raw heart. Why didn't he see it was her? How could he have lost her again? "How could I not have recognized her?" he muttered. "I mean, sure her hair and eyes were different, but… why didn't I realize it?"

"I don't know. Maybe because she wasn't her, not really."

Opute frowned.

Lilfor continued. "I saw from your memories the kind of woman she was as your wife, as Mahri. That woman wasn't Exarth. The woman who died two weeks ago had ten years of terrible deeds built up inside her. Maybe that made her different."

"I still should have known. And now she's gone…again."

Her eyes shined with tears and Opute knew she felt Mahri's death as badly as he did.

Go away," he told her, turning his head. He didn't want her pity, her sorrow. He didn't even want his own. "Leave me alone."

"Opute…I—"

"Just leave."

Lilfor left quietly, head bowed. He saw her wipe tears from her face before she moved out of sight.

Opute knew she just wanted to help, but he didn't care. A gaping hole in his chest seemed to fill him up and suck him dry at the same time. He thought his wife had been killed all those years ago and then he found her only to watch her actually die…

The hole in his chest widened. He fell into it, into the darkness.

* * *

Opute lived in a world of grays. He didn't speak when Lilfor came into the room. He mechanically put food and drink in his mouth when she brought it and relieved himself when he needed the washroom, but otherwise he stayed laid out flat on the bed, staring at the ceiling or the walls. The food did nothing except sit in the pit of his gut, reminding him of his agony, reminding him he was still alive while Mahri wasn't.

One morning, the black hole in his heart as dark as ever, he looked over at the soup Lilfor had brought him. His stomach growled in hunger, but Opute ignored it. He wasn't getting better. And he didn't want to get better. He deserved this pain, this torture.

Ignoring the soup, he turned over and stared at the wall next to the bed.

A quiet knock sounded and the door to his room opened.

"Leave me alone, Lilfor."

"Mister Opute?" The voice sounded soft and hesitant.

He rolled his head toward the door. "Coresque?" he asked.

She glided into the room and stood serenely next to the bed. "I am glad you are alive."

"Yeah," he said, turning his head away again. "Alive."

"This place," she continued, "makes me very happy." She spoke as if she were lost in a dream, her words light and fluffy. "I feel as though I could stay here, now that my family is gone."

"Your family?" Opute asked, in spite of himself. He could see her in his peripheral vision. A grinding noise ensued, which accompanied her attempt to nod.

"Exarth and Iry. I was taken from my parents at a young age, barely remembering my mother crying when the hospital took me from her clutching hands. I was raised there and underwent experiments, torture if you prefer, since I can recall everything they did to me. I escaped with the aid of Exarth and Iry. They became the closest thing to a family I had."

"Stop calling her that!" Opute said.

"But that is her name. She adopted the name 'Mahri' as a cover, which is when you met her. She fell in love with you, Mister Opute, and kept the name to keep you from knowing who she really was."

"And who was that? A murderous, back-stabbing, double-crossing, lying..." Opute trailed off. The intense anger he had proved too much for his weakened body to handle. Sweat pinpricked his brow and his teeth chattered.

"Yes, Mister Opute, she embodied all those things. Betrayed at a young age first by a family who gave her up, and then by someone at the hospital who she believed cared for her, but really used her. She was on a path of self-destruction until she met you."

"Let me guess. Her love for me saved her." Sarcasm dripped off the words.

Coresque took a moment to consider his words. "Why, yes. That is precisely it. You created hope inside her, Mister Opute. But Iry's jealousy, to lose her in the power triangle he sought to create, made him want to destroy you. So he told Exarth you betrayed her and made it appear she died. A simple solution, actually."

"Too bad it backfired."

"That it did. Iry did not realize how strongly you felt for your wife. He believed he would find you and finish the job by murdering you. He did not think you'd continue to search for your wife's murderer.

"Iry was an intellectual," Coresque continued. "He did not understand emotions, not like you and Exarth did. But I understood. I believed you could save Exarth if I could get you two together."

"Great job."

Coresque frowned. "Things did not work out well, no. I am very good at concepts, but my execution of them is wanting. And I feared Iry. I still didn't know why he lied to Exarth and I never confronted him. After all, he represented the intelligence behind our operations. How could I know what he planned? But with Lilfor's help and the files Iry left behind, I sorted out the truth."

"Why are you telling me this?" Opute growled. "I don't care about any of it. I just want to be left alone."

"You have suffered," she told him, placing one of her hard, cold hands on his. "We have all suffered. I did not want to continue living after what I had been through at the hospital. The doctors spent days hitting me, cutting me, beating me to see how much my hardened skin could take. They did not care that I felt the pain of the injuries. When I escaped, living with those memories tore at me. They invaded my dreams. But that only made up a portion of my life. It helped create what I am today, but it does not define me."

"And what am I supposed to take from this situation? That I shouldn't get close to anyone because they all just die horrible deaths? That happiness is fleeting and should be cherished? What kind of cliché response are you going to give me?"

"None."

Opute looked at her, surprised. "What do you mean, 'none?'"

"There is no cliché that will help you through this. There is no reason or rhyme to how this is supposed to benefit your life. Because it does not. The things that happened to you were horrific and should not happen to anyone. But they did. And you can live with it or end your life. But if you live with it, you have to remember it, and that is something I would not wish on anyone."

"Why bother remembering it?"

"Because if you forget the negative, you cannot keep the positive. You will erase Mahri. I never met her, but she sounds wonderful. She deserves to exist. I would like to know her."

Images of Mahri flooded his mind, her smile, her kiss. But then the pain doubled and he pushed his face into the pillow. "I don't know if it's worth the trade."

"Understandable since you are still entrenched in something so horribly fresh. But your passion for your wife gave you strength to fight for her even after you thought she had been killed. Your friendship with Lang stayed so strong it led you to help fight when the Aleet Army resurfaced. Your connections with Nuis and Zarsa were so pure they drove you to escape prison and finally complete your quest for justice. And your unique history with Lilfor made you let her come along in the end, which not only saved your life, but mine as well.

"Each negative thing had a negative consequence, but it has also shaped your life so you could affect others in a positive way. Your pain has driven you to do great things you would not have ever accomplished without it."

He turned his head slightly, looking at her through tear-rimmed eyes. "But if I'd just let things go ten years ago I would have been happy and my friends would be alive."

"Perhaps. Or perhaps Exarth would have succeeded in her alliance with the Aleet Army and killed thousands of innocents in the process. Perhaps Nuis and Zarsa would have lived if they had not known you, but then you never would have uncovered Iry's plan and he eventually would have killed me and Exarth and taken over everything and you would have never known the truth about your wife."

He felt like a child, gripping to any sense that somehow, this statuesque woman, would have the words to comfort him, to make his pain end. He wanted her to say that this outcome was inevitable, that he didn't need to feel guilty. "So this would have happened no matter what?"

Coresque sighed. "No. Each choice led to this. If you'd have made other choices, things may have been different. We will never know."

These words hurt deadlier than a thousand knives.

Coresque paused. "May I tell you one last thing?"

He turned away from her again, letting the gray overtake him once more. "I don't care."

"She felt happy to see you, in those final moments."

He snorted a laugh. "How could you possibly know that?"

"Did you see her eyes? Blue and green?"

"Yeah. So what?"

"Exarth's eyes changed color depending on her mood. As an adult, she always wore colored contacts to hide this feature. She believed it to be a weakness. Even when involved with you, she wore them. But I knew her before that, during our childhood. And those colors, blues and greens, represented happiness. I almost never saw her happy.

"I believe she felt happy with you again. Happy to die in your arms."

Opute heard Coresque glide from the room. Her words burned into his heart, his soul.

EPILOGUE

XANA UNCURLED HER long fingers and stretched them out in front of her, relishing the feeling of their elasticity. She felt grateful to be corporeal again. Surprisingly enough, she missed eating food the most. She'd be eating soon enough.

She sat on a small sandy beach, watching the waves lap up against her bare feet. The warm breeze caressed her face, the sand felt soft, the water silky.

Breathing in a large gulp of salty air, she let it out slowly, relishing its briny flavor. The sound of soft steps moved behind her in the sand.

A young woman, completely void of pigment, sat down beside her. Three standard months had passed since she came to these shores, along with Lilfor and an unconscious Opute. Each needed healing in their own way.

"Hello, Coresque," Xana said.

"Hello, Xana."

"How does your body feel today?"

Coresque took a moment to bend her wrists, her fingers, her toes. "A little more flexible than yesterday. I am still not quite used to the idea of being able to bend. Sitting, for example, is wonderful."

"I'm glad to hear this place has helped to restore some of your flexibility."

Coresque nodded. "My skin is still rock hard, but the joints bend more easily."

"The hardness is a part of you. But this place allows you to soften yourself."

Coresque paused to watch as the sun blossomed into the morning sky. Golden rays lit up the undersides of the clouds. "Do you think Opute will be okay?"

Xana looked over and saw him walking on the beach with Lilfor, trailing behind Xera and Xutu, his once muscular frame withered, his steps unstable on the warm sands. The family, with Coresque included, decided to have a sunrise picnic. At that moment Opute watched the sun come up. He looked over at Xana, as if he felt her gaze upon him, and gave a slight nod before turning away. His eyes still looked hollow, dark, but without the shadow of death like before.

"He will never be okay," Xana said, answering Coresque's question. She took in another deep breath of sweet air. Warm rays of light filtered through the clouds and shone in stripes across the sandy beach. One such strip danced across Opute's face, showing it half in light, half in darkness.

"But he will find balance," Xana continued. And although she barely knew him, Xana felt glad.

Thank you so much for reading
COILED VENGEANCE!

If you enjoyed this book, try another from author
Christa Yelich-Koth, **The Jade Castle,**
Book 1 in the *Land of Iyah* trilogy

Here's a sneak peek!

CHAPTER 1

Bekk chased after her as she flitted through the dense foliage. She flew so fast, streaking through the dark green and silver leaves. He clambered over fallen logs and broken twigs, nearly slipping into the firestream next to him. Its heat pulsated in waves as the flames danced toward the edge of the cliff before tipping over and cascading down into a firefall.

Sweat dripped from his forehead, stinging his eyes.

They headed deeper into the forest. Broad, leafy, fern-like plants thwacked at his legs, leaving his olive-toned skin red and stinging. He pushed aside thick, black branches covered with what looked like a soft blue mold, but were in fact tiny flowers called Fairy Flits, the nectar inside them a fairy equivalent to a Greek god's ambrosia. Their sweet scent, like honeyed lilacs, hung in the air around him.

Oh Bekk! Please hurry! The fairy's voice sounded soft, but urgent in his head.

"I can't navigate through this forest as well as you can, Ryf," he answered, panting. Green sunlight slanted through the treetops, casting patterns of light and dark in his wake. It made it difficult to see the rough terrain.

I know, but we're almost out of time. Yir's life is at stake! And if we get there too late...

"We'll make it," he reassured her. "She saved my life. We aren't going to let anything happen to her." He ignored a sharp twig that cut into the sole of his foot.

Why didn't I think to wear shoes? he thought.

We still have a ways to go until we get to the castle, she said, her voice so high with panic he could barely hear her. She blasted off ahead of him—a red firework burst of sparks where she'd just been.

"Wait, Ryf! It's too dangerous!" He upped his speed, skirting around a group of Pepper Pot flowers as they sneezed their spores into the air. But then he accidentally kicked a second collection of the bell-shaped black flowers and received a face full of their discharge.

He coughed through the cloud of black mist, sneezing sharply four times in a row. His eyes burned and he slowed, raking his sleeve across his face. It came away wet, full of perspiration and the tears trying to clear away the infiltrating pollen.

"Ryf," he called out, hacking again. Air forced its way in and out of his lungs and he waited for his eyes to clear. They did, slowly, but he couldn't see Ryf anywhere. Sweat dripped down the sides of his face and collected in pools under his skinny arms. His T-shirt stuck to him like a layer of wet paint and his own stench wafted up his nostrils.

Regaining his breath, he jogged a bit further, but he'd lost his bearings. The castle he ran toward, its familiar spires like jade ice crystals under the world's deep green sun, remained lost behind the thick forest.

Bekk took a moment and rested against a tree, his hand sinking into the bark as if into a dense sponge. But the longer he stood still, the harder it became to breathe. Was this a side effect from the Pepper Pot spores?

His breathing shallowed and his vision blurred. Far in the distance he could see a tiny sparkly red dot, flying toward him.

Moments later Ryf came into view, terror in her eyes. *Bekk?* she said. *Bekk? What's happening?*

"I don't—I don't know." He was huffing now. "A Pepper Pot. I just—I can't seem to catch...." He leaned over, lightheaded. As his head dropped, he watched his hands blur.

"No."

He rubbed them across his face. Everything tingled. Pinpricks of needles danced across his skin.

"No," he cried out. "Not now!" A ringing in his head made him cover his ears. The sound intensified, like repeated gongs—electronic, horrible gongs.

Ryf sparkled in his face. Her red light dimmed. She began to fade. *Please Bekk. Please don't leave. He'll kill her!*

But the blurring intensified. Bekk's body vibrated. He could see Ryf call out to him, but her voice had been drowned out by the deafening noise.

With a yell, Bekk awoke.

Salty sweat stung his eyes, dripping from his dark hair. After a deft swipe across his brow, he turned and slammed his hand down on his alarm, silencing the noisy culprit.

"I have to save Yir," he muttered, laying his head back down on the pillow. Its soft contours wrapped around his moist face.

"You have to get your ass out of bed." A shadow stood over Bekk.

"You don't understand," Bekk said to his older brother, rolling onto his side. "I am the only one who can save her." His eyelids drooped, his breath slowed. He could see the red sparks from Ryf's fluttering wings...

WHAM!

Bekk bolted into a sitting position. "Jesus, Shon!" He rubbed his raw face. "What? Did you line that pillowcase with quarters?"

"It's next on my list," his brother grumbled, throwing the squished pillow to the floor. "Seriously, Bekk, I'm tired of these games. You are going to get up. You are going to go to school. And you're not going to be late. Why? Because it's *my* ass on the line if you don't. You know that bitch from Social Services is just itching to prove I suck as your guardian."

"I know," Bekk answered through a yawn. "I don't try to be late."

Shon sat on the edge of the bed, its rusty springs creaking. "I know you don't. But how many times can your excuse be falling asleep on the bus?"

Bekk pushed back his blue comforter and sighed at his sweat-soaked sheets. "I just can't seem to stay awake lately."

"Drink a FlySky." Shon glanced at the soiled bed. "And you're on laundry duty tonight."

Bekk plopped his feet on the beige carpet and ran his fingers through his damp hair. "Caffeine doesn't help," he said, ignoring the order to do his least favorite chore. He paused, grabbed a black, rock band t-shirt from the floor, and shoved his upper body through all the correct holes. "Maybe there's something wrong with me?"

"Yeah," his brother replied, tossing him a pair of dark jeans. "It's called post-traumatic stress. Remember? Your insightful school guidance counselor who thinks she's a real psychologist told us so."

"Shon, Mom and Dad died a year ago. It's not that."

Shon let out a sigh, his brows knitting together in a moment of concern. "Well we can't afford to send you to a real doctor to find out, so in the meantime, drink two FlySky's." He sniffed. "And put on some extra deodorant."

The Jade Castle is available now at all retailers.

ABOUT THE AUTHOR

Christa Yelich-Koth is the award-winning author (2016 Novel of Excellence for Science Fiction for ILLUSION from Author's Circle Awards) of the Amazon Bestselling novels, ILLUSION and IDENTITY from the Eomix Galaxy Novels collection.

Aside from her novels, Christa has also authored a graphic novel, HOLLOW, and 6-issue follow-up comic book series HOLLOW'S PRISM from Green-Eyed Unicorn Comics. (with illustrator Conrad Teves.)

Originally from Milwaukee, WI, Christa was exposed to many different things through her education, including an elementary Spanish immersion program, a vocal/opera program in high school, and her eventual B.S. in Biology. Her love of entomology and marine biology helped while writing her science fiction/fantasy aliens/creatures.

As for why she writes, Christa had this to say: "I write because I have a story that needs to come out. I write because I can't NOT write. I write because I love creating something that pulls me out of my own world and lets me for a little while get lost inside someone or someplace else. And I write because I HAVE to know how the story ends."

You can find more about Christa and her other books at: www.ChristaYelichKoth.com

Made in the USA
Columbia, SC
31 July 2019